Fuse
Samantha M Thomas

Contents

To the speed bumps, the unexpected, and the hard times.

Fight like hell through them all to get what you want.

Content Warning

It is important to take care of yourself. Please read these content warnings and make the best decision for your mental health.

Chemical pregnancy (past event, discussed and worked through within the book)
Pregnancy after miscarriage (discussed in full)
Alcoholism, addiction (shown on page)
Detoxing from alcohol (shown on page)

Chapter 1

Tomic Unconscious in US Race in What Is the Worst Crash in Modern Times. Will He Race Again?

Shocking events at the United States Grand Prix this weekend. Last year's Driver's Champion, Luka Tomic, has ended his season early, it seems. What has been a disappointing season for Tomic has turned into a nightmare. It appears no one was around him when he crashed hard into the barriers, his car immediately erupting in flames.

The FIA stated that Tomic is in a serious but stable condition and is currently being treated at Dell Seton Medical Center, Austin for a concussion and severe burns. Empress Racing has already issued a statement in support of Tomic, stating they will be pulling David Acevedo up from Formula Two for the remainder of the season in place of Tomic.

Tomic's wife, Daisy, was in attendance at the time of the crash, and fans witnessed her running to the ambulance to join him. She was described as "inconsolable and frantic" as she waited for him to be cut from the wreckage.

Is this the end of Luka Tomic's Formula One career? Can he rebound and come back stronger next season? Only time will tell.

Chapter 2

Daisy

I sent everyone home. They were suffocating me, and I didn't want to take everything out on them when I couldn't even verbalize what I was feeling.

But now it's just me in the hospital, in this isolated waiting room, trying to make sense of everything.

Luka crashed.

Luka was unconscious and had to be dragged out of his car that was engulfed in flames.

Luka has third-degree burns on his hands and forearms.

I have no idea what this means for his future, for *our* future.

"Mrs. Tomic?" the nurse calls from the barely cracked door.

Looking up, I wordlessly arch an eyebrow in response. I'm not sure if the words will come, so I don't even try.

"The doctor is on his way to Luka's room to discuss treatment and progress," she says softly.

I nod, slowly standing up and bracing myself for more bad news. That's all that seems to be coming nowadays, so I might as well start expecting it, right?

I follow her down the desolate hallway, and we arrive at my husband's room. A deep breath is all I have time for. One breath to calm my nerves and put on a strong face for the man who's been through more in the past three days than ever before. One breath to push down all the feelings of resentment and anger I had toward him before the accident.

My head is a chaotic mess, filled with too many feelings—both pre- and post-accident. I can't sift through them well enough to express any sort of outward emotion. Grabbing a surgical mask from the station beside his door, I place it over my face to decrease the risk of infection, just as I was instructed the first time I was allowed to see him.

He barely glances at me as I enter his room. His arms are elevated and bandaged, but otherwise, he looks just like the gorgeous, grumpy man I've come to know over the past few months. His hazel eyes, more golden than brown or green, flick to me and quickly look away.

My heart clenches so hard in my chest that I briefly consider whether it's a heart attack or not.

"Mr. and Mrs. Tomic, good to see you this morning." Dr. Branch startles me as he walks in.

"Good morning," I mumble.

Luka grunts and shifts up in the bed as much as he's able to.

"So, everything is progressing well—"

"Sure doesn't feel like it," Luka growls.

"Luka..." I gently scold.

"It's fine," Dr. Branch reassures me. "The fact that you are sitting up, and tolerating the pain and medication, is good progress. Obviously, due to your loss of consciousness, the burns on your hands are worse than if you had been able to get out of the car sooner. I want to schedule you for surgery tomorrow to debride all the burns, take a deeper look to make sure everything is free of infection, and assess to what extent we will need to apply grafts. We're still monitoring that fifth digit on your left hand closely, but at this stage in the healing process, I can't yet determine if it will remain viable."

"Is that the only ... appendage you have major concerns about?" I ask as delicately as I can.

"Currently, yes. But there are a couple of spots around his right thumb that I want to watch as well. We won't have a clearer picture until I get him into surgery, due to the severity of the burns. We are anticipating you're in for a couple of skin grafts at least, and following that, it's just a waiting game."

"Fucking awesome," Luka snips.

"I know it's not the news you were wanting, but this is a slow healing process. You'll be here for a couple more weeks at a minimum post-operatively, then we can discuss specific wound care as the grafts settle and the lesser of the burns start to heal, and then what your rehab will look like post-discharge." Dr. Branch looks at me sympathetically.

"Thank you for your help. We really appreciate it." I nod at him as he takes his leave.

The nurse follows behind him, and then it's just me and Luka.

"I know you're frustrated, but taking things out on your doctor is not a great approach. He's just trying to help and get you out of here as quickly as possible." Sitting in the chair off to the side, I tip my head back and sigh.

"How the fuck am I supposed to act, Dais? My season is done. I have no clue if I'll have a contract after this shit, and now we're talking about not even keeping some of my fingers?" His voice gets louder as he adds more fuel to the fire.

The fact that his thoughts are solely on his job is what hurts the most, I think. It's not as though everything has been sunshine and rainbows between us lately, but it wasn't all dire.

I'd still had hope that things would get better once the season was over. That we could work on us before the next season and everything would be back to how it was before.

But now, his physical recovery and his mindset are the only things that matter. Even as I acknowledge that, sadness works its way through my veins at the knowledge that we'll be put on the backburner for an unknown amount of time.

"I know, and I'm sorry," I murmur. I know anything I say won't really matter and won't mean much right now.

Looking down at my hands, I blink back tears. I've cried so much over the last three days that I can't imagine there are many more tears left. But I can't cry in front of him. I can't make him feel worse than he already does.

A heavy sigh from the direction of his bed draws my attention.

His voice is soft with regret. "I'm sorry, *hercegnőm*." *My princess.*

"Nothing to be sorry for. This is ... so shitty. You're allowed to feel how you feel." And I mean it. I may be a veritable mess, but everything about this situation sucks for him, and I get it. There is no light at the end of the tunnel in his mind right now, and I can't fault him for reacting as he is, without thought.

"I want to get the fuck out of here," he says with so much vulnerability in his voice that it cracks my heart even more if that's possible.

"I know, and we will, but after surgery and when we can be sure certain you are out of risk of infection."

"You should just go home," he says, gruff but firm in his words.

"Sure, let me just go home to our empty house and continue to worry about you." I scoff.

"Daisy. Go. Home," he grits out.

"No." My eyes drill into his, matching his stubbornness as only I seem to be able to.

"I don't want you here." The anger in his voice shocks me to my core, though it shouldn't.

"Too fucking bad." With every ounce of energy in my body, I try to hold back the crack in my voice. To stop the tears from falling. The best way to fight Luka when he's being stubborn as fuck is with fire, and I've got plenty of it. I just need to find it again. I need to dig deep and find who I used to be before things started falling apart for us. Before the beginning of this season and certainly before this crash.

Plopping down in the recliner that's far too nice for a hospital chair, I cross my arms and stare him down. He wants to wallow in misery and sink into depression? Fine, but he's going to do it under my supervision so he doesn't become fully lost to me.

We made vows almost two years ago, and I won't be the one who breaks them. I'll fight like hell to bring him back to me. To fight his fights, to be his support and just hope we come out the other side better than we were.

God, I hope we can make it to the other side.

"You're as stubborn as a mule," he grumbles, but there's no heat in his words.

"Takes one to know one, hubs." I sigh, tipping my head back against the headrest.

We'll be okay. Luka will be okay. I hope.

I just can't figure out if I will be.

***

Murmurs jolt me awake in the hospital chair. It takes my hazy brain a minute to understand what I'm seeing, but then it registers. Luka is fighting like hell to not show his pain. His head is tipped back, eyes closed, and his teeth are clenched so tight that his jaw looks like it's about to pop.

The night nurse is attempting to take off the bandages on his hands, moving slowly and apologizing quietly. He hisses as the last of the bandages come off of his right hand, blowing out a steady breath as he picks his head up. I can see sweat dotting his forehead even from across this hospital room.

"Alright, I just want to do a rinse on this one, then we'll move to the next one. Once that's done, we can move you to pre-op and get things going." The nurse speaks softly, but tears fill my eyes at the thought of not only the surgery but the amount of pain he is in.

Luka grunts, but there are no other outward signs that he's freaking out about the impending operation.

The nurse looks up and spots me watching them. "Good very early morning," she says softly.

I nod to her, but my eyes quickly shift back to Luka.

His eyes stay locked on the ceiling, and it shouldn't hurt so much, but being shut out when he's struggling is killing me.

Hell, it feels like the last six months have been trying to kill me. All I want to do is be his support system, but he won't even let that happen right now. There's no confiding in me about the accident; there's no talking about it, period.

The nurse moves to his other hand, and I spend the next ten minutes agonizingly watching my husband suffering through the pain. Eventually, numbness sets in—for me, not for him—but I can only handle so much. It's not just the pain; it's the graphic nature of his burns right now. I can handle a lot. I watch surgery videos all the time with no issue, but this is someone I love—my partner, my other half—and I can't reconcile how bad his hands truly are.

"Okay, worst part is hopefully done. I'm going to loosely wrap these and keep them protected while I roll you to pre-op. Once there, things will move pretty quickly, and you'll be back here before you even fully wake up." She gives us a smile, but neither of us returns it. "I have to ask you to head back to the waiting room so we can thoroughly disinfect everything before he returns, Mrs. Tomic." She bows her head apologetically, but I'm learning quickly just how much of an infection risk burns really are.

I stand up, suddenly emotional over the fact that I can't kiss him before he goes in. I missed my chance because I fell asleep. Hovering by his side but far enough away to avoid a lecture from the nurse, I wait until he glances over at me.

"I love you." I try to throw every ounce of truth into the words. We may be struggling. We may have a bunch of shit to work on, and that's not even touching on the last forty-eight hours. But I love him. Desperately. I can't let him go into surgery, no matter how low risk, without him knowing it.

His eyes soften, and I see a glimmer of emotion behind them.

"I love you too, *hercegnőm*," he whispers before shutting down just as quicky.

Chapter 3

Luka

Crashing my Formula 1 car sucks. Catching on fire sucks more. Surgery, where they go in and cut your dead skin out of the burn on your hands, sucks so bad that I don't have enough descriptors to say how fucking bad it sucks. But not remembering the full day of the crash because of a concussion is possibly the most annoying.

The FIA has called to do their post-crash interview, and I don't have jack shit to tell them. It cements the fact that I'm most likely done in the sport. Not that I should be surprised. My friend, Beck, said I'm being dramatic, but what does he know. He's about to take my championship—not that I gave him a run for his money this season.

Fuck.

Everything feels ... wrong and distant.

The sport I've worked my whole life to be in. My friends carrying on with their lives like mine didn't just stop in its tracks. Daisy.

God, *Daisy.* I don't deserve her right now. I haven't deserved her in months, but I'm a selfish prick. She's the only thing keeping me some semblance of sane right now, and even I know I have a short leash on her generosity.

"Dr. Branch is on his way in, said he has an update." She breezes into my room, beelining it to the line of flowers on the windowsill to adjust them and avoiding my gaze. It's a nervous habit, I've noticed. She rearranges the flowers every single day when she doesn't know how to handle me, when I'm being too much of an asshole to deal with.

I can't really blame her.

I just have no clue how to get the fuck out of this endless, shitty cycle of doubt, sorrow, grief, and humiliation. It goes around and around in my head every single day. Taunting me. Telling me how big of a failure I am.

Lord knows why this perfect woman is still with me after everything I've put her through lately.

The heavy weight of my wedding band sits on a chain around my neck. It's something she added when I came out of surgery. Mine had to be cut off when I got to the hospital after my hands had burned to shit in the car. And instead of cursing my name, she went out and got me a new wedding band because she hasn't given up on me.

She should.

I've proven to be the worst kind of husband material, and yet she's still here. Still by my side, every single day, as I damn near cry my way through therapy. Still taking verbal beatings as I lash out at her. And all I want is a fucking drink, but I can't even indulge in that.

Fuck, I've done so much wrong.

"Good morning, Tomics, how are we doing today?" Dr. Branch strolls into my room like it's the best day ever.

I grunt. He's used to it, and it means I have to talk less.

"Well, and you?" Daisy asks in her bubbly tone that I know she's faking. Her smile doesn't reach her eyes like it always does. Well, used to always do.

It hasn't since that day over seven months ago.

But now is not the time to think about that, especially when I can't drown myself in booze to numb it all.

"Great, thank you. I wanted to stop in and give you the good news myself. We're letting you out of this joint." He smiles and holds his hands out like he's just performed a magic trick. Never mind that I've been here almost a month. Never mind that my healing still has months if not years to go. But sure, going home sounds great. I almost roll my eyes.

"That's wonderful news," Daisy says genuinely. Her shoulders drop a couple of inches, and I can see the relief on her face.

"You should be good to continue with wound care. I know the nurses have been observing you for the last week or so," he says to Daisy.

She nods, making me hate how they just talk around me. Like I'm not here, not able to hear them or join in the conversation.

But that's my fault too. It's not like my face or grunts have displayed anything other than a big "fuck off" sign to everyone. Feeling helpless has reduced me to a man who can't articulate anything, apparently.

"Yeah, I feel comfortable with it." She sits in the chair she's lived in since they started letting her stay for longer stints as my level of care gradually decreased.

"Great. They're working on the paperwork currently. We've listed appointments that you will need to schedule for physical therapy and the plastic surgeon. And from there…" He looks over at me. "It's about regaining strength and making your hands as functional as possible. You are officially out of the burns ward." He smiles like we should celebrate, but all I hear is more work and more surgery.

"That sounds great. Thank you so much for everything. Your entire team has been the absolute best." Daisy stands up quickly, holding her hand out to shake, but he draws her into a hug instead.

"Call me if you ever need anything. Questions, concerns… We're always here to help, even if you are no longer in our care." He grins down at her, and I get a hit of jealousy straight to my chest.

Which doesn't make sense. He's in his fifties, and married if the ring is anything to go by, and Daisy would never think about anyone else like that. She's too pure. But it doesn't stop my heart from racing and a red haze from blurring the edge of my vision.

I wait for them to separate and watch him leave before I turn to my wife.

"You want to just go home with him instead?" I growl.

"Are you kidding me with this shit, Luka?" She rolls her eyes as she starts gathering random stuff around the room.

"You seemed *chummy*, that's all." I shrug, annoyed with myself more than anything. The fact that I couldn't just shut my fucking mouth, instead accusing her of things I know she wouldn't do, just goes to show what a fuck-up I am. The minute we get home, I need that drink.

"I'm not even dignifying that with a response." She shoves everything into a bag, zipping it up as the nurse walks in with my discharge paperwork.

The process is pretty quick, considering I've been here almost a month. Just like that, they kick you out and say, *Good luck with your fucked-up hands.*

I'm silent during the entire process—as they wheel me out, and as I climb into the car that Daisy's pulled around to the entrance.

Once she's shut my door and walked around to the other side, closing hers as well, I finally take a full breath.

"You're a dick some days." Her voice is soft, but it doesn't lessen the bite of her words.

"I know." And I do. The problem is I'm not sure how the fuck to stop being one. How to get out of this funk, this ... this ... depression. I actually don't want to stop and think about any of it. Numbing the pain sounds much safer.

I pound my head against the headrest a couple of times in frustration. I've never been good with emotions, and it only seems to have gotten worse over the last month if that's possible.

"Please just let me get us home, then we can do whatever you want. Talk about whatever you want. But I just want to go home." Her words trail off to a whisper, and for the first time in ... I have no clue how long ... I really look at her. The heavy, dark bags under her eyes.

The gauntness in her face is almost alarming. Has she not been eating? Why haven't I noticed?

I nod in agreement before turning my focus to the blurring skyline of Austin. It was lucky I crashed in my home away from home, I suppose. It was Daisy's home base when we got married, and we had just started alternating where we stayed when I wasn't racing.

Walking into our house is foreign. Like this isn't my home anymore, and yet nothing has changed.

"I ordered food. Should be here soon," Daisy clips as she heads to the bedroom to drop off our bags.

Sighing, I walk to the couch, dropping down, careful to keep my hands clear of touching anything. They may be healing well, but they're still so fucking sensitive, and hitting anything hard will drop me to my knees.

Daisy joins me moments later, sitting on the far edge of the couch, away from me.

"What now?" I ask dumbly.

"Now, we relax in our own home for the first time in a month."

"Daisy—"

"Honestly, I don't want to talk about any of it. I'm exhausted, hungry, and in desperate need of a shower." Her head tips back against the edge of the couch.

"Okay," I whisper. There's so much to say, so much to talk about, but I can't lie—her giving me the out is an easy take. If I can avoid talking about it for as long as possible, I will. I know I can't hide from all this shit forever, but maybe for another week? Or longer if I can swing it.

Doubtful, but I'll stick to my delusions for now.

I mirror her, closing my eyes and trying to clear my head of everything.

The next thing I know, she's touching my shoulder to wake me up.

"Food's here," she says softly.

Jerking up, I see goulash from my favorite restaurant. Instant comfort flows through me.

"You're too good to me," I murmur as she helps set me up. It'll take me forever, but I've been practicing holding utensils for the last couple of weeks. It'll hurt like a bitch, but I refuse to have anyone else feed me anymore.

A folding tray gets put over my lap. A spoon is added, and the cup of soup is placed on top. Her hand hovers, hesitating, before she cups my cheek. My eyes close, and I lean into her touch. It's something I feared I wouldn't get again. I *shouldn't* get her comfort again, not with how I've dealt with everything.

"We'll be okay," she whispers.

"How can you be so sure?"

"I just ... do. We got married for a reason; we just have to find it again." She sniffles.

I think I'll always remember this day as the day my heart completely shattered, the organ I didn't think could have so much feeling suddenly crumbling in my chest at my wife's words. I've done so much wrong and very little right in the past seven months. I'm not even sure *how* to change things, but I know I need to.

I can't lose her.

Clearing her throat, she abruptly stands and moves to the coffee table to pull out the rest of the food.

To my horror, tears fill my eyes. *What if I can't fix this?* It's a question that's on repeat as we eat, nothing but the television droning on in the background.

Once she's done, she gets up and goes to take a shower. I half-ass cleaning up before clumsily reaching toward the top shelf over the fridge. My hand painfully catches on the bottle, jolting pain through my body as I grab it. But it doesn't matter. I just need a couple of drinks to dull the pain.

It takes me longer than I want to take the top off. I resort to using my teeth, but once I do, I take one long swig of the tequila we got at the Mexican Grand Prix this year. One becomes two. Two become five before I'm finally feeling numb enough.

The overwhelming feelings are finally quiet.

I go to bed that night alone. It's what I deserve, and Daisy deserves a break from it all, but it doesn't hurt any less knowing that.

Chapter 4

Luka

The soft sounds of the British announcers reporting who has overtaken whom and which driver is in the lead pound in my head like an ice pick. The tequila I finished off before the race has run through my system, not doing its job of helping me ignore the pain in my chest as I watch this.

"Beck Davis is having the drive of his life!" The words are as clear as day as I look to the ceiling and exhale slowly.

That should be me. I should be defending my title. I should be *winning*. Instead, I'm sitting on my couch in Austin, a glutton for punishment, watching the last race of the season.

I should have made an effort to be there in person, to support my team and my friends, but I can't peel myself off the couch for longer than it takes to shower and eat. And sneak drinks when Daisy isn't micromanaging me.

"Just shut it off, Luka." Daisy's soft voice sounds from behind me.

"No."

Her sigh is a thousand unspoken words of disappointment. I can see her out of the corner of my eye, with so much sadness on her face.

"You're torturing yourself."

"Yep," I clip. It's my self-induced penance for failing so miserably at everything in my life lately.

She throws her hands up in exasperation and heads to the kitchen. It's for the best. It's not like I'm good company right now, and she'll only try to talk me off the proverbial ledge as I watch my championship title slip away lap by lap.

"...Alejandro Suarez will not give up the lead easily..." The broadcaster continues his rant, but I tune it out. My skin feels too tight for my body, my heart is pounding, and my breathing is shallow.

I should be there.

I should have won this season.

I should be fighting with Beck for the win.

I should. I should. I should.

I *should* be so many things, but I'm none of them.

Failure.

Disappointment.

Terrible friend and husband.

Useless.

Probably a drunk.

My self-doubt has never been higher, and there is no light at the end of the tunnel.

Lifting my deformed hand in front of my face, I look at the damaged skin. The pits where the fire burned the muscle away. The strange texture of the skin graft that's still healing. Luckily, I kept all my digits, but my hands look no less ruined because of it. Ugly scars that will never go away. Nerve damage that will never heal. This is my new reality, and it's one I don't want to face. I don't want to accept the fact that I have nothing going for me anymore. I don't want to face the fact that my racing career is over.

So I just ... don't. I avoid it all instead.

"...Beck Davis passes Alejandro Suarez on Turn Five! Could this be it?" The voice is getting louder and louder with excitement.

Dropping my hands to my lap, I tune back into the last handful of laps. I watch as Beckett finds an inner strength I don't have, as he increases the gap between him and Alejandro. I watch the camera pan to Sydney, with tears rolling down her cheeks as he turns onto the final straight.

Daisy looked like that last season. Her heart so pure and happy for a stupid race that now means nothing.

I think that's the last time I remember her being that happy.

Now, my career racing fast cars means jack shit, forever tainted by a stupid crash that never should have happened.

"Oh my God, he's going to do it," she murmurs from the kitchen.

I peek over at her to see her hands covering her mouth with that same happiness she had for me last year. I keep watching her face as he crosses the finish line. As they play his team radio transmission, tears are audible in his voice and Sydney's. Daisy swipes at her eyes, radiating pride and delight.

Can I even remember a time those emotions were directed at me? It'd be just under a year ago, when I won the Driver's Championship, I think. Before things went to shit almost eight months ago.

Picking up the remote, I shut the television off, dropping it to my side.

"Are you kidding me right now? You torture yourself the entire race and then shut it off when your best friend wins? Can't even feel an ounce of happiness for him?" Daisy says accusingly.

She's right. I shut it off to be a dick, to prevent her from watching what could have been and remembering that I'm no longer a good partner. I don't even have a job right now, and I'm sneaking in a drink every chance I get.

Degenerate party of one.

"I didn't want to watch it anymore."

She walks into the living room, standing in from of me, not saying anything. "What?" I ask.

"I know you're struggling. I know you have so much built-up frustration inside of you right now, but taking it out on me is not going to help matters. I can only be a punching bag for so long, Luka." Her voice strains as she attempts to hold back the tears.

She angrily swipes at her cheeks like the tears that she couldn't hold back have personally wronged her.

When, really, it's me that's done nothing to support her.

"Daisy..."

"Nope. I need" —her eyes shift between mine, and I see the moment her decision takes root— "time. I need time, Luka. I need a break and space because I think I'll break if I keep this up."

She closes her eyes, so much pain in them, and she attempts to hide it all for me. It's like a gut punch.

"Stay, *hercegnőm*." The Hungarian endearment slips out as the blood drains from my face. All I feel is panic at the prospect of losing my wife. "I promise I'll work on things." Even I can hear the lack of conviction in my voice. I want to work on things, but I'm not even sure where to start.

"I'll be back and ... around. But I need a break. I'm at my limit, Luka." She walks to our bedroom, shoulders shaking as she cries, and I do nothing but sit here. Wondering if I can have a new bottle of anything one hundred proof delivered as soon as she leaves.

The easy out she gave me when we first came home from the hospital turned into over a month of silence. A month of not talking about anything real. All surface-level conversations with zero solutions as to how to move forward.

And it's all my doing. I let things get brushed under the rug because it was the easy option. I let us drift even further away from each other because putting in the work felt too hard. It's easier to numb it all and act like nothing's wrong. Like we can go back to our life as if nothing at all happened this last year.

I'm paying the price for that now. As I watch her pull down a bag and put it on the bed, throwing in clothes, I realize I'm on the verge of losing everything.

Driving feels like it's already gone. My future job is in limbo.

But I've always had Daisy.

Watching her pack an overnight bag drives a stake into my heart with the realization. She's leaving me. Maybe not permanently, but it sure as hell feels like it. A switch in my brain seems to click.

I'm losing Daisy.

Fuck racing, fuck my job, and fuck everything else.

I can't lose her. She's the only thing worth a damn in my life.

Panic hits me full force. Nausea isn't far behind, forcing me to swallow down my unease.

Things need to change. I need to change. But I'm so fucking scared. I don't know how to be anything other than Luka Tomic, Formula 1 hotshot.

Who am I without that?

A drunk who does nothing but sit around all day and pout? A deformed husband?

How can I be a good partner to Daisy if I can't answer that?

She rushes out of the bedroom, with her head down.

"Daisy—"

Her head jolts up, devastation in her eyes.

"I just need time," she whispers.

"I know," I concede, reaching out before my bandaged, mangled hands stop me in my tracks. "I know, and I want to give you that. But, Dais... I promise I'll work on it." It's the best I can give her right now, even if it feels inadequate. Even if it feels impossible.

Her sad smile lets me know she doesn't believe me, but that's expected. I haven't shown her any reason to believe me for a long while. Hell, I don't believe me, not really. It doesn't change the fact that I *need* to work on it, though.

With a newfound need for change, I watch the love of my life walk out of the door, with no return on the table.

Running to the bathroom, I puke up all the tequila I've drank today. My stomach contracts painfully from the lack of anything substantial, and I fall to my knees in shame and pain.

As I sit on our bathroom floor like a college frat guy who can't handle his liquor, I reflect on what I need to do.

This is a wakeup call if ever there was one.

It's time to stop wallowing and put in the work. Living life like I have been isn't worth living at all, and Daisy deserves a husband who is willing to fight tooth and nail to keep her. To show her she is the most important thing to me and nothing will change that.

A headache pulses behind my eyes. If I wasn't already seated, the intense pain would bring me to my knees. Falling onto my side on the bathmat, I curl up in a ball and let one tear fall down the side of my face.

This isn't how I thought my life would be.

This isn't how I *want* it to be.

I know this won't be an easy process. God knows I'm in for the fight of my life, but I have to do it.

I have to get healthy and win back Daisy. I can't live with myself otherwise.

Chapter 5
Daisy

Something in me snaps.

The minute he clicks the television off in a tantrum, I snap. The eggshells I've been walking on for long before his accident finally catch up to me.

As I walk out of our front door, I shoot off a text to my boss and best friend.

Me:

Can I crash at your place for a little while?

Sydney:

Of course. House is yours as long as you need it.

God love her because she doesn't ask any questions.

Me:

Thank you. I owe you!

Sydney:

Never. You know that.

Throwing my bag into my car, I climb in and pull out, heading the fifteen minutes to Sydney and Beck's house. Being her assistant and having keys to her house comes with perks, apparently. Once I get situated in their guest bedroom, I plop down onto the bed and pull up my oldest sister, Heather's, number.

The FaceTime connects instantly, and whatever she sees on my face gives away how dire the situation is.

"Shit, hold on. Let me get everyone."

Within seconds, my two younger sisters' faces grace my tiny phone screen. Our matching wild blonde curls cover most of my screen.

"Are you okay?" Ruby asks, her brows furrowed in concern.

"Of course she isn't okay!" Autumn, the youngest, scolds.

"I'm right here." I roll my eyes.

"That doesn't actually answer the question." Heather winces.

I give her tiny face in the left corner a "shut the fuck up" look.

"Did you watch Beck win?" Ruby asks, and for whatever reason, that's the thing that causes tears to fill my eyes.

"Fuck," Autumn whispers.

"I watched it, and then Luka shut off the TV and I didn't get to see the celebrations or Sydney and Beckett be all adorable and in love," I wail as the tears fall.

"It's okay, Dais," Ruby says in a panic. She hates crying. Or any outward emotions, for that matter.

"It's not okay." I prop my phone up on a pillow and throw my hands up. "I've been walking on eggshells since the accident, and he's just acting like things are normal. Like him acting like an ass all the time is completely fine. I don't know how to help him." I sob.

What I don't mention is the empty alcohol bottles I've been finding in the trash. I'm not sure why I keep that information to myself, but divulging it would feel like an admission of failure. Like I couldn't help him, like I wasn't enough, so he turned to drinking to ignore his life completely. To ignore *us* completely.

"Do we need to come out there?" Heather asks.

"No." I sniffle.

"Dais…" Heather pushes.

"I'm at Sydney's house. I left." I barely get the words out through my gasping sobs.

"Oh shit," Autumn says, her eyes comically wide.

"You left for good?" Heather questions. Ever the mother of us girls and our brother, Adam, she tries to get to the heart of the issue so she can find a solution. The problem is I don't think there is a solution right now. The ball is in Luka's court, and only he can turn things around. Should I have confronted him about the drinking? I honestly have no clue. It could have made it worse or been the thing he needs to take back control; who's to say.

All I do know is that I needed to get out of that house.

"Not for good. I don't think," I whisper. "I honestly don't know."

"Okay, we can work with that," Heather says, and I just know she's pulling out a notebook right now.

"Is this only about his accident?" Ruby asks.

"I mean, he did burn the shit out of his hands, Rube. Of course that's a huge factor." Autumn rolls her eyes.

"Can you two just not right now?" Heather interrupts.

"What? It's an honest question!" Ruby exclaims.

"I shouldn't have called you," I murmur, annoyed that they are already arguing.

"Bullshit. You absolutely should have called me," Heather says. "So, are you just staying for the night or longer? What's the plan?" She stares a hole through her camera lens.

"There is no fucking plan!" I throw my hand up in frustration. "Something just snapped in me, and I walked out because I can't handle being in that house right now. He's so angry at everything. I don't know how to help him."

Marriage isn't supposed to be like this. We're supposed to work through things together, be strong together, and he won't let me. I don't know how to have patience when he doesn't seem to give a shit about his future. When he is apparently fine drinking his life away.

Well, I'm not okay with that. Not anymore.

"I'm sorry," Heather mutters.

I sigh, wiping my tears. "It's not your fault. I just don't know what I'm supposed to do. How can I help him heal and process the accident when he barely looks at me? When he shuts down every single time I try to talk to him about it? I can't force someone to move forward."

The hard truth sits deep in my chest. *I can't force Luka to move past the accident. I can't force him to stop drinking.*

"What can we do?" Autumn asks.

"Talking helped." I smile sadly at her. "I think I'm going to go take a bath and sleep. Maybe that'll help give me some clarity in the morning. Thank you, guys."

"Call us if you need anything. One of us can be on the next flight," Heather says as Ruby and Autumn nod. They're only five hours away, but it's nice having an airport there to cut down on the commute if we really want to see each other.

"I will. Love you."

"Love you too," echoes from each of them before I hang up.

As I shuffle to the ensuite, my thoughts are running a million miles per hour. Tossing a bath bomb into the oversized tub releases a soothing lavender scent. I dip my toe into the steaming water and then melt in up to my chin. The hot water and bath bomb mixture release a little of the tension I've been holding onto.

The question now becomes how I can help Luka. It's not just the accident either. We were having problems long before that. This whole season has felt ... off, and there is only one reason for that and his actions after. Both of our actions, really. I'm not innocent in this either, and I need to take some responsibility.

A chemical pregnancy in February changed the course of our marriage. A fluke I shouldn't have even known about, not really. I was feeling off, and I was checking things off the list of potential causes. A pregnancy test was logical to rule it out.

Then it popped up positive. I remember feeling shocked. Unsure. Scared. This wasn't what we had planned. Hell, we didn't really have plans. Luka and I lived life as it came. Until that positive test.

Luka's reaction was not what I had expected. He paled, stumbled out of the bathroom, and then refused to talk about it. I went to the doctor alone to confirm things, and that's when I learned about chemical pregnancies.

Before it really even set in, it was over. I barely knew about it—I wasn't even five weeks—but it didn't change the grieving. Hell, did I even really grieve?

I'm still not sure how I feel about it all. If I even want kids, if I want to try again. I felt like I didn't have time to process it all because the Formula 1 season started and Luka was having a terrible season, so that's where my focus landed. *Shit, is that why he started drinking then?* I realize I don't know when the drinking started, but it would make sense, considering his performance this year.

Not to mention, Sydney getting a Formula 1 team courtesy of our big boss-man, Pierce Vanstone. In the span of a couple of months, my job changed, my husband changed, *I changed*, and nothing felt safe anymore.

I shoved down any feelings I had for something that never was and focused on other people's problems.

In hindsight, it was probably the wrong approach—never dealing with how *I* felt about the pregnancy, just acting like nothing happened.

I've accused Luka of burying all his feelings and letting it all pile up when I'm just as guilty. That's just hypocritical and makes me equally as fucked up.

How can I help him heal, get through this devastating crash, when I'm also not in a good headspace? When I can't even pull myself out of this funk that's overshadowed anything good this year?

Closing my eyes, I slide down until I'm completely submerged.

Clarity. I need that ever-elusive clarity.

The biggest question is where do I go from here? What do *I* want in my life? And does that include Luka?

The lack of oxygen helps me focus. Opening my eyes under the water, I try to imagine life without Luka, and every version I see is awful. It's lonely and boring and *hard*.

Surging up from the water, I gasp for air.

My mind is pinging with a hundred thoughts, but the biggest of all is that I want to be with Luka. I *need* to be with him. We may have rushed into dating, into marriage too, but I firmly believe he's my soulmate.

Being with him means we both have a lot of work to do. I need to work on healing myself before I can help him. I can't be his support system if my foundation is cracked.

I soak for a few more minutes as the exhaustion sets into my bones.

By the time I'm dry, and dressed in one of Luka's Empress T-shirts and a pair of boy shorts, my eyes are barely staying open.

The last thing I do before sleep finally takes over is pick up my phone and send a message.

Me:

I'm sorry for walking out. I want to work on things. Not just us, but me. I know I've contributed to all the problems this year, and I'm sorry for that. I love you so damn much, Luka. Please meet me halfway and help me fix us.

Chapter 6

Luka

I reread the text Daisy sent over and over again.

She isn't asking for anything that I haven't already come to terms with, but *how* to meet her halfway is the hard part.

How do I take that step into the darkest, deepest cave, with no guarantee I come out the other side intact? With no assurance that I get to keep Daisy when this is all said and done? It's all too overwhelming. I know for a fact that it's going to take time. Whatever I need to do to get her to believe I'm ready to change, to work *with* her instead of against her, isn't going to be an overnight fix, but I have to try.

Tomorrow, I can start putting together a game plan. Tonight, I'll wallow in self-pity for a little bit longer. The whisky bottle sitting next to me is a testament to that.

***

Three days later, I'm no closer to figuring out how to start fixing things, but I am out of easily opened food. I've ordered a ton of delivery, but the only things I can open without issue are tacos. Everything else has come in those plastic containers that are impossible for me to open. Now, I'm sick of tacos.

That's a problem I didn't see coming. The fact that I have next to no dexterity in my hands right now because of the skin grafts and how tight all the skin is. It's painful as fuck and putting me in an even shittier mood, if that's possible.

Alcohol can be opened with my teeth, luckily, but if I truly want to start making changes, that probably needs to stop sooner rather than later.

It's a hell of a lot harder than I thought it would be, though.

Pacing the length of the living room, I debate my options. This close to Christmas, everything is limited. If I was in Monaco, I'd have friends available to help me, but I'm in Austin, where I have no one except Daisy.

Plopping down onto the couch, I grab my phone and take a quick picture of the empty coffee table. I pull up Daisy's number, attach the picture, then pull up the voice-to-text feature.

"I'm hungry, and I can't open anything currently in the house. And I'm sick of tacos." I hit send before I overthink it.

Do I have my shit figured out? No, absolutely the furthest thing from it, but if this pitiful display of ineptitude is the sword I need to throw myself on, to crack the thick sheet of ice between us, then I'm running with it. It's not that I really need help with food; it's that I want to talk to her, even if it's about something stupid and inconsequential.

Daisy:

> **Sounds like a you problem.**

That brings a smile to my face.

"I was hoping you'd take pity on an injured, hopeless man." *Send.*

Daisy:

> **Best I can do is send a cheesesteak from Hoppy's.**

"I'm sorry." *Send.* "I've been ... a really shitty husband, and you don't deserve the way I've been treating you." *Send.* "I'm not even sure where to start, but I know I need you here to help me." *Send.*

I sound so damn desperate because I am. The last three days have been pure torture without her. I'd call them barely functioning at best.

Holding my breath, I wait for her response. The minutes tick by with no response, and my heart sinks deeper into my gut. My phone buzzes on my thigh, and I fumble to pick it up.

> I need more than words, Luka. I'll go grocery shopping and stock you up with easy to open things, and be by to pick you up for your appointment on Friday, but I'm not ready for more than that.

I stare at the phone for too long. Daisy has never been shy about voicing her opinions and thoughts, but this might be the first time she's ever had to really put me in my place. It's eye-opening.

Pulling up the browser on my phone, I search therapists, and pick the first one who pops up and has immediate openings. Filling out the intake forms takes a few minutes, but within fifteen minutes, I have my first appointment booked in two days.

Daisy needs action, and I need Daisy.

Switching over to our text thread, I let myself be vulnerable with the one person I feel safe doing so.

"I have a therapy appointment on Thursday at 10am if you could take me to that as well." *Send.* "I promise to try, *hercegnőm*. Just give me time." *Send.*

> I will be there at 9:30.

> And thank you … for putting in the effort.

***

Thursday comes too quickly. My deformed hands are sweating, creating a mess of slick skin and aggravated wounds, and making me grumpy as fuck.

Daisy dropped me off as promised, telling me she'd be back in an hour. She'd barely looked at me, only answered direct questions, and didn't initiate conversation at all. Her sterile reaction combined with my insecurity have panic welling in my chest, so I guess it's a good thing the therapist just called me through.

"Good morning, Mr. Tomic. I'm Dr. Mason Tate. What brings you in today?" He's a middle-aged guy in good shape, with a warm and welcoming face.

I instantly feel at ease. Well, as at ease as I can feel right now, I suppose.

Clearing my throat, I decide to go for broke. "I need my wife back."

"And you think I may be able to help with that?" he asks.

"Yes. Well, I hope so. I, umm... I recently had a major accident at my ... job, and I've pushed her away." My mind races as I try to come up with a way to make me sound less like an asshole.

"I'm sorry to hear about your accident Mr. Tomic. It's evident you have been through a lot," he says, glancing and gesturing at my hands. "Why don't we start at the beginning. What do you do for a living?"

"I'm a Formula 1 driver—well, I was." I cough into my mutilated hand.

"And you're not anymore because of your accident?"

"No. Yes. Well, I'm not sure. That's up in the air, currently." It takes me a minute to realize he probably knows what I do for a living and I didn't need to try to hide it from him because it was on my fucking intake form.

"And how do you feel about that?" I roll my eyes at his very scripted therapy response, but he smirks in return. "It seems cliché, but it's really helpful to understand the heart of the issue. We naturally put up barriers, especially with people we just meet, and something as simple as figuring out how we feel about the situation can help us find a way to move through the situation, if that makes sense."

I nod, digesting his words. "I feel ... crushed." I look up at him. "I don't who I am if I can't race."

"It's understandable you feel that way, given your current circumstances." He pauses as though to let me ingest his words. "And what about your wife? You said you're here to get her back. Why do you feel like you've lost her?"

There's one major event I don't want to get into right now—the one I've pushed so far down it's like it didn't even happen. Bringing it up would lead to talking about my drinking, and I'm not so sure I want to face that quite yet. So, instead, I look to more recent events.

"She walked out a few days ago. Staying at her boss and my best friend's house for the time being. She's the type of woman who is there for everyone. Goes above and beyond for everyone except herself, and it was no different with me. When I crashed, I'll admit I was an asshole. I pushed her away and didn't let her in. Didn't talk to her about how I was feeling, about any of it."

"And why do you think that is?"

"Because I feel weak," I whisper. "And inadequate." I hold up my hands as though it's obvious.

"All very valid feelings, considering what you've been through. Is the decision to pursue therapy your own?" he asks.

"It is."

"Well, that's a great first step. Wanting to change or work through things for yourself is usually a more powerful motivator than doing so for others. Now, if you don't mind, I'd like to hear a little about your injuries and how extensive they were, to gauge medically where you're at from a recovery point of view. Burns can cause a lot of hurt beyond the physical, and I think that might be a good starting point for you."

I nod and proceed to tell him how long I was in the hospital for, my future planned surgeries, and how much mobility I'm expected to be able to recover. It's cathartic to just run through the injuries with no pressure to provide anything more. I don't think I've simply told anyone about what exactly I went through. Most people were there, to an extent, so they feel like they know what I went through, but I'm realizing what they witnessed and what I experienced are entirely different animals.

It takes me the rest of our session to recount my crash and subsequent injuries. By the end, the pressure on my chest eases ever so slightly, making me breathe a little easier.

"Thank you for being so open with me. I'd like to get you on the books for once a week and see if we can help you make progress toward your goals."

I nod, looking over at the clock to see our time is already up.

"Thank you for your time." I stand up, head to the door, and attempt to open it but struggle with my lack of dexterity.

Dr. Tate saddles up next to me, turning the door handle and ushering me out. His sympathetic smile doesn't piss me off like it normally would. Instead, I start to see it for what it is—empathy for my situation, not pity.

We schedule my standing appointment as I thank him again before heading outside. Daisy is waiting out front for me, watching me with curiosity as I get in the passenger seat.

"You going to ask me how it went?" I grumble.

"Nope. If you want to talk about it, you'll talk about it. Otherwise, it's between you and your therapist," she says simply.

I'm not sure if I expected her to show more interest or if I'm just disappointed that it's not making more of a dent in the hard outer shell she has now. Either way, her neutrality shows just how far I need to go before she'll open back up to me.

But I'm working on it, and that's the best I can do right now.

Chapter 7
Daisy

Words won't come. Luka walks out of his first therapy appointment with visibly less stress carried on his shoulders.

And it makes me think.

There's a certain part of my head that tells me I'm being too stubborn, too harsh on him. But it's the other part, that knows we both need to work on things, that keeps me distant from him. His slumped shoulders when I didn't ask him about his appointment damn near make me cave, though. With no family and the bulk of his support system on the racetrack, I know he's likely feeling alone.

But I need time to work on me, to figure out how to be assertive with what I want. For us to be on the same page with all the major things in our lives.

One therapy appointment doesn't change everything.

It certainly doesn't stop the drinking, not if he doesn't want to make the change.

It does make me realize I should probably find a therapist too, though. Doing this alone, when I don't really know how to move forward on my own, probably won't give me the progress I'm hoping for. I make a mental note to seek out an appointment as I drive Luka back to our home.

We part ways in the same boat we started the day in. A promise to see him tomorrow for his physical therapy and an awkward wave goodbye add more hurt to the mix, but it's all I have to give right now.

***

The drive to Luca's physical therapy session is filled with tension.

When I pull up to the front of the building, Luka opens the door but pauses, turning back to me. "I should only be an hour today." His voice is soft.

I nod, staring out the windshield, waiting to hear the slam of the door. Instead, I hear Luka.

"I'm going to fix this, Dais. I promise. I don't know how long it's going to take, but I'm going to fix this."

Then the door shuts, and I'm left drowning in too many emotions. Driving over to the parking lot, I park and make an impulsive decision.

Trying to find Luka in the mixture of patients on the physical therapy floor proves harder than it should be, but once I do, I realize this was the right move. He's sitting in a chair, with a grimace on his face that shows every bit of the pain he's in. His physical therapist is manipulating his right hand every which way, and Luka is gritting his teeth through it all.

I wave at the office manager and point to a chair, questioning if I can take it. She nods, so I grab it and set it next to Luka once I reach him.

My hand moves to his, intertwining with his left hand and startling him. He looks over, and pure relief spreads over his face. His hand squeezes mine tight as they continue through his exercises. As they progress through the motions, I realize something with startling clarity.

This is the hardest I've seen Luka work since well before his accident. The effort he's putting in right now is a testament to his will to succeed and perhaps even to change. I didn't expect to see something so obvious so soon. It's even more of a reason for me to see a therapist too. If he's able to make this much progress in a few days, what can we accomplish if we both put this much effort in?

I'm lost in thought when a tap on my shoulder startles me. Looking up, I see Dave, the physical therapist, smirking at me.

"I need to switch hands. And probably don't let him grip you that hard with his right hand. He just did a lot of work, and it's going to hurt like hell if he clenches up that tight." His easygoing smile is low pressure, and I appreciate it.

"I'm right here," Luka mumbles, but there's a twinkle in his eye that hasn't been there in so long. It's distant, but even that little spark gives me hope.

"Yeah, yeah. You don't exactly have the best track record of listening," Dave says.

Chuckling, I move my chair to the other side and hold my hand out to my husband.

Shaking his head subtly, he puts his hand—palm down—on his thigh. *Stubborn mule.* This time, I'm not annoyed, though; I'm more shocked he's listening and attempting to be compliant.

Who the fuck is this therapist of his? A miracle worker, clearly.

These may not be huge changes, but dammit if it doesn't feel like they are.

Luka powers through the rest of his PT, gritting his teeth and working through the pain, and collapses in the car once we get there.

His head lulls to the side. "Thank you for coming in."

"You're welcome."

"You want to grab some lunch?" The hope in his voice has my heart hurting.

"Not today, Luka." I internally cringe, but I know I need to stick to my guns. It's important for both of our futures.

He nods, sadness written over every inch of his face, but there's a determination there as well.

The drive home is quiet. I can tell his hands are hurting him, but I'm not sure how to comfort him without sending the wrong message.

By the time I get back to Sydney's place, my head is a mess of confusion. Sydney calls me just as I'm walking through her front door.

"Hey, how's the celebrating going?" I ask her.

"So fucking good! How are you? Are you okay?"

"I have no clue," I huff out.

"Totally understandable. What can I do?"

"Give me a distraction. Something to work on, maybe? I know there's a ton of shit that needs to happen now that the sale of Empress Racing is finally public." The level of begging to work on anything I'm hitting is a little sad, yet here I am.

"You're supposed to be on break," she lectures.

"There is no break when we need to get the best team together. So, what can I do? I can take a break once the season starts or something." I won't, but whatever gets the job done today.

"I really need a list of contenders to keep an eye out for our new team principal. I don't want to necessarily hire anyone right now, but I need some people in the wings. And see if you can pull Eli or Cruz—or both—from Legacy. I already poached Nina, and Felix is so fucking pissed about it." She actually giggles.

"I thought you two were friends," I deadpan.

"Felix and me? Oh, we totally are. That's why he didn't fight when Nina left. He knew I was the better option for her to grow as something other than his assistant. But I swear Cruz and Eli are the last ones I'm after. They can lead the garage, get us quick pit stop times. They have the kind of analytical brains I want on the team."

"And it doesn't have anything to do with matchmaking Nina and Eli, right?" I chuckle.

"Shit, I forgot about that. Is he still crushing hard? Do you think that's going to be a problem? I mean, they work for the same team now and it hasn't been an issue..."

"Syd. Take a breath."

"Sorry. I feel like there's so much to get done, and with the usual Idaho trip, Beckett made me promise not to work, so I'm attempting to get some ducks in a row before that."

"Consider it already done, Boss Lady."

"You're a lifesaver, Dais. You need anything?" Concern laces her voice.

"Nah, I'm good. I'm going to jump on this and probably organize some of the financials for you, so you have it at your convenience." I walk to the kitchen and snag a notepad off the counter, making a list of everything I want to try to get done.

"Well, you're the best assistant ever. Actually, we need a new title for you because that's a dumb title," she ponders.

"Whatever you say. Call me if you need anything else." I hang up without another word and head to the office to get to work.

Hours pass before I pull my head up long enough to see dark skies. Grabbing my phone, I see it's already 8pm and I've been working far longer than I intended to. I also see way too many missed texts.

Most are in the group chat with my sisters. I won't even pretend I'm going to read them because the last message was about how many pieces of pie Autumn can eat.

There are three from Luka, though.

Luka:

> Thank you again for coming to PT today. It kicked my ass, and I really appreciated the support.

Luka:

> I'm sorry. I know it's not enough right now, but I am, Dais. I'm going to make you believe it.

Luka:

> I love you. Never forget that.

I reply back but have every intention of heading back to Sydney's, taking a hot shower and calling it a day after.

Me:

> I know, and I love you too.

After my shower, the doorbell rings. I wrap myself in my robe and check the peephole. I see a retreating figure, and wait until they are in their car and driving away before I open the door.

Food from my favorite Italian place is sitting on the front steps. My eyes well up with tears, knowing it was Luka's doing.

Damn him.

He's trying, and that's all I've asked for. Now, it's my turn to put in as much effort as he is.

Chapter 8

Beck Davis Marries Sydney Johnson After His Surprising Retirement

The world learned of the couple's nuptials when Davis stepped out of his Monaco apartment, wearing a new piece of hardware. It's said that their close friends were in attendance, including Legacy team principal, Felix Karlsson, Vanstone Properties CEOs, Pierce and Jane Vanstone, and longtime trainer, Nate Murphy, among others.

One couple not in attendance were Luka and Daisy Tomic. It's said he's been released from the hospital and is resting comfortably at home, but no one has seen him in public since the crash. Is there trouble brewing for the golden couple?

We want to send out congratulations to the Davises and wish them a long and happy marriage. Stay tuned to see if Mrs. Davis poaches Mr. Davis for some work at Empress Racing.

Chapter 9
Luka

Fucking F1 pundits are as bad as the gossip columns and need to mind their own business. I throw my phone onto the couch, annoyed I even looked at the article.

I watch Daisy stock up the kitchen with groceries and pray she doesn't open the cabinet above the fridge. I should have moved the bottles, but I didn't think about it. It's been a couple of weeks of the same: therapy, physical therapy, and Daisy avoiding any real connection. Not that I blame her. We didn't even spend Christmas together; she went off to be with her family, and I stayed here … alone. I've been trying to slow down on the drinking, but my crutch to it seems stronger than I realized.

My anger gets the better of me after seeing the article.

"You tell Sydney we couldn't make it to the wedding?" My voice is low and irritated.

"Why yes, thanks for asking. Who would want us there to ruin a beautiful day for our best friends," she says sweetly as she pours coffee. We may have recently had a few bright moments in the darkness that is our marriage right now, but we are still a long way off from being what anyone would consider good.

"We wouldn't have ruined it," I grumble, knowing full well I would be the one to ruin it, just like I'm ruining everything else. Hell, I probably couldn't have hidden my drinking, and everything would have gone to complete shit.

"Sure, the 'I hate everything' look on your face would have filled them with love and support." She rolls her eyes with that hint of mischievousness.

The corner of my lip tips up in a smirk. Even now, after so long of being an utter asshole, she puts me in my place like she knows it's just a waiting game.

One day, she'll make me laugh and she'll think it's all worth it. But she deserves more than this, a better husband than me. I'm trying so hard to be one. I'm just not good enough yet. Progress is too slow for my liking.

"You could have at least asked me before making the unilateral decision."

The sound of her coffee mug hitting the counter hard draws my attention.

"And tell me, how that would have gone? Should we role play that?" She arches her eyebrow, anger written all over her face.

"I just would have liked to be included in that decision. I didn't even know they were getting married," I sulk.

Her sigh reaches my ear before she walks over and sits next to me.

"I think we need to talk—really talk. This, what we're doing, isn't solving any problems. And I am sorry I didn't tell you about Beck and Sydney; that was a dick move from me."

The earnestness in her eyes catches me off guard. I decide right now to stop holding on so tightly to my anger. It's something my therapist has talked about with me, but it didn't really hit me how tightly I cling to it until right now.

"I probably wouldn't have told me either. Did you send them something?" I ask.

"I did and then got promptly yelled at by Sydney." She smirks.

"Good. That's good," I mumble.

"They're worried about you. Beck said he hasn't heard from you in a few weeks."

I reach over to grab her hand but quickly pull it back. How easy is it to forget how fucked up my hands are? It should be impossible to forget how mutilated they are. My jaw tenses with regret that I can't even comfort my own wife properly.

To my surprise and disgust, Daisy reaches over and gently holds my hand.

"Dais, please don't..." My breathing is getting shallow, and I feel the panic rising up in me.

"Does it hurt?" she asks with caution.

"No, but it's so ... bad." The lack of a better word shows how conflicted my head is. It's obvious I haven't come to terms with any of this, even with therapy.

"It's not. It's our new normal, and it's something we—*you*—need to get comfortable with. I know you have more surgeries ahead to correct some of it, but you haven't even let me touch you since the accident, except to change your bandages. Even mostly healed." Hurt coats her voice, and my heart pounds harder.

"How?" My voice cracks.

"Time. Talking. Therapy will probably help with that. I don't know, but I also know I can't help you if you just shut me out. It's almost worse than you being a jerk." Her half-attempt at a joke falls flat.

I heave in a deep breath, taking a leap of uncomfortable faith and maybe, just maybe, a first step to the land of the living.

"I'm so fucking angry all the time," I say, barely louder than a whisper.

"I know."

"I wake up, and I'm so mad that I'm not racing, training, doing interviews—anything."

She nods but doesn't say anything.

"And then here, I'm scared to do anything too invasive with my hands and busting open the skin or something. I don't even know if that can happen because I've been so scared to do anything, but it freaks me the fuck out." All the air leaves my chest as I voice my simple truths.

"I understand that. I can help with that," she offers.

"I've been annoying the physical therapists lately," I add.

"I know. I've been getting strongly worded emails about them on the verge of quitting or pawning you off to someone else."

"Shit." I haven't looked at her this entire conversation, afraid of her judgment and disappointment.

"Yeah. We should probably work on that one first. You need physical therapy to make sure you keep mobility in your hands. The last time I went, you were doing well." Daisy is so business-like that the pull to look at her is just too strong.

Pure sadness. That's all I see on her face. It's a knife to my already tender chest.

"I'll really put in effort from now on," I murmur. The last time she came was the last time I really felt the need to push. To show her I was doing it. Then, I just fell back into old habits of resisting the progress, as exhibited by the stacked bottles in the cabinet she knows nothing about. No one said this shit would be easy or quick, I guess. One step forward, five steps back.

"I'm going to keep you to that." She holds my gaze.

A beat passes, then two, before I get the courage to ask a question I've held onto for so long.

"Are we going to be okay, *hercegnőm*?" My hand gently squeezes hers as a lifeline.

Tears fill her eyes, and her chin wobbles. "I really hope so."

Testing the strength in my hand, I pull her to me and wrap my mangled hand around her shoulders as they shake with her cries.

"I'm so sorry, Dais," I whisper into her hair. "I'll work so damn hard to do better. You should have better."

We hold each other for hours, the closest we've been in months. The closeness is something I desperately needed.

Even though I'm scared shitless, even though I know there's so much work to do and the least of it involves my hands, I think I finally believe that I'm redeemable after all that I've put her through. With time, I can win Daisy back. I can prove to her that she married the right man. The amount of work I have already done in therapy feels trivial, like there is so much more to work on, but I have to. I can't lose her.

Life won't be worth living without Daisy. I'd rather drink myself to death.

Chapter 10
Daisy

The shift is immediate. The air around us is less stifling, easier to breathe. I'm still leaking tears like it's a full-time job, but for the first time in almost a year, I understand more of how Luka feels.

I've been flying blind for so long that I forgot it wasn't how things *should* be.

Him simply telling me he's angry is more progress than we've had in the three months since the accident.

"I'm sad," I say through my tears. "So damn sad all the time."

"I know, and I'm so sorry for being the cause of most of that," he whispers into the crown of my head.

"How do we move forward?" I sob, barely able to get the words out.

"I keep going to therapy. Work through … hopefully everything, and keep trying. I'll put in the work, Dais. I'm trying to put in the work," he adds. "You want to see a couples' therapist? Sign me up. I'll do anything, *hercegnőm*."

"I started seeing a therapist last week," I whisper.

"Yeah?" No judgment, no inflection, just genuine curiosity in his voice.

"Yeah. It was really hard," I hiccup through a laugh.

"It fucking sucks, right?" He chuckles, squeezing me tighter.

"It really does." Taking a deep breath, I sit back up. "Thank you. For talking. For listening. For being more open."

"I know I'm not good at it, but I'm always here for you. If I'm being an asshole, call me on it please. I feel like for every big step forward, I end up taking ten steps back when things get uncomfortable again. I need you to help pull me out of that. And I know that's not fair to ask, but I need you."

The earnestness in his eyes pulls more tears to the surface.

"Will this ever not be hard? Are we destined to just … struggle?" I ask.

"I … don't know. I can't promise you one way or the other, but I will fight like hell for you, for us, every single day. Even if I'm not good at it some days—most days—know that I'm still fighting for us, okay?"

"I want to fight too, but I'm so damn tired." My voice cracks. "Everything is so hard. And now, I've got to jump into Empress Racing shit and that's going to be time consuming, and I'm scared that means I put us on the backburner," I ramble.

"Hey," he says softly, drawing my attention back to him. "There will be good days and probably a lot of bad days, but I won't ever leave your side. I'll be here when you need to cry, when you want to yell at me—all of it, okay?"

I talked a lot with my new therapist about when I would feel comfortable moving back in, if I ever did. And this conversation, this honesty, is exactly what I need. I'll hold off, though. I need to make sure this isn't a one-off. I don't think it is, but I need to work on things as much as he does. I need to know he's stopped drinking too, but that seems to be something we aren't talking about. I'm just as chicken-shit as he is about it because it's just another black hole to dive into, and I'm not ready for more hurt right now. Proving that we are both putting in the work isn't going to happen overnight. I need to remember that.

"Okay," I say, swiping at the tears on my face.

"I have an idea." He sits up straight.

"What?"

"I want to take you on a date."

"A date?" I'm confused. We're married.

"We've sort of lost the fun in … all the things, so what if we go back to basics?"

"You want to date me?" I repeat, dumbfounded.

"Yes." He smiles that blinding, cocky smile of his I haven't seen in too long.

Date. My husband. I don't see a negative to it. From where I'm sitting, maybe this will help us move forward instead of rehashing the past. I mean, I know we need to address that at some point, but up until now, we've barely been able to be in the same room together. Maybe this will give us the opportunity to lessen the pressure of … everything in our lives.

Take a step back in order to revive our marriage.

"Okay," I say cautiously.

"Yeah?" The excitement in his voice and on his face is the most I've seen from him in over a year. I just want to bottle it up.

"Yeah. Let's date."

"How does Friday sound?"

Four days. It gives me four days to prepare myself for what this looks like. Prepare myself to hold true to what I want out of our relationship. Yep, totally easy.

"Friday sounds great. I need to get back to Sydney's, so I can get some work done," I mutter, already wanting to stay longer than I should.

"Of course," he says as he lifts his hand up toward my face before jolting it back down. The sharp mental pain on his face, because of his hands, nearly brings me to tears again.

As much as we both want to say "fuck it" and move forward, we know we can't. Our marriage won't survive, and that is something I won't let happen. Strengthening our base is more important than ever.

"I'll talk to you later, okay? Call me if you need anything."

He nods, but the sadness is back on his face.

"I love you, Daisy," he says softly.

"I love you too," I whisper before turning and walking out the front door of our house.

***

I haven't been back to the Vanstone offices in a long while, but I needed to get away from it all. Being at Sydney's place is great, but it's not my house and I'm not ready to be at my house yet, so here I've landed. Being in limbo in every sense of the word.

"Well, hello stranger," a deep voice calls from the doorway of Sydney's old office.

"Hello yourself," I say to the owner, Pierce Vanstone himself.

"Not that I'm not glad to see you, but what are you doing here?"

I laugh at his words. "I am here in an attempt to get work done without distractions," I say before turning back to the job listing I'm proofreading.

"How is everything?" he asks, changing his tone to one of sympathy, and by everything, he means Luka.

"Everything is in progress. I wouldn't say great, but it's not awful either."

"Good. That's good. You know we're here for you if you need anything," he says with a nod.

"Thanks, I'm already crashing at Sydney's, so I should be fine. How was the wedding?" I ask before I realize my words.

"You moved out?"

"Uh, just temporarily. It's fine, honestly. For the best, really." I don't think I sound believable at all, but what can I say? Luka and I hit our limits and needed to physically take a break from each other while we figure out all the hard shit? That I don't know if we'll ever get back to what we were? No, he may be a good guy, but I'm not drama dumping on my boss's boss.

"If you're sure. And the wedding was wonderful. I'm really sad you missed it, but I'm sure Sydney will have a million pictures to show you when they get back."

"No doubt about that." I chuckle.

"How's the team going? Any major snags?" he asks.

"So far, just what we expected. I'm working on a couple of job listings to try to poach some people from Legacy, but we'll see if that happens. Otherwise, outside of watching the team principal and most likely having someone ready in the wings, things have been pretty smooth so far," I spout off the major things we've been doing.

"That's good to hear. And you'll keep an eye on Sydney? I know Beckett is going to be extra protective, but you know the job and how she works. She still needs to take it slow."

Sydney was diagnosed with rheumatoid arthritis not that long ago so, as a group, we're trying to rein in her inability to slow down.

"I am. I'm sure I'll get lectured multiple times when I steal some shit off her plate to take care of." I smirk.

"Good. You two are a great team. Well, I won't distract you anymore, but it was good to see you. Don't be a stranger, even if it's to have a quiet place to work."

"It was good to see you too! Tell Jane I said hi," I sneak in. We may not be the best of friends, but his wife and her best friends are somewhat legendary in these parts, and Sydney introduced me a few years back. One day, I'll grow a pair and take her up on the invitation for brunch, but that day is not today.

I turn back to my work as Pierce leaves, looking into personnel and making sure we aren't missing any key players. I also spend an obscene amount of time looking into potential jobs for Luka. Places where he could fit without being resentful that it isn't driving. Sydney has said from day one that he could come to Empress, but I'm not sure that's a good plan right now.

I don't find anything immediately, but I tuck it into my back pocket to keep an eye out for anything that looks up his alley. Or, who knows, maybe he will want nothing to do with Formula 1. It would be problematic since that is now my full-time job, but I could deal with it ... hopefully.

For now, it's time to turn my attention to this date. What do I wear? Where are we going? Do we kiss?

God, it truly feels like a first date all over again.

I kind of love it.

Chapter 11

Luka

When I came up with this date idea, I didn't anticipate the fact that I can't drive yet, which means I can't pick up Daisy like she deserves. My insecurity heightens ten-fold as I wait for her, the ever-present worthlessness in the background rushing back to the surface. It's something I've been working on in therapy, but clearly, I still have a long way to go.

As I pace the living room, I try an exercise my therapist gave me for when I start to get overwhelmed: breathing in to the count of ten, then exhaling to the same. I repeat that a couple of times until I feel my heart rate settle down. I look at the cabinet with the bottles I'm trying desperately not to rely on and debate a little pregame to help get me through. But then I hear my thoughts and realize how horrible that is, and decide against it.

One of the hardest things for me to come to terms with, outside of the injury to my hands, is just how out of condition my body is and how little control I have over it. I'm used to being in peak shape, my body doing exactly what I needed it to and always being strong. Now? It's weak, it doesn't respond when I need it to do something, and it freaks out at the slightest inconvenience. I'm sluggish, thanks to the alcohol, but it's hard to just shift everything. It's a complete one-eighty, and figuring out how to deal with it is akin to torture. I don't think puberty treated me as unkindly as my body does now.

A knock at the door gives me mixed feelings. That she even feels like she needs to knock pisses me off, but excitement for our date soon overrides my anger.

This is step one in winning her back. To show her I'm not totally broken, not a complete asshole.

Baby steps.

"Hi," I say softly as I open the front door, relieved that my hands have managed to do so. Over the last couple of weeks, the mobility in them has really progressed.

"Hi." Her small smile is a balm to my soul that I hadn't realized I needed. Her wild blonde curls are piled on the top of her head. The dark-green, loose-fitting dress she wears just emphasize how damn gorgeous she is. Although she's not tall, her legs look long as hell in the heels she's wearing.

My mind flashes to the not-so-distant past when I would have had those heels by my ears, balls deep inside of her, showing her exactly what I can do for her. My dick twitches, and I suck in a breath to hopefully calm myself down.

But that time isn't now. It hasn't been for a long while. Hopefully, tonight is the first step in changing that.

"You look beautiful."

"Thank you. You look good as well." She looks me up and down, and I preen at the attention.

The shyness between us is new. Neither of us ever claimed to be shy, especially with each other, yet it's almost refreshing. A new landmark in our relationship, which has me thrilled for what's next.

"You ready to go? Wait—" I spin around and move to the kitchen to grab the small vase of flowers I ordered for her. She's not big on flowers, but it felt appropriate to get her *something*.

Quickly making my way back to the front door, I awkwardly hold out the vase. I concentrate on keeping my grip while her eyes shift between the flowers and me.

"If you hate it, I'll just keep them … here," I say, gritting my teeth as I feel my hands starting to weaken.

"Oh no! I love it, sorry. You just caught me off guard." She rushes to grab it from me, and I blow out a breath and flex my hands. "Shit, sorry. Are your hands okay?" She moves to set the vase down on the entry table.

"Good. They're good," I clip.

"I'm sorry. I just wasn't expecting that, and I should have grabbed them sooner," she rambles as she twists her hands together.

"*Hercegnőm.*" I pause until she looks up at me. "I'm fine. You are fine. They're just flowers." Her nervousness eases mine ever so slightly. We're both fumbling our way through this, it seems, so at least we're on equal footing.

"Okay," she whispers.

I reach for the door, opening it and gesturing her through. I get her situated in the driver's seat before walking around the car and getting into the passenger seat.

"Have they said when you can start driving again?" she asks as she waits for me to enter the address of our destination into the GPS.

"No set date. Just until my muscles get stronger. Hell, by that time, I'll probably need another fucking surgery." It's something that weighs heavily in the back of my mind. Will I ever be able to drive again? Or is it going to be years down the road when all my surgeries are complete before I even get the chance to try?

"I think you'll surprise yourself," she says as she pulls out to the main road.

Luckily, our destination isn't far. There are perks to living where we do. The lake is just blocks away.

"Are we going to the lake?" she asks as we get closer to it.

"We are."

"And what are we doing at the lake?"

"I rented a boat," I say simply. I wanted to go *do* something, take her out on a real date, but my scars, barely healed, have to me too self-conscious. This felt like the next best thing although, now, I'm not so sure.

"Sounds fun." Her tone is non-committal, but I'll take that as opposed to her outright hating it.

We step on deck, where I get her settled in one of the loungers before going to find the captain.

"Hey, I think we're good to go," I say with a nod rather than taking the hand he holds out to shake.

"Perfect. Just sit back and relax, and we'll take care of everything else," he says instead of judging me for not shaking his hand.

I head back up the stairs to find Daisy gazing up into the evening sky, with a glass of champagne in her hands.

"Is this okay?" I ask with a look that really asks if this is too much.

"It's great, Luka. Come sit." She pats the seat next to her.

Silence that is both comfortable and just a tad awkward surrounds us. I know I'm overthinking everything. This date was my idea, and now I don't know what to say or how to talk to her—none of it.

"Sydney is probably coming back in the next few weeks," she says into the still air.

"Oh yeah?"

"Yeah. It made me think about what needs to happen for me to come back."

My heart drops at her words. Of course I want her to come back home, but I also don't want her to be forced into it just because her crash pad will no longer be available. The idea of trying to hide my drinking is still in the back of my mind too.

"If you don't want to come back home by then, I can set you up in a hotel," I offer.

She turns to face me, her face unreadable. "Is that what you want?"

I sigh but hear a clattering coming up the stairs. The caterers show up and start setting up the table across from us, stopping our conversation entirely.

We both watch as they efficiently set things up before bringing food and quickly clearing the area.

I stand, holding my hand out to her. There's not a moment of hesitation before she takes it, letting me lead her to the beautifully made table.

"This is gorgeous, Luka," she says earnestly as she sits down.

Once I've joined her, we pick up our glasses, holding them out to each other. It's something we've done since we met, toasting at every occasion.

"Thank you. To tomorrow," I say. "A day to be better, stronger, and hopefully the person you want to spend the rest of your days with."

Tears well in her eyes before she clears her throat. "That's never been in question. You know that, right?"

I stare at her, trying to process her words. Of course I don't know that. She left, which means everything's up in the air.

She puts her glass down and sighs. "Never have I stopped loving you. I just... Everything got so overwhelming, you know? It was like all these events happened and I didn't have time to process anything. Everyone needed more attention, more of my time, and I just ... got pushed to the background. You and I aren't the only thing that's gotten to me, but it was the last straw."

"Okayyy," I draw out.

"It's"—she huffs—"so complicated. I feel like we've gotten away from what made us us, and I just needed a break from always being the one you took your anger out on. Your very valid anger." She holds up her hand to stop me from talking. "I'm not saying you can't be angry. You should be angry—hell, I'm so damn angry for you—but it's like stone after stone piled up on my shoulders, and I broke." The strain in her voice gets to me.

"How do I fix it? How do I make it so you can come back home?" I ask.

"I'm not sure. I know I want to be out of Sydney and Beckett's house before they get back to town, but I'm not sure if I can just move back into our house."

"What if I take the guest room?" I offer against every bone, nerve, and instinct in my body. I absolutely don't want to move into the guest room, but if it brings her one step closer, I'll do it.

"I..." Her eyes shift between mine. "I'll think about it. I know that's not a real answer."

"Hey, it's okay. There's no pressure. We don't need to make all the big decisions now. Let's just enjoy the boat and dinner." I gesture to our untouched plates while my heart splits into shards. It's not a lie—there is no pressure—but *fuck*, I wish it hadn't come to this. I wish I saw that she was struggling before it got this point.

But no. I was Luka *fucking* Tomic. Self-centered. Too focused on myself, my reactions, and how it would affect my driving that I didn't even care enough to make sure my wife was okay.

She starts taking bites of her steak while I sit stock-still. The glass of red wine I just set down calls to me. It's saying I can numb this feeling a little bit and make everything more manageable. So, I bring it to my lips and drink most of the glass in one go. Luckily, she doesn't notice.

The revelation I just came to hits me like a pounding wave. It keeps pushing me under, the pressure making it hard to breathe.

I made everything about me. Not once did I stop and ask myself how Daisy felt during it all. Not when she ... had the positive pregnancy test, not with the aftermath, and sure as hell not after my crash.

Have I ever put her needs, her wants, first?

Holy shit, I'm such an asshole.

"Hey." Her soft voice pulls me from my spiraling thoughts. "You okay?"

"Umm, no, I don't think I am. But I think I will be," I tell her honestly. Grabbing her hand from across the table, I squeeze it as much as I can with the tight skin there. "I'm sorry for so much, but I think I see it now. I'm going to show you, Dais. You're the most important thing to me, and I'm going to prove it to you."

It's a promise I'm not entirely sure I can keep, but I'm going to fight like hell to keep it. I hope she can see the determination in my eyes because I don't think I've ever been more serious in my life. And that includes the drinking.

She holds my eyes for a moment before shoving her chair back and standing, her hand still holding mine. I help her shift my chair enough for her to sit in my lap.

"This is a damn good start." She places a gentle kiss on my lips then presses her forehead to mine. We spend a minute just soaking each other in.

I know in this moment that I'll do anything to keep Daisy, anything to make sure my wife is my number-one priority from now on.

Chapter 12

Daisy

Time is a funny thing. It can seem like a day or a week is never ending, and then you blink and a year has passed.

After our date, my mind seemed to only focus on time.

The bathtub seems to be my space for reflection, and Lord knows I need it after the therapy session I just had.

The hard-hitting questions came out...

What do I want within my relationship with Luka?

Where do I see myself in the future?

Am I going to bring up his drinking?

Do I want kids?

The last one is what I'm stuck on. I never had an inflection, one way or another. Hell, Luka and I didn't even talk about it. I was on birth control, and we never looked back. But then, one moment changed everything. My therapist suggested that I haven't really healed or, in fact, processed that time period. Pushing down how I felt about it was easier than coming to terms with wanting something that Luka maybe didn't. He wouldn't talk to me, so I assumed that meant he was happy things didn't work out.

In hindsight, not talking things through with him was a terrible decision. He's my husband; if I can't talk to him about everything then should we even be together? And if I can't talk to him, whom can I talk to? My sisters are great, sure, but I wouldn't say I spill my guts to them on the regular.

More questions with no answers.

Sinking deep into the steaming water, I hold my breath.

I know I want Luka in my life. But past that, what does our life look like in my ideal world? Is it us traveling the race circuit still with Empress? Is it making a home base and getting a dog? Kids? I think I'd like to create a home base. I don't even care where, honestly. Just a place to be stationary, create *good* memories.

That's what's been missing in the last year. Good memories. Our date on the lake reminded me of that, of how good we are together. It hasn't been that way in too long, and it felt so damn good to get back to that. The only downside to our date on the lake was Luka chugging wine when he thought I wasn't looking.

Gasping for breath, I surge up through the water.

I want more dates. I want stability within our relationship, which means being together more and having the hard conversations. Probably stepping up and addressing his drinking too, no matter how much I don't want to.

Let's not even mention our non-existent sex life that is slowly killing me. I've been pushing that into the background too.

Haphazardly reaching for my phone on the edge of the vanity, I snag it and open up our message thread.

Me:

> What would you say if I said I wanted to move back home?

Luka:

> I would say get your ass over here.

Me:

> On the condition that one of us is in the guest room until we get … more figured out.

Luka:

> I will make sure our room is cleaned and ready for you.

Me:

> I'm being serious, Luka.

Luka:

> So am I, *hercegnőm*. I know we're not there yet, but I

want you home. No. I need you home.

I stare at his message for a long minute. For the first time in too long, I don't feel dread or panic at being around him. I'm not unsure of how he'll react. Hope—and mostly missing him so damn much—takes its place, and I know this is the right decision.

Me:

I have to get some work done in the morning, and then I'll be over after that. Is that okay?

Luka:

You want to come over tonight instead?

Me:

Well, I'm in the bath and about to do my twelve-step skin care routine before crashing in bed, so I'm going to say no. Tomorrow. I promise.

Luka:

Pics, or it didn't happen.

I burst out with laughter at that. I've missed this playfulness. This easiness between us.

Me:

I don't know if you're that lucky.

Luka:

Ah, that's where you're wrong. I'm the luckiest man in the world. I've done a terrible job of showing you that, but I will.

Luka:

Seriously, though, you could send a picture. Just saying. I love you. Get some sleep, and I'll be counting the seconds until tomorrow.

Gah. How can he go from utter silliness to melting my heart in a nanosecond? Life has been so damn hard, but when he says stuff like that, I remember why it's all worth it.

Because he's my person. I knew it the second he took me out for our first date. His cocky outer shell melted away—just for me—and showed me this Luka.

***

A shitstorm just dropped on my desk, and I'm buried in financials that Sydney wanted me to look at. This isn't my expertise by a long shot, but she wanted a second pair of eyes on it, so I'm trying my best.

My phone buzzes on the wood of my desk, with a text, but I ignore it.

Today was supposed to be easy, just a half-day to catch up on emails then moving back home. Now, God knows what time it is.

I vaguely hear my phone vibrate a couple more times, but I tune it out. If anyone needs anything, they'll call me.

By the time I'm on the last page, fatigue is catching up to me. I rub my eyes, take a deep breath, and buckle down to finish this so I can reclaim some of this day.

"You're supposed to be at home." A gruff, oh-so- familiar voice works its way down my spine, making me shiver.

I look up to see Luka, one foot crossed at his ankle, with his arms crossed in front of his chest hiding most of his hands. His jeans sculpt around his thighs, and the T-shirt he's wearing is one of my favorites. Worn and faded.

"How did you get here?" I ask almost unconsciously because he can't drive and it's the only question registering in my very Luka-hazed brain.

"Uber." His arched eyebrow accompanies his words.

I glance at the time on my computer, and see it's almost six in the evening and I've been here far longer than I intended. What I didn't expect was my husband showing up here to, I assume, bring me home.

"I lost track of time."

"Clearly. I've been texting you. I called you a few times…" he trails off and looks to the side like he's embarrassed, but all I see is his worry.

He was scared I changed my mind.

"Luka … I'm sorry," I say softly.

"It's fine," he grumbles.

It's clearly not fine.

Shoving my chair back from my desk, I make my way over to him. He still won't make eye contact with me, but I cup his cheek, forcing him to look at me.

"It's not fine. I should have at least texted you to tell you I was swamped. I didn't even realize how late it was."

"I thought…" He sighs. "I thought you gave up on me."

I don't think I've ever heard this much vulnerability in his voice, this much doubt. My heart hurts so much for him, especially because I'm the cause of it.

"Never," I whisper.

His eyes shift back and forth between mine. "I miss you." He says it so quietly I almost miss it. But I don't, and it makes the pounding in my chest almost painful.

"I miss you too." I stroke my thumb across his cheek. "Can you give me, like, five minutes to finish up, then we can go home?"

He nods as he turns his head, placing a gentle kiss on my palm before unwrapping his arms and pulling me in for a hug. The strength and comfort he's always given me—except in the last year—are a pillar of support, and I didn't realize I was missing it so much.

"Five minutes," I whisper into his chest.

Nodding, he steps back and sits in one of the visitors' chairs. There's a tension to his body, one I wish I could absorb, but that's half our problem. We both do a shit job of acknowledging our own feelings, of dealing with our own problems; instead, we take on someone else's in order to distract us from our own. Or just bury them underneath the guise of being normal.

Releasing all the breath from my lungs, I inhale to calm my racing thoughts then move back to my desk.

At least I wasn't lying about how much work I have left.

Five minutes later, I close up my laptop and shove it into the bag I brought with me.

"Okay, I think I'm done." I look up to see him watching my every move. There's a heat in his eyes, one I've missed more than I want to admit.

"Good. Let's go home." His voice is gravelly, just like it is when he's about to lose control in the bedroom. It makes my thighs clench together, but I will myself to keep focused.

We wordlessly walk to the elevator and down to my car, and climb in. Tapping my fingers softly against the steering wheel, I patiently wait for Luka to buckle up, immediately impressed with his progress. I've missed a lot in the last few weeks since our lake date, apparently.

I glance at the clock and realize it's not only dinner time, but I forgot lunch too. A well-timed grumble from my stomach fills the car.

Luka arches an eyebrow at me before both furrow together. "Did you eat lunch?"

Shaking my head, I choose not to give him an explanation.

"Pick somewhere for food, and I'll call in an order. We can pick it up on the drive home." He leaves no room for argument, but dammit, I want to give one.

"I can handle food myself. I don't need you micromanaging me," I huff. The need to control things, anything, rears its ugly head.

"The fuck you don't. You didn't eat lunch—don't deny it—and now your stomach is eating you from the inside out. You're clearly not taking care of yourself." He throws his hands up in exasperation, but his words have me heated.

"You're one to talk. You want to go over who isn't capable of taking care of themselves? It sure as hell isn't me, Luka. If I remember correctly, you texted me a fucking picture of a bag of chips you couldn't open not all that long ago. So, yeah, let's not throw fucking stones." Gripping the steering wheel hard, I make my way onto the main road. I almost throw in his drinking but catch myself just in time. That would surely ruin any progress we've made.

We were doing so good. But I should have known it wasn't going to last. We have so much to work through still, and it's a gut punch, really, that we can't just have a simple conversation.

"Pull over." His voice is deadly calm.

"No."

"Pull the fuck over, Dais."

"Absolutely not."

"I swear to God, *hercegnőm*... Pull the fuck over before I do it for you."

I wrench the car to the side of the road, where there is luckily some on street parking.

"What?" I yell as soon as I put the car in park.

It takes all of two seconds for him to come across the center console and grip my hair in his fist. His lips make contact before I register what's going on, and the hand in my hair makes sure I'm placed exactly where he wants me.

My brain finally catches up, and I instinctively try to push him away but he's too strong, which shocks the hell out of me. Guess he has been working out lately.

Breaking the kiss, he presses his forehead to mine. "Take everything out on me, Dais. Lord knows I deserve it. But never put yourself in danger again."

"When was I in danger?" I murmur, confused.

"Driving angry is a fast track to not paying attention, and I can't... Just please give me this." His eyes flutter closed, but I don't miss the pain in them.

"We need to have a real conversation." My whispered words are followed by the welling up of tears in my eyes. I hate this. I hate that a simple statement has me so angry that he feels unsafe. I hate that I'm the one who put that worry on his shoulders. I hate that everything is so fucking hard all the time. And I hate that I'm a broken record every time we're together. The never-ending cycle, it seems.

"Yes. We do. When we get home."

I nod against his forehead, breathing in the smell that is purely Luka, and it somehow puts me at ease.

"Now, tell me what you want for dinner, and please don't be stubborn. I've been worried sick all fucking day, and I'm starving now." He presses one lingering kiss on my lips before his grip in my hair tightens to the point of pain as he tips my head back more. His kisses trail along my jaw, the scrape of his teeth sending arousal through my body. When he clamps down on that spot on my neck, right where my shoulder meets, I whimper. He knows every single trigger point for me, and he's not afraid to use them against me.

The instant he releases me, I feel the loss. It's like all the sunshine left, and now I'm left with gray skies and thunderstorms.

"Pad thai," I whisper, trying desperately to calm the blood rushing through my body.

I draw one more deep breath as I hear him dial the number, and I hit the road once more.

Chapter 13
Luka

The parallels between watching Daisy driving angrily and me crashing my F1 car scared me more than I want to admit. It was like watching my crash through her eyes, and I couldn't handle it. No wonder she's struggling. She had to watch me self-destruct in the worst kind of way and couldn't do anything to change the course of events.

I call our favorite Thai place and quickly put in our order. She drives that way without any fight, thank God, and before long, she's parking in the garage.

We eat in silence. The kitchen island feels more like the Grand Canyon as we're both lost in our heads. Once she's done and pushes her plate to the center, I stand up and take our plates to the sink. I start washing them when she cuts in.

"I thought you weren't supposed to submerge your burns."

"Graduated this week. Granted, the surgery in three weeks will put me back to square one for a while," I say plainly.

"Three weeks?" she whispers.

It's hard to remember how distant we truly are. It's easy to push it all down and act like nothing happened. That we've still been involved in the happenings in each other's lives, but it couldn't be further from the truth.

I rinse off the plates before putting them in the dishwasher and turning to her.

"Next batch of skin grafts are in three weeks. It'll mostly be on this big patch." I hold up my right hand, the back of it a huge, angry-red patch where the worst of the damage is. My pinkie is a special project that they may or may not get to on this surgery. "He did say recovery should be easier this round since everything else is well on its way to being healed."

She opens and closes her mouth a couple of times before slumping in her chair.

Walking around the island, I hold out my hand to her—quietly congratulating myself that I don't instantly flinch at the contact—and lead her to the living room.

"I think we should have that talk," I murmur.

She sighs, resting her head on the back cushion. "I'm sorry I scared you. Multiple times."

"I'm sorry I haven't talked to you about it at all." It's the truth and a hard one at that. My therapist, God bless him, has to pull these revelations from me, and it still doesn't really sink in until something happens with Daisy and me.

She turns her head to look at me. "What are we doing?" Her voice cracks as tears fill her eyes.

"I don't have an answer to that, but I'm fighting like hell, *hercegnőm*. I just need you to not give up on me."

"Never," she whispers. A couple of tears drop from her eyes.

I lean over, swiping them with my mangled thumb.

"How's ... everything?" I ask, going vague and not talking the deep stuff yet. What we need to work through is more than a one-conversation thing. This is a huge fucking start, but it's more than that. It's making an effort with each other every single day. I see that now.

"Everything is ... hectic. Taking over Empress is so much more work than I was anticipating initially, although I shouldn't be surprised with Sydney at the helm. She's bugging me about bringing you on. In whatever capacity you want."

"She is? I've been an asshole," I say in wonder.

Daisy emits a giggle of laughter, and it is like sunshine on the shittiest of days.

"You have been. But you've had reason to be."

"Don't excuse my behavior, Dais. Starting today, I want honesty between us, even when it's hard as hell. Even if it's mean or hurtful. I think I need that the most." My words register, and I realize being honest means broaching my drinking. I almost flinch at the thought.

"Fine. You've been an ass since long before your accident."

I bark out a laugh at her bluntness, but I also love it. She's never been shy, never had an issue calling me out, until a year ago. This little glimpse of our version of normalcy makes me think anything is possible.

"But yes, for some reason, she thinks you'll be a 'great addition to the team'—her words, not mine." She grins over at me.

"God, I missed you." The words slip out without my consent, and judging by the look on her face, she's not completely ready for them either.

"Luka..."

"I know. But I did and I do, and even though we aren't there yet, I want you to know that in the back of your head when I undoubtedly fuck this up again."

"Who are you right now?" she whispers.

"I am ... trying really hard to be the husband you deserve."

"Off to a stellar start." She sniffles.

I don't hesitate, even though I probably should. Instead, I drag her over to me, getting her situated on my lap and holding her tight.

It takes a minute, but her body sags in relief as she cuddles against my chest.

Minutes could pass—hell, hours—but it doesn't matter. Daisy is in my arms, and I'm in heaven.

We both doze off, taking comfort in each other for the first time in too damn long.

***

Daisy had to run to the office today ,so I'm taking the chance to do something I haven't done in almost six months.

As the rideshare pulls up to the center, I reflect on the fact that I haven't been here physically for anything recently. Sure, I've funded a ton of shit, but coming here and helping the kids has always been a priority for me. One that no one knows about, not even Daisy.

Come to think of it, I'm not sure why I've hid it from her. Embarrassment?

Keeping up the cocky Luka appearance, maybe? Who knows.

After a very long talk with my therapist, he decided this would be a good exercise for me: get back to something familiar and something that gives me motivation. I wanted to do it before I have my next surgery tomorrow and won't be able to for a while. I also haven't had a drop to drink today. A first since ... the hospital, probably. So far, so good, though. I've been slowly attempting to wean off of it.

"Luka! It's so good to see you!" Mary comes around the front desk of the Boys and Girls Club.

"Hey, Mary. Sorry it's been so long." I give her a hug, shocked at how much I missed her motherly attention.

"Nonsense. You've been here in other ways, and it doesn't go unappreciated."

I nod but don't agree with her.

In every city I spend a fair amount of time in, I find a place like this. A place that helps the kids in need. A place that helps them when they have no one else in their corner.

I may have the public image of a pretentious, cocky asshole, but deep down, I'm not sure that's who I really am. I've only recently come to that realization. Even getting married to Daisy didn't change my reputation in the media.

"Well, we set up an art project for you today. I hope that's okay. I wanted to do something lowkey. I wasn't sure how well you were healed up."

I give her a small smile, glad she isn't shying away from my burns.

Everyone else avoids them like the plague.

My angry thoughts start to pull me from the reason I'm here, and I shake myself from going down that road.

"Sounds perfect. Are they in the main room?" I ask.

"They are. Make sure you find me before you leave. I've got something for you," she says as she hustles back behind the desk to answer the ringing phone.

I wave her off and make my way to the kids. I can hear them the second I turn the corner, and a genuine smile stretches across my face.

I think this is exactly what I need.

Time to remind me why I do these things. Time to remind me where I came from and what's really important.

"Luka!" A couple of the kids yell when they see me.

In an instant, I'm almost knocked to the ground, but I plant my feet to keep us steady instead. "Hey, guys, how are you?"

"Good!" A chorus sounds once they finally free me.

"Great. Miss Mary said she set up some art today. You guys ready for that?" I ask, hoping to move things along and distract them from all things crash related.

"Yeah!" they yell again, except ten times louder.

I've been alone in a quiet house for too long, apparently, because it feels like they almost burst my eardrums.

I sit down and take a look at all the supplies: paint, paper, and some glitter which will likely be decorating my house and clothes for the foreseeable future. Thinking about what to suggest to prompt them into action stumps me for all of a half a second before I find it.

"How about we draw or paint something that makes us happy?" I tell the group as they start to settle down.

"I'm going to paint a rainy day."

"Well, I'm going to paint my sister."

"Eww, you actually like your sister?"

The conversation carries on, and I have to stop my chuckle. No need to encourage the "hating on the sister" argument, not when it's Sean who will stand up for her.

Picking up my own paint brush, I decide to go with a field full of daisies. I'm not going to try to paint my wife, inevitably butchering the shit out of it, so this is the safer option.

Little Rose's pipsqueak voice silences the whole group, though.

"What happened to your hands?"

I freeze in place, panic taking over my body. I flush, the blood draining from my face. My gut reaction is to lash out. I can feel it welling up inside of me, but I force myself to count to ten and take a deep breath.

Rose is barely six years old. She's curious, not malicious, and I need to remember that.

Clearing my throat, I go for the condensed version, hoping it's enough and that I can get through it.

"I, uh... I got into a crash at my job. A fire broke out, and it burned my hands." The croak in my throat as I speak is dangerously close to becoming a fully-fledged breakdown. But I hold my breath and hope I don't need to go into more detail.

I could use a drink right now. My hand starts to shake at just the thought of a shot. Sweat breaks out on my forehead, and I can't figure out if it's the lack of alcohol or the line of questioning.

"Oh no! You crashed? Are you okay? Were you in the hospital? We didn't even get to send you a get-well card!" Rose's assessment is nothing like I imagined.

No. It's kind, thoughtful, and so damn sweet it steals my breath. I've been so worked up about *anyone* asking me about the accident, and her concern wasn't what I was expecting.

"I am doing better now, thank you, Rose. It's very sweet of you to think about sending a card, though," I offer to her instead of breaking down in tears and stealing a hug like I desperately want to.

A little kid's simple words of support have burrowed their way into my head, and I can't shake them. They're making me think about not just the crash but before that too. Everything I've done wrong with Daisy simply because I couldn't talk about it, too scared of the repercussions. But little Rose's care and concern are making me reevaluate everything.

She smiles at me, then promptly goes back to her painting like she didn't just blow my world apart.

It's strange what breaks through when you're stuck. Never in a million years did I think painting a field of daisies, with a group of kids that need all the support they can get, would be the thing that opens my eyes a little bit more. Letting me see that taking the first step to opening up, simply talking, might solve more problems than I thought it would create.

It's also made me realize how bad my drinking really is. It's easy to feel like it's just been recreational, that I have control over when and how much. But my reaction to having to talk about the crash, even to a child, showed that I *needed* a drink. And that's not something I'm comfortable with, let alone like. My reliance on it is worse than I thought, and it might be time to talk to my therapist about how to stop completely—or my dependence on it, at the very least.

Admitting I have a problem is really fucking hard, though.

The rest of the time at the Girls and Boys Club is spent talking about everything I've missed lately: new friendships, old friends leaving, and everything in between. It makes me sad to think that I've been avoiding this place for months. The kids never deserved that. They probably felt like I abandoned them.

And, in a way, I did.

As I walk out, after four rounds of hugs and a promise to be by in a couple of weeks after my hand heals up a little, I walk out to the front and catch Mary.

"How'd it go?" she asks with a gleam in her eye.

"Really good. I'm sorry I haven't been around more lately."

"Oh, nonsense." She scoffs. "It's not like you haven't had a good reason." Her motherly look would send even the strongest of people withering, and I'm no different. "Anyway, I have something for you. Stay right there."

She heads to her office while I pace the entryway. Pulling up the rideshare app, I order a ride before Mary comes back out.

"Here you go." She holds out a rectangular box, with an arched eyebrow.

"Thanks," I draw out, but I'm not sure what this is.

"Open it." She huffs in annoyance that I'm so dense as to not do the obvious thing.

Carefully taking the lid off, I pull the protective paper to the side and read the writing.

"'The Girls and Boys Club of Austin's Person of the Year'?" I look up and can barely keep a hold of my emotions.

"Thank you. For all you do here and for being present with the kids. They love you," she says.

"I ... I don't know what to say," I whisper, knowing if I say any more, I'll have a full-on breakdown in the lobby.

I'm wholly undeserving of this. Hell, having a drinking problem should automatically disqualify me from any recognition.

"You don't say anything." She shrugs. "We're all just sorry you couldn't make it to the banquet to make a real shindig of it. You never did like the spotlight with all of this, though." She smirks knowingly.

Even if I was healthy, I probably wouldn't have come. I don't do this for the clout; I do it to help the kids. Recognition has never been a part of it.

Setting down the placard on the counter, I walk toward Mary and encase her in a crushing hug.

"Oh!" She fumbles at the unexpected move before wrapping her arms around me. "You're a godsend, Luka. Never forget that."

I hold her for a long moment. A mother figure I've never really had. Then, I let go and step back.

As I attempt to clear my throat, she gives me a knowing look before nodding back to me.

I nod in return before picking up my award and heading outside, right as my ride pulls up.

Mary knows my gratitude, not only for what she's done for me but the kids as well. The fact that I didn't have to spell it out tells me she's held a bigger part in my life than I've ever given her credit for.

Another day full of guilt and revelations.

Sitting in the back of the car, I stare at the award then pick up my phone to call Daisy.

"Hey, you okay?"

"Can you be home in thirty minutes?" I rasp, my voice still caught in my throat from all the emotions.

"Umm, yeah. Absolutely. Are you okay?"

"I don't think so." It comes out in a whisper. "I'll see you in a little bit," I say before hanging up. I don't need to lose my shit in the back of a rideshare. I need to get home and lose it with the one person whom I know will support me through anything, even if none of it makes sense. My head is too full, too overwhelmed with a myriad of memories and thoughts, but I know talking it out with her will help me figure things out.

Huh. Wanting to talk things out with Daisy. Maybe I am making progress.

Chapter 14

Daisy

I'm fumbling with my computer, throwing papers around in a mild panic. Luka doesn't just call me and ask me to come home; I don't think he ever has during our relationship. So, yeah, I'm panicking.

I finally make it out to my car, but I slow my pace once I'm driving, remembering the night a couple of weeks ago when I scared Luka. Nothing good would come from putting myself at risk while driving.

Twenty-six minutes later, I'm racing through the garage door and sprinting to the living room, only to stop in my tracks at what I see.

Luka is sitting with something in his lap; his shoulders shake, and he's sobbing. I also see a bottle of tequila on the coffee table, but it's full.

"Oh shit," I whisper as I rush over. "What happened?" My eyes move frantically over his body, triple-checking his hands, and see no new injuries.

"I-I-I want to talk." He heaves in a breath. "But I need to cry."

Nodding, I sit next to him, wrapping my arm around his shoulder and pulling him to me. I have never seen Luka like this. Hell, I don't think I've ever seen him cry, and that includes our wedding day and the aftermath of his crash. It's jarring, to say the least.

It takes him far longer to calm down than I expected. I feel helpless, enough so that my own tears joined his. There's a pain in him, in this emotional release that I can't help but feel responsible for in some way. If only I wasn't so stubborn. If only I made sure he knew that he could talk to me about anything. If only things had been different.

"I can hear you overthinking and blaming yourself." His gravelly voice startles me as he sits up.

"I—"

"None of this is on you."

I shift my eyes between his, looking for an answer to a question I'm not even sure I know.

"You scared the shit out of me," I say instead, going for honesty like we've promised each other.

"I think I scared myself too." He gives me a small smile. Sighing, he shifts back on the couch. "I went to the Boys and Girls Club."

My brows furrow in confusion. "For what?"

"I volunteer there and any other similar place that helps kids. When I wasn't on the track, it's where I spent a good chunk of time."

"What?" Shock radiates through my voice. How could I have been with this man for the better part of three years and not known this about him?

"I don't … tell people about it. Never have, and I don't plan to in the future," he says stiffly.

"Okay, but me? I'm your wife, and I had no clue." If I dig deep enough, I'm hurt. This seems to be a big part of his life, and he's hidden it from me completely. My eyes shift to the bottle on the table. Kind of like his drinking.

"We've established I'm an asshole." He smirks, but I'm not having it.

I throw a pillow at him. "This is not a time to joke around. Jesus, Luka. What else are you doing that I have no clue about?" I don't mean to throw the accusation around, but his answer will tell me a lot.

He turns to face front, his eyes on the bottle, and I hold my breath.

"I think I have a drinking problem." His voice so low that I only just hear it.

I don't know what to say, so I wait him out.

"I've been drinking since … since you got pregnant."

I suck in a breath, shocked by the timeline, to say the least.

"I—" He sighs. "I don't know how to talk about it. But I need to talk to my therapist. Is that okay? I don't know why or how it got this bad," he admits, and I have to say I'm proud of him for at least recognizing it, even if it doesn't give me any answers as to why.

"Umm, yeah. I think so." How are you supposed to respond this this? I have no clue, so I do what I seem to do best—downplay the obvious to give him time.

My head shakes in disbelief at all the new information, so I focus on why he originally called me. "What happened at the center that upset you so much?"

He heaves in a breath and hands me the box on his lap that I had forgotten about. I open it up and read it, jolting up in surprise.

"How? W-why?" I stutter out.

"Apparently, my volunteer work and donations have made an impact. I didn't ask for this," he says defensively, and it's then I realize that my tone is a little harsh. My distrust is making me impersonal, and it's throwing him.

"I know. I'm sorry. I'm just … so shocked. I had no idea."

"And that's my fault. I'm trying to tell you now."

"This is huge, Luka," I tell him in an effort to dial back my accusations.

"It is."

"This upset you this much?" I'm trying to piece things together, but I still don't understand.

"No. Yes. It's part of it. Mary, the coordinator there, gave it to me when I left, and I didn't know how to just accept it, you know? I don't do this for the recognition. I do it because giving back and helping kids is the only thing that makes me feel like I'm doing something worthwhile and good in the world."

My heart splinters at his words. I know he didn't have a great childhood, but he's never gone into detail about it, and now I'm regretting not digging deeper.

"Today, I painted with the kids. When we started, one of the younger girls asked me about my hands, and I freaked out."

Shit.

"Oh, Luka, I'm so sorry," I murmur.

"It was strange. I panicked for a split second, thought how much I needed a drink, then gave her the bare minimum. And you know what she said?"

I shake my head.

"She was worried about me. Upset that they didn't get to make me a get-well card. No judgement, no disgust over my scars, just concern for someone who doesn't deserve it."

"You deserve it." My throat closes up with unshed tears.

He looks over at me sadly. "I really don't, but she made me realize that by not talking about it—hell, about everything—I wasn't helping anyone, especially not myself. Just telling her the simple version felt so … cathartic. Like the guilt and shame somehow lessened just from unloading on a six-year-old."

"I think we're both probably guilty of doing that."

"Probably explains the last year," he comments, and it's like a knife to the gut. I know that's not how he means it, but it doesn't hurt any less. All the new information and how much he's hidden catches up to me in an instant.

Clearing my throat, I stand up. "Umm, I just need a minute or a couple." I rush off to our suite, closing the door behind me, and walk into the bathroom. Turning on the water as hot as I can stand it, I wait until there is a couple of inches of water in the tub before stripping and sinking into it.

I ran away.

Between the stress of the phone call, the new knowledge about his charity work and his drinking, and the unexpected pain of the truth of Luka's words, I can't handle it.

It's a fault I know I need to work on, but the pain in my chest won't subside. I need clarity and less anger, and this is the only thing that helps. I won't be helping us achieve any progress in my current mindset. I'll only make things worse, and no matter how hard I try to do otherwise, I'm not there yet.

I turn off the water before sucking in a deep breath and submerging myself.

Luka opening up and talking to me is a good thing.

So why did I freak out? Why do I feel so hurt at the knowledge that he kept something from me?

Because I'm supposed to be the one he can tell everything. And yet he didn't. The fact that he feels he can now is great, but past hurts don't just disappear.

Then there's a word I don't know how to process: addiction. How do I help him with that? Should I? Or does he need to do this on his own? I've known about some of his drinking, but not to the level he is describing. But then, I don't think it registered how bad it really was.

The only way past this is through it, and I don't know how to make that happen.

How do you disconnect the pain from progress? The past from the present?

I surge up from the tub, no clearer than when I came in, and scream when I see Luka leaning against the vanity.

"You scared the shit out of me." My hand is on my chest as I breath rapidly.

"Sorry. This is usually where you come when you're overwhelmed, and I just wanted to check on you."

"I don't know…" Gulping, I try to articulate how I'm feeling. "I don't know how to not be hurt that you never told me about all the charity work. Or the drinking," I add in a whisper. Why my mind is hung up on that, I'm not sure, but the dam breaks and the tears flow.

I cover my face and my shoulders shake, and I just let it all happen.

I don't hear Luka move. I don't notice him getting undressed, but a gentle tap on my shoulder has me scooting forward without thought.

He climbs in behind me, getting situated before pulling me back to him.

"I'm sorry, *hercegnőm*. It's what I've always done, not that it's an excuse, but I didn't even think about it. It was thoughtless on my part. And the drinking… Can we press pause on that until I can wrap my head around it more?" he murmurs in my ear as his arms tighten around my middle.

"I just don't understand how our marriage can survive if things like this aren't out in the open. How can we move forward when I feel like I don't even know who you are?" I hiccup.

"You know me, Dais. I promise you know me better than anyone ever has. It was my fuck-up, and I'm working on it. I promise. I just need professional help to actually get it all straight in my head."

I cry harder because I hear him, and I know he's right. He is working on it—it's as plain as day—and yet here I am, so stuck on this that I don't see a way out.

"Talk to me. Even if it's to call me an asshole. Even if you need to yell at me."

"I don't want"—I breathe in to try to stem my tears—"to yell at you."

"I mean, I can do it for you if you want." He sucks in air. "LUKA, YOU'RE SUCH A DICK!" he yells, making me smile.

"Stop." I tap his arm.

He presses a kiss to my temple as his thumb strokes my stomach.

"I was scared. When you told me about the pregnancy."

I suck in a breath, not expecting this.

"I never wanted to be a parent. I had shit examples, and I still don't know if I can be a good father. I didn't know how to tell you that. Numbing myself to those thoughts was easier." His voice trails off.

"I was so sad," I whisper. "I didn't know how you felt, and then it was just over and we moved on like nothing happened." More tears fall freely.

"It affected me more than I wanted to admit. I drove like shit, couldn't get my head on straight, and drank most days," he says.

"Everything is so overwhelming. Like the bad stuff will never end, and I can't see the light at the end of the tunnel. I just want a pinprick of light, Luka, but it's not there." I sniffle.

"We're both trying. I'll bump up my therapy appointments and see if I can go twice a week. Get a handle on my drinking even if I need to go somewhere to do so. Does that sound like a decent plan?" he asks, still stroking my stomach.

"Yeah." Silence takes over before I speak again. "I'm sorry for running away."

"I get why you did. As long as you let me chase you, I'll always come for you."

"Promise?" Vulnerability leeches from my question.

"Always, *hercegnőm*. It's going to take time. We're both probably going to take a ton of steps back before we take one forward, but I'm here. Together, we can figure it all out, okay?"

I think on his words. They aren't sugarcoated. They're real and *hard*, but they are also honest. We need honesty more than anything, and he's proving that it's a priority for him. Now, I just need to meet him halfway. Face the problems instead of avoiding, instead of running.

"Okay," I whisper as I sink deeper into him. "I miss you."

"I miss you so damn much." He presses another kiss to my temple before moving to my cheek.

I soak in the feel of him against me as he kisses my jaw. On his next kiss, I turn my head and meet his lips.

It's soft, gentle almost, but no less intense. The connection after a hard conversation proves to be exactly what we both need. A simple kiss. A brush of his knuckles against my stomach. A slide of my hand against his thigh.

But we don't do anything more than kiss.

We breathe each other in until the water takes on a chill. When goosebumps pop up on my skin, I finally pull away.

"You have surgery tomorrow," I say.

"I do." He nods, looking a little dazed.

"Stay with me tonight." My words are barely loud enough to hear.

His thumb brushes against my cheek. "I'd love nothing more."

It takes us a minute to get up and dry off. I don't bother with clothes, just head to the bedroom and curl up under the sheets. It feels like any clothes will be too much between us when we finally made a step toward *good*. My eyes are starting to swell and hurt, and sleep is calling my name.

Luka joins me, curling up around me, touching every inch of skin he can.

"I love you so much, Dais."

"I love you too," I whisper as sleep starts to pull me under.

Chapter 15

Daisy

Sitting in waiting rooms has quickly become the bane of my existence.

I swear that every time I sit here, it takes me at least an hour to calm down. Fight or flight kicks in, as though Luka just crashed all over again and I have no clue what's going on. It's exhausting.

Then, my mind wanders. A dangerous thing when life has been so up in the air lately.

Last night was hard. A mixture of old comforts and hurts with new connections and vulnerabilities. It's like whiplash.

Sharing a bed again with my husband soothed so much of my uncertainty, but it also made me realize how selfish I was last night. Hindsight and all that.

Luka was wide open, telling me about something he held so dear to him while also acknowledging a huge problem he's been ignoring, and I turned around and made it about me. I was hurt. I had a knee-jerk reaction to his words and ran away from them. I didn't try hard enough to work through it. Eventually I did, sure, but it took Luka coming to me in order to do so. He seems so much more ... advanced than I am, and I don't know how to get there with him.

Throw in work on top of it all, and I feel like I'm drowning. My stress is at an all-time high. I'm having trouble sleeping—hell, eating even. I know talking about it all with my therapist and with Luka will help, but shit, where do you start?

And the start of a new season is just around the corner. What if I can't be home all the time to fix this? What if he doesn't want to wait for me?

The self-imposed knife to my heart digs in deeper.

Stop. Take a breath and stop spiraling.

My usually sarcastic inner voice might be on the right track this time.

Another yawn hits me as Dr. Branch comes out from behind the theatre doors.

"Mrs. Tomic," he says with a smile.

"Hi." I stand up, wringing my hands together. A smile is usually a good thing, but I've come to expect the worst in hospital settings.

"The surgery went well. We were able to do some work on his pinkie as well because everything went a lot smoother than we had anticipated. The grafts look great, and I don't expect any problems with them or the healing. I know we discussed our expectations for the healing progress, and I think it'll be much improved over his first grafts when the area around it was healing as well. He'll have full use of his other hand, but the repaired one will be bandaged, so it will be wise to give it a bit of time prior to resuming using it, and make sure he doesn't go in the sun with it for a few weeks. The nurses will get you on schedule with physical therapy again as well."

"We already are." I smile at him. Lord knows the amount of physical therapy Luka has to do is damn near a full-time job.

"Right, of course. Do you have any questions for me?"

"Just when I can go see him."

"They're waiting for his room to open up and for him to come out of the anesthesia, but they should have you back there within the hour." He smiles at me, holding his hand out.

"Thank you so much. I appreciate everything."

"Anytime. You have my number if you need anything."

I nod and watch as he walks back through the door, taking the surgical cap from his head as he does.

I slump back in my chair, tension releasing from every muscle in my body, before I pull out my phone and text my sisters.

Me:

Luka's out of surgery. Everything went well.

Heather:

Great to hear. Are you okay? Do you need anything?"

Me:

No, I'm okay. Plus, you're five hours away from me; what are you going to do? Drive here?

Ruby:

Umm, yes. We would. We're your sisters, you crazy woman. If you need us, we'll be there ASAP.

Autumn:

I have a hookup with a pilot. We could fly.

Well now, this is interesting.

Me:

A hookup, you say? Would you say his plane is of average length? Is it one of those double-decker ones? A tight fit?

Ruby:

And she's back, ladies and gentlemen.

Heather:

Well, I was worried, but now I'm not. But I would like to know who this pilot is…

Autumn:

God, you guys are the worst. Firstly, no, I'm not hooking up with him. Secondly, who the hell makes the size of an AIRPLANE a sexual inuendo?? You have real problems, Dais.

I chuckle but see the nurse coming out and heading my way. I do have real problems, but my usual sarcasm is making me feel more like myself.

I don't wait for their response, instead standing when the nurse comes my way.

"We just got him set up. You ready?"

"I am." I follow her back.

"He's still pretty out of it. We like to keep him pretty sedated at first, so he doesn't try to rip off the bandage or anything. With you there, it should be easier to get him to understand not to touch it."

"Makes sense. Put all that effort into a graft, and then the patient rips it to shreds because they're so high." I let out a weak chuckle.

"Exactly. He should be fine in a little bit, though." She smiles over to me as she Vanna White's her hands to the door in front of us. "I'll be by in a few to check in on him," she says before walking away.

I try to settle my racing heart before I step in. The last time I had to do this, he was hooked up to so many machines and had so many bandages that the image still haunts me.

This time, it's not anything too bad. His hand is bandaged and he has an IV, but that's it. I can handle this.

I pull the visitors' chair over next to his bed, the sound jostling him.

"*Hercegnőm?*"

"Hey, love," I whisper.

His eyes part, just enough to see through, and the smile he graces me with blinds me.

"You're so fucking pretty," he says.

A burst of laughter comes from my chest. "And you are very high right now."

"No, no, I'm fine."

I smile but don't respond. It's kind of adorable; I'll give him that.

"Best thing I ever did was marry you." He slurs a little.

"Oh yeah?" I play along.

"Oh yeah. You're so fucking gorgeous and smart. And pretty, and wayyyyyyy too good for me. Had to lock you down quick." His head lulls over to look at me.

"Is that what you did?" I try to hold in my laughter.

"Oh yeah. I mean, you wanted me. I just sealed the deal." He gives me a lopsided grin.

My heart skips a beat at not just his words but how carefree he looks right now. I know he's drugged up, but it's been so long since I've seen this lighthearted, cocky version of my husband. I've missed him.

"*You* sealed the deal? I seem to remember me being the one who made the first move." I may have done some light stalking, but whatever. Semantics.

"Yeah, you did. It was hot as fuck too."

I don't try to hide my chuckle, but his face turns serious in a nanosecond.

"I was scared."

"I know," I murmur.

"No, not of that. The baby." I suck in a breath as he echoes his words from last night. "I never planned for kids, ya know? Not dad material, don't have good examples." He says it like he's telling me what he doesn't like when it comes to food, not talking about something that I still haven't come to terms with.

"Yeah," I whisper.

"You ... you're too good for me. You'd be so good as a mom. So damn good, Dais." He slurs a little more as his eyes slowly blink.

"I'm not, Luka."

His eyes shoot open. "You'd be the best mom. I'm sorry I'm so scared of it. I don't know if I can do it, though." There's so much clarity in his words. Then his eyes close again and don't open until snores sound from him.

He just falls asleep after words that I can't process.

He's never spoken a word to me about any of this before, and now he's said something two days in a row. He gave me a hug when I told him I was pregnant, and then was distant and apparently drinking. And then, after the doctor's appointment that he couldn't come to because of a race, relief was the only thing on his face. I've assumed this whole time it's because he just didn't want kids, but this is so much more than that.

It gives me both hope and fear that we may not be able to figure this out. It's clearly something we should have talked about before we got married, but we're nothing if not a whirlwind couple. Talking about serious stuff wasn't really on our agenda.

And now, we're both forced to do so.

I still don't know how I feel about having kids. I used to think I'd eventually get the mom bug once I was settled down. But we weren't settled. We hadn't even discussed it.

I didn't get the chance to grieve something that never really was. It doesn't make it hurt less. Doesn't make it *feel* any less real, tangible.

I intertwine our hands together—his good one—and put my forehead against it.

Luka was right when he said one step forward, ten steps back. This somehow feels like both.

Seeing happy Luka, goofy Luka, lets me know that we'll somehow be okay.

I don't even have the words to say how much I missed him, missed this. Between last night and this high, honest version of him, I want *us* back. I know we may never get back to where we were; too much has happened to both of us for that. But maybe this new version of us can be just as good.

My phone dings. Lifting my head up to check it, I see it's Sydney.

Sydney:

How's he doing?

Me:

Out of surgery and high as shit, but doing good. Doc said everything went well, and Luka will be up and running in a couple of weeks.

Sydney:

That's good to hear. When are you guys going home?

Me:

No clue. I didn't ask. When we talked before the surgery, they said he would probably be good to go in a day or two. Since it's on the main part of his hand and not between the joints, they said it won't be a "complicated heal", whatever that means. They did some additional repair on his pinkie, though, so that might change.

Sydney:

Okay, well, text me when you guys are leaving, and I'll have some food delivered to the house. Is there anything else you need?

Me:

You don't need to do that.

Sydney:

Daisy, I love you, but shut up. We may not be there, but we can help however we can. What kind of shitty friend and boss would I be if I left you to fend for yourself? Seriously, let me send dinner or whatever meal you're home for. Selfishly, it'll make me feel better about not helping you more.

Me:

You're the boss. But thank you, I appreciate it and the flexibility with work.

Sydney:

Love you, and keep me updated.

I keep a hold of Luka's hand and sigh as I lean back into the chair.

If the last couple of months have taught me anything, it's that my support system is better than I could have ever hoped for. I probably did myself a disservice by not relying on them more. Sydney forcing me to accept it might just be what I need to realize I'm not alone in all of this.

Chapter 16
Luka Tomic Seen Leaving Hospital

Formula One driver, Luka Tomic, has been quiet since his horrific crash that was felt by the entire racing community. His usual fondness for the media has been absent since and has left the sporting world wondering what the future holds for its one-time playboy racer.

Today, he was spotted leaving St. David's Medical Center in Austin, Texas with fresh bandages on his hand. It is speculated that this was a planned surgery, with no comment issued by his team, Empress Racing. Requests were made to Sydney Davis, formerly Johnson, the new CEO of Empress for the latest update on his status ahead of the upcoming season, but she declined to comment.

Is there trouble brewing between the team and Tomic? Has he already lost his seat on the Empress team? Will his hands ever heal enough to get back into a car again? Seems we'll all have to remain not-so-patiently waiting for any news regarding the former champion of Formula One.

Chapter 17

Luka

The good news is that I was only in the hospital for two days before they sent me home. The drive home was quiet, but Daisy seems ... different, in a good way. She seems lighter. She's also been a lot more physical. Little touches here and there, more than she's initiated in a long while.

I'm not sure what happened between pre-op and now, but I'm not questioning things.

Currently, I'm sitting on the couch, watching the car unveiling for Empress. Beckett and Sydney are there but not on camera. Their new drivers, Sawyer Joseph and Malcolm Acheson, look all too pleased with themselves. They're soaking in their new fame, grinning from ear to ear, and all I want to do is chuck the remote at them.

"You okay?" Daisy's soft voices calls from the hallway.

"Yes. No." I sigh. "I am. I'm just annoyed." *And I want a fucking drink so badly.* But I'm staying strong. Luckily, the pain meds have helped distract me up until now.

"Understandable. I'm shocked to see you watching it, honestly."

"That makes both of us." I tap the seat cushion next to me with my non-bandaged hand.

She joins me readily, sitting so our thighs are touching. "I'm proud of you, though."

"Thanks," I murmur, still terrible at taking praise. She spent thirty minutes, once we got home, emptying every bottle above the fridge at my urging. If they are there, they're a temptation and I don't want that in the house.

"Beck said the new guys are acting like scared little newbies." She smirks over at me.

"They look like they're letting the promotion go to their head. I'll be interested to see how they do because I know Sydney won't give a shit how popular they are if they aren't producing." Something as simple as talking about the upcoming season used to send me into a spiral, literally weeks ago. But now? It feels good. I mean, I'm still annoyed with these young assholes, but I can talk about it. No panic attack, no depressing thoughts about what I'm even good for now. Those thoughts are still there, but I'm trying so hard to move past them and look to the future. To attempt to figure out where I go once my hands are healed. The alcohol is proving to be the worst part, and maybe that's distracting me from the rest of it. But having an ounce of clarity about my future has been a nice change in pace.

Is that in a car driving? I'm starting to think no.

Daisy snorts. "Yeah, she's already annoyed with Sawyer because he's supposed to be 'seasoned' enough to not pull this shit."

"They have to learn the hard way. It takes us all a while to understand we still need to be professional and prove that we deserve our spot every single race. There are many who don't cut it anymore, but that also depends on the team. Sydney will want results ASAP, and she won't accept anything less," I say.

"You know there's a job waiting for you whenever you want it." She arches an eyebrow at me. "Your analysis is spot on, and I didn't even think you were keeping up with things."

"I don't think Sydney wants me around right now. I'd be a distraction to everyone in that garage. And I can't even write or type." I hold up my bum hand.

"The option is still there," she says before leaning her head onto my shoulder. We watch the rest of the unveiling before I feel her posture relax. She's asleep.

I slowly try to untangle myself from her as much as I am able to with one good hand. It takes a few minutes, but I finally get her laid down and covered with a blanket before heading to our bedroom.

I need some Tylenol or something because my cravings for alcohol are hitting me with a force I didn't count on.

Between surgery and getting the good drugs in the hospital it hasn't been an issue, but I'm suddenly drenched with sweat and shaking as I collapse into bed.

My head starts pounding, and I curl up in a ball, trying to fall asleep so I don't have to suffer through this.

I'm vaguely woken up by a body wrapping around me and a cold cloth on my forehead, but nothing really registers.

***

Searing heat wakes me. I thrash around and around, trying to get free of it, only to realize I'm wrapped in the comforter as well as Daisy.

I need to get away from it, though. My breath is coming in short bursts, panic making its way through my body as I roll over and fall onto the floor, right onto my hand.

"FUUUUCKKK!" I scream as I collapse onto my back.

I barely hear Daisy's freaked out, "What the fuck?" I'm too consumed with pain.

Her hand touches my shoulder, and I flinch.

"Hey, it's just me." Her calm voice pulls me from my confusion enough to figure out what's going on.

"I was too hot." My throat is so dry that I can barely get the words out.

She presses her hand to my forehead and stands up in an instant. I can't see where she goes, but the sound of the shower turning on helps me get more grounded.

"Up. Come on," she says once she comes back.

I struggle to stand. The sharp pain in my hand is concerning, but my brain can't focus on that. The cold sweat causing me to shiver is the only thing I can think of.

Daisy supports most of my weight as we walk to the bathroom. Not bothering to undress, she walks us both under the spray of the shower. We're lucky there's a bench in here, so she can put me here and not try to support me the whole time.

The cold water drenches me fast, but I welcome the shock. Hell, I need it.

I hardly notice Daisy rushing around, grabbing things, until she is right in front of me and taking my hand.

"Let's check this first," she mumbles. With the utmost caution, she moves my hand out of the spray—another fuck-up on my end—and unwraps it.

I open my mouth and close it a couple of times, trying my hardest to be present, but I can't focus.

I want a drink so badly. It'll help all of this go away.

No.

I'm doing this for her. For my *hercegnőm*, my princess. For me and our future.

She dabs something on my hand, startling me, which makes me yank my hand from her.

"Stop," I grunt.

"I need to rebandage it. You fell hard on it, but the graft still looks okay."

"Just leave, and I'll do it later," I growl, anger spreading deep within my body. I'm not sure why I'm even angry. I just know this intense rage has taken over, and I can't see anything but red.

"Luka..." Her words are like a warning growl before she sighs and grabs my hand again with more strength than I give her credit for. "I think you're detoxing, so I'm not going to take any of this to heart, but I do need to clean this up and cover it. Please."

I say nothing. How can I when the shaking and nausea hit me full force?

I didn't think it was this bad.

I didn't think it was this big of a problem.

I didn't think I was *addicted.*

Puking in the shower while my wife bandages my freshly grafted skin says it's way worse than I thought.

Falling to my knees after she finishes so I can dry heave is my low point.

In a T-shirt and shorts, drenched with cold water, with my head pounding so hard it feels like it's going to explode, I hit rock bottom.

Once the nausea subsides a little, I sit down on the cold tiles.

I don't realize I'm crying until Daisy sits next to me, protecting my hand from the bulk of the water, and wraps her arm around my shoulders.

My body shifts, curling in on itself and laying on her lap as the sobbing starts.

Failure.

Addict.

Worthless.

Weak.

I am so fucking weak. It's a gut punch because I really thought things were getting better, that *I* was getting better.

It was all just masked by the ugly veil of alcohol.

Daisy whispers words of positivity, of hope, as I break down in her arms.

Maybe this is the real start to healing. God, I hope it is.

Chapter 18
Daisy

We don't sleep.

I do manage to get him to bed, but not without a ton of effort and yelling from him. *It's the alcohol*, I keep reminding myself. He doesn't mean to be hurtful; he's detoxing, and this comes with the territory. At least, that's what I've read since I realized his drinking was a bigger problem than either of us wanted to admit.

He's sweating, dry heaving, and shaking all night long, and I can do nothing but try to comfort him.

I cry. For him, for us, for what is happening to him, and for how we'll make it out of this intact. It seems like there is so much against us and we aren't able to catch a break.

I just need a break.

The next twelve hours are just as hard, but his symptoms seem to be petering out. I'm scared to leave him, though. I fear that he'll relapse somehow—even though I dumped all the booze—or that he'll have a seizure when I'm not here. Too many things could happen, so I stay glued to his side.

When dusk hits the sky, the last dredges of sunlight streaming through our window, sleep finally takes him. His fever seems to have broken, and he isn't sweating like he was. The shaking has gotten a lot better too. But he's worn out, understandably. Exhaustion finally wins now that it seems like the worst of the withdrawal is over.

I wish exhaustion would take over for me too, but it seems like I'm destined to remain awake for a while yet. My mind is racing with too many thoughts.

Is the worst of the withdrawal over?

Should I have taken him to the hospital?

Am I doing enough?

Can he stay sober?

Endless loops of hypotheticals, of replaying conversations and events that should have shown me that he was this far down the path of addiction. Thinking of things I should have done differently. Minutes, hours... They all blur together.

"Did you get any sleep?" His sleep-roughened voice startles me.

"Uh, no. Not much." I turn to see him staring at me with so many emotions on his face.

"I ... umm. I'm sorry," he croaks.

Nodding as tears come to my eyes, I don't think I could talk if I wanted to.

"I feel a lot better."

"That's good," I say on a broken whisper.

"I didn't think it was that ... bad."

"I— You scared me," I finally say after a beat.

"I think I scared myself too, honestly." He chuckles, but there's no humor in it. "I'd like to shower and change the sheets if that's okay." He's so shy right now that I'm not sure how to respond.

"Of course. Go shower, and I can change the sheets." I shoo him out, even though he has that look on his face that says he wants to push to do both.

Watching him walk, I can already see how much steadier he is, which is a relief. It takes me no time to change the sheets and snuggle in to wait for him.

I jolt awake when I feel his body wrapping around mine.

"Shh, go back to sleep," he whispers.

"I'm okay." I roll over to face him. "Are you okay?"

"I feel better and will be okay, I think."

"Can—"

"Dais—"

We speak at the same time before he nods for me to continue.

"Can we just maybe wait to talk about everything? I need time to process." I'm trying to keep my emotions and tears at bay.

It's not that I don't want to talk about it. It's more that I want to talk to my therapist and really take time to come up with how I want to respond. How I really feel about all of this. I don't want a knee-jerk reaction that could cause more harm than good.

"Of course." I see the sadness in his eyes but also relief. His left hand moves to cup my face, the metal of this wedding ring cold against the heat of his hand. "I am so damn sorry, Dais," he whispers.

My eyes shift between his, and I'm not sure what comes over me, but I need to know there's hope at the end of the road. That we still have the connection that got us to this point in the first place. Turning my head, I kiss the palm that was holding me. Just a soft kiss, testing the waters.

"What are you—"

"How's your pain?" I ask.

"In my hand? Head?" Confusion swirls in his eyes. Maybe I'm taking this a step too far, and he doesn't want anything like the closeness I need.

"Yes, in your hand."

"Umm, fine. Twinges every once in a while and itches like a mother fucker, now that I think about it, but it's fine. My head is a lot better too, but I did take some Ibuprofen."

"I have a thought." My fingertips brush along the hem of my shirt, my one-track mind saying 'fuck it'. Desperation is making me lose my damn mind, apparently.

"Oh yeah?"

"You can tell me no."

"I won't ever tell you no, *hercegnőm*." He gives me the look he used to. The one that says he'd do anything for me, and my fragile little heart grips onto it so hard.

"I think we both need a little distraction."

"Yeah?"

"Yeah." I move my hand up his abs, and they contract at the softness of my skin against his.

I tuck my legs underneath me before swinging one over his hips and settling my weight against him. He reaches for my hips, but I shake my head.

"No touching. Not with your hand. It's too fresh."

"I have one … mostly good hand." He holds up his left hand.

"Nope." I slide my hands up to his chest, playing with the little bit of hair he has there, before I slide his shirt completely up.

"Daisy…" He sighs and moves forward so I can remove the shirt. This may be a terrible idea in the light of day, but right in this moment, it feels like a necessity.

"Shh, I think we both need this." I lean over, pressing a kiss to his heart, before I move up his neck and jaw.

Leaning back just enough to look into his eyes, I press a soft kiss to his lips. "We're going to work through this together." Another kiss. "We're going to get healthy together. Mentally and physically."

"Promise?" he murmurs.

"I promise on the vows we said over two years ago. I'm not giving up on us, but we both need to want it."

"I promise. I want to be and stay sober. I need *you*, Daisy," he chokes out.

"Then let's forget about the hard stuff for a little while."

I shift my hips on him and feel him hardening beneath me.

"*Hercegnőm*, you don't need to do this," he says on a groan as my hips move again and his head tips back.

"I know, but it's been so long," I breathe. The horniness I've pushed way down deep has gotten a taste, and now I need it. To go from a very, very voracious sexy life to nothing in the span of a couple of months has gotten to me more than I thought, and now it doesn't matter how inappropriate the timing. Bigger issues have been at the forefront, but now I can't reel it back in. "Tell me no, and I'll stop." I give him an out, even though I'll burn through a ton of batteries if he does.

"Fuck no. I told you I won't tell you no." He arches his hips as much as he can.

"Then let me lead. Let me get us there." I shift to shove down his shorts before stripping out of my oversized shirt. My panties are a little harder to finagle, but I manage with little fanfare.

Once we're both naked, I look him over. A little leaner, less tanned for sure, with angry red scars winding up his forearms. Slow to heal, but a visual sign that he survived. And he more than does it for me. He's still the most handsome man I've ever seen.

And I've missed him so fucking much.

I glide my clit against him, my head tipping back on a sigh. I continue that at a leisurely pace, not in a hurry for release, just desperate to connect.

He stays true to his word and keeps his hands down by his side, even when I hold him in my hand and notch him at my entrance. Slowly, so damn slowly, I slide down onto him.

I'm so turned on that I have to take breath just to gain my bearings again.

"Holy fuck," Luka growls and thrusts his hips a little. It sparks my movement, but I keep things slow and deep.

Intense.

So fucking intense it's like the universe opened up and swallowed me whole.

My nails dig into his chest as I sink down on him and circle my hips.

Luka's good hand moves to cup my cheek like he can't stand not touching me. I'm not sure what comes over me, but I grab his hand and shove it down by his head as I lean forward.

"I'm in charge. You don't touch me unless I tell you to," I growl against his neck, all the while swiveling my hips so my clit gets some friction.

"Oh my God," he murmurs. "Keep talking like that, and I'll come in two seconds."

I smirk before pulling back to look at him. "You like it when I boss you around?"

"I think I fucking love it when you boss me around," he says with an arch of his hips.

My grip on his wrist tightens, and my eyes roll back at how good it feels.

Hearing him say that brings out something new in me, something I didn't realize I needed.

Control.

I've lacked control in every facet of my life lately, and this one act of it is giving me the confidence to regain more.

To take back my life and turn it into something I can be proud of, be happy with.

And that starts with fucking my husband so well that we both finally get some relief.

Chapter 19
Luka

Never in my life have I had a submissive bone in my body.

That all changed about five minutes ago.

Daisy in charge of both of our pleasure is a sight to behold. She looks like a goddess riding me as if she owns me, which she does. It's not that we've had a bad sex life—it's been the best sex of my life—but this is somehow different. It's *more.* It's powerful and hot as fuck.

Her taking what she needs from me is also helping to distract me from the fact that I just detoxed from alcohol. Am still detoxing—a fact that I'll have to deal with later, but not right now.

Right now, the feel of her clenching against me sends a tingle down my spine. My jaw locks as I try to hold my shit together, but her wet, searing heat is pulling me under.

"Fuck, *hercegnőm.* I'm so close," I grate out.

She eases her pace, leaning forward to kiss me. The lazy, languid kisses take the edge off. When her hips start moving again, I bite her bottom lip in an attempt to slow her down.

I don't want this to stop.

It's life affirming after so much doubt.

This is making me wonder why I used alcohol to cope when I could have had Daisy this whole time. She could have soothed my soul and kept me on track instead of falling so far off the path.

But sex with her is what started this entire spiral.

I won't let my head go down that road right now, though. There's more to it; I know that, and it's not fair of me to lump all of my issues down to one event that was, technically, the result of us having sex. To blame Daisy at all doesn't address my part in any of it.

She leans back, pulling me out of my head, and moves the hand that was holding mine down to her thigh and up to her clit.

My head tips back as much as it can, as I try desperately to not come on the spot. Watching her masturbate does me in every single time. I'm just a mortal man, after all.

"Jesus, Dais." My body clenches so tight that my muscles start to ache.

"Oh God, I missed this so much," she whimpers.

I flex my left hand, wanting so badly to grab onto her hips and slam her down onto me, but I stay strong. It's my new life's motto: Stay strong and don't cave.

"Get there, please. I'm so fucking close." I close my eyes against my better judgement, but the sight of her rubbing her clit, her face pure ecstasy with my cock spreading her, is too damn good to resist.

I feel her pace stutter as her knees clamp onto my hips. My eyes pop open to watch her come right as my orgasm hits hard.

Heaven.

No, utopia—that's what this is.

This is what life should be like, what it should feel like.

She collapses on top of me, and I finally wrap my arms around her. If I were to jeopardize this, it would be my biggest mistake. If I manage to fuck it up? No. No more drinking. No more pushing her away because I can't handle the hard things.

No. It's me and Daisy against the world.

✳✳✳

I've been sober for three weeks.

My therapist has been a life saver, taking my calls whenever I need help, upping my appointments, and giving me resources like AA to help connect with other alcoholics.

It's been hard; I won't lie. Once the worst of the detox was over, the cravings came, and they have yet to go away.

But every time I have a craving, I look at Daisy, and the sight of her solidifies my resolve to stay strong.

Daisy's in Bahrain this weekend for the first race of the Formula 1 season. I could have gone, but I just don't think I'm there yet. She understood, but I kind of wish she would have pushed me harder to go. I'm too chicken-shit to push myself, so maybe she could do it for me. Which is a dick way of thinking and something my therapist will probably have a field day with on Monday, but whatever.

I am pushing myself to watch the press conferences and practices, though. Baby steps with low stakes is what Dr. Tate said.

The Empress drivers are about to hit the press conference, and I'm eagerly waiting to roll my eyes at their arrogant asses. Their canned responses will be predictable, but I'll be interested if either of them gets ballsy enough to go off script.

Malcolm stays on the straight and narrow, but Sawyer goes off script in a big way, and I swear I can see Sydney's head about to explode all the way on the other side of the world. I'm sure Beck is handling it, but that isn't the way I would want to start out my F1 career under new ownership.

I pull out my phone and text Daisy, my hand finally at the point where I can finger-peck at texting. My physical therapist said it was good practice, even though I hate it.

Me:

> Is Sydney about to go ballistic on Sawyer?

Daisy:

> I think Beck is because, holy shit, what was that?? I mean, you're cocky, but you've never been stupid. At least not in a press conference.

I burst out laughing at that.

Me:

Thanks for the clarification.

Me:

Seriously, though, how are you? You doing okay? Not working too much?

Daisy:

So far okay. I'll withhold the answer for the rest of your questions until after Practice One. That'll tell me what kind of mood Sydney will be in for the weekend and how much work I have to do.

Me:

Keep me updated, and I can send food to your room if you need me to.

Daisy:

Thanks. Gotta go. Love you!

Me:

Love you too.

I relax back onto the couch and fidget before pulling out the journal my therapist has been hounding me about starting. No time like the present, I guess.

***

My phone rings on Friday, ten minutes after Practice Two ends.

"Hello?"

"Thank God you answered. I need inside your arrogant brain." Sydney's voice is rushed and exasperated.

"Umm, okay?" I guess I'll take that as a compliment.

"How the fuck do I tame Sawyer? He was supposed to be the easygoing one, and now he's a giant … asshole who's about to wreck a car in the first week."

"Shouldn't you be talking to Gavino about that?" I ask because the team principal should be the one who deals with these issues, not a washed-up old driver.

"Don't even get me started on him," she growls—actually growls—and now I'm a little scared.

"Umm, I guess you could put him on notice. If he can't get his shit under control, he'll be out of a contract. Threats usually get the job done."

"I didn't want to be a huge bitch when I took over, but damn." She sighs.

"You're not a huge bitch if you're trying to prevent your two drivers from being at odds all year, along with crashing cars left and right. That's the worst situation for everyone. Just sit down with Sawyer and ask him what the hell his problem is."

"Beckett said the same thing."

"Well, he does know a thing or two about racing fast cars." I smirk, even though she can't see me.

"Hey, Luka?"

"Yeah?"

"It's good to hear that sarcasm again. Whenever you're ready to get back to the sport, let me know. We'll find a place for you."

My throat closes up, and I try to clear it, but my voice just comes out as a croak. "Thanks."

I quickly hang up, but my mind doesn't stop racing. I'm not sure what's next for me, but I do know that my friends, my *family*, have my back with whatever direction I decide to go.

The rest of the weekend is spent talking to Daisy when I can, and watching Malcolm and Sawyer fuck things up royally. Malcolm places seventeenth, and Sawyer doesn't even finish the race. I don't hear from Sydney again, but I know she's more than disappointed with her debut as the new president of Empress Racing.

My phone rings at almost four in the morning on Sunday, after the race is over.

"Hey, *hercegnőm*."

"Hi. I'm at the airport, about to board, but wanted to call you before I'm in the air," Daisy says. She sounds exhausted.

"You okay?"

"I'm just tired. My plan is to sleep most of the flight, even though I should be working."

"Sydney will tell you to sleep," I tell her.

"I know," she says quietly.

"I will also tell you to sleep. Get some rest and come home safe to me. I'll have food for you when you get home."

"Thank you. I love you," she whispers.

"Love you too. Be safe."

I crash while she's in the air, then make sure I have pancakes and bacon ready for her when she gets home.

Chapter 20

Daisy

The first race weekend was abysmal.

Sydney, Beckett, and I didn't expect our drivers to turn into smug little divas with very little to back it up. At least Luka had the skill to back up his attitude.

Luka.

Things have been, dare I say, better since he detoxed and we had sex. We've been cordial, more like roommates who sleep in the same bed now. But no more sex. I'm honestly not sure how I feel about it all. I haven't had time to think about it with the season starting, and now it's all I can think about on the trip back to Austin.

The car Sydney hired to take us all home from the airport just dropped her and Beckett off, and the drive to my house is short, luckily. Because I miss Luka. I miss the connection we had a few weeks ago, even if it was the worst possible time for it.

As we pull up to the house, I see a figure standing in the doorway. Strong and steady. He looks healthier than he did when I left just days ago. More color to his face, along with some stubble on his jaw that makes my thighs squeeze together.

Walking up with my suitcase behind me, I tuck my blonde curls behind my ear.

"Hi." Shyness I've never experienced with him before is thick in my voice.

"Hey, gorgeous. I missed you." His Luka smirk is on full display, and it makes my heart pound in my chest.

I was so scared to leave him for the race because he's so newly sober, but it seems I worried for nothing. He looks damn good.

"I was told there would be breakfast." I tilt my head.

He chuckles before moving to the side and leading me in. I leave my suitcase by the door, to deal with later, and head to the kitchen but stop in my tracks at what I see.

"How does a date sound?" Luka says from behind me.

"A date," I say dumbfounded as I look at the multiple vases of flowers on the island. All of my favorites in abundance: tulips, sunflowers, and peonies. Our dining room table is covered with food that looks incredible.

"It's from Lucy's," Luka says softly. He hasn't taken over, instead letting me take it all in.

"You've never wanted to do brunch at Lucy's," I say. I've tried for months, but he always told me he didn't do brunch. That it was full of food that didn't fit into his strict diet.

"Well, I want to now. We were due a date, and although the diet thing is true, I was an asshole for not taking you anyway."

I look back at him, at the earnest look in his eyes, and I swear I fall even more in love with him.

He's making an effort—one hell of an effort, actually—and I need to be able to take him at his word. Holding grudges, and only focusing on the past and what we've done wrong, won't move us forward. Trust. I need to trust him.

Walking up to him, I wrap my arms around his neck and rise up on my tiptoes to press a kiss to his lips. "Thank you."

"Let's eat before it gets cold." He pulls away and leads me to the table.

We stuff our faces with decadent stuffed French toast, eggs Benedict, and enough pasties to last us a week. Sipping my London fog, I peak at my husband from over the lid.

He looks content, maybe for the first time since I've known him. The thought sends unexpected sadness through my body. He's never been this content with me, this *happy* with me, before. Maybe that says something? Or were we like this before? It feels like so long ago that I can't even remember.

"You're thinking too much." His smooth voice pulls me from my head.

I look over at him, his brow furrowed as he picks at a Danish.

"I... Are we wrong to hold onto this so tightly?"

"Hold onto what? Us?" he asks.

I nod, and his face transforms into a mask of anger, but not at me. "What did I do to put your head there?" he asks with surprising calmness.

"Nothing! It's just that you look so healthy and happy, and I've been gone, and we haven't done anything else since..." I ramble, so confused by my own thought process that I'm not sure where I'm heading.

"Hey, hey, slow down. Come here." He shoves his chair back and beckons me to him.

I settle on his lap, trying to figure out why everything has taken such a turn.

"First, let me ask... Did you get some sleep on the flight?"

My cheeks heat as I shake my head.

"Okay, so sleep is definitely needed. Second, I had to call my therapist while you were gone. I won't lie and say that having a drink wasn't tempting as hell with you gone, so I did what I could to not relapse. That meant reaching out to people for help when the cravings got too strong. If I look happy, it's because you're home. If I look healthy, it's because I'm doing everything in my power to get there for you, for us. And—and this is really fucking important—don't ever think I don't want you. I want you every second of the day. Every single day. That's never in question. What is in question is if I can do right by you and not just have sex to take the edge off. I don't ever want to put you in that position. And I know I'll fuck this up, but I don't want you to give up on me when I do."

"Why didn't you reach out to me?" My voice is small and on the verge of tears. During that amazing speech, all I could think about was that I didn't know he was struggling with not drinking. I guess I expected him to call me when he had a craving. My selfish thoughts are a sign that I need to call my own therapist because damn... All that sweetness, and I'm still focused on me.

"Oh, *hercegnőm*, I didn't want to put more on your plate. God knows I've done nothing but put more on your plate recently, and I just wanted you to have a weekend to focus on your job and not worry about me."

"I always worry about you," I murmur as the exhaustion I've been fighting starts to take over.

"I know, Dais, I know. But now, it's time to let me worry about you, okay?

How about we get you to bed, and we can talk more when you wake up?" He presses a kiss to my temple before patting my butt.

I stand up, and the full force of the weekend hits me hard. Luka wordlessly leads me to our bedroom, stripping me out of the clothes I flew in and putting one of his T-shirts over my head. There's no hesitation when I curl up into bed. When I feel the bed dip and Luka's arm comes around my middle, my brain finally shuts off, and I fall into a dreamless sleep.

***

I got one day to do nothing before work called again.

Luka and I spent the day binge-watching movies and relaxing. It was a silent truce that we'd get to it eventually, but not that day. We both needed a break, I think.

Now, I'm rushing to get dressed as Luka watches me from the bedroom.

"Why do you need to go in right now? I thought you guys had a couple of days before you needed to regroup." he asks.

"So, funny story. I put out feelers for Team Principals, just to have in our back pocket, but after this weekend's showing, Sydney is pushing that to a main priority. She wants me to interview—or talk to, I guess, since it's not that formal—a couple of the candidates, with the idea that we bring them in before summer break." I shove my legs into my favorite pair of dress slacks.

"Sydney doesn't fuck around."

"No, she doesn't. But she's also not feeling great this morning after all the travel, so I'm filling in for her like I have any fucking clue how to interview a Team Principal," I mumble as I toss on a pink silk shirt and fluff my blonde curls.

"Make Beck come. He can help you," he offers.

"I think he is, but who knows how comfortable he'll feel actually interviewing since he just retired. It's like a driver interviewing his boss, you know?" Picking up the watch Sydney gifted me when the Empress deal went through, I clasp it on my wrist and slide my feet into my favorite power stilettos.

They'll give me a much-needed boost of confidence and height.

"You're nervous," Luka observes.

"Well, no shit!" I throw my hands up. "I'm just an assistant. I'm not the one who's supposed to be interviewing for possibly the most important position on the team outside of drivers!"

Okay, so maybe the stress is getting to me a little, judging by the shrillness of my voice.

"Hey." Luka's soft, calming voice pulls my attention. "You're not just an assistant. And I know for a fact that Sydney would say the same, so if you get stuck on that, I will be calling her to make her lecture you." He smirks.

"But what if I fuck this up?" I ask as I walk over to the edge of the bed.

He pulls me between his legs and hugs me to him, enveloping me in his arms. "You won't. Sydney wouldn't give you the responsibility if she didn't think you could handle it. Besides, a team principal isn't just about their capabilities; it's about how they'll fit within the team. You have a great sense of judgment when it comes to people. Except for me." He winks.

"You're ridiculous." I roll my eyes. "You are good people, but I don't have time to fill your head with praise."

"That's a damn shame because I could go for some of that right about now." The twinkle in his eye almost gets me.

I shove him back against the bed. "Too bad I have to go be a boss bitch, then, isn't it?" I whisper before kissing him with a little more tongue than I intended.

"I have so many things I want to say, but then you'll be late," he murmurs against my lips.

Smirking, I stand back up and throw my hand up as I turn around.

"I love you, and you can tell me all about all those things when I get back home."

"You're a cruel, cruel woman, *hercegnőm*!" he yells as I make my way to the garage.

The entire drive to Vanstone Properties home base, I think about the playfulness Luka and I had. How much I miss it. How much I wish I could play hooky and screw his brains out.

But the real world calls, and I need to do exactly as I said—go be a boss bitch and channel my inner Sydney. It doesn't matter that she hates that nickname; she's fucking incredible, and I've always looked up to her. I guess, today is the day I see if I can really cut it in this world.

I'm scrolling through emails as I head into Sydney's office. Walking around to sit in the chair behind the desk, I scream when I finally put my phone down and see a man sitting in the chair across from me.

"Jesus, Beck, you're going to give me a heart attack." My hand is on my chest as it heaves from the scare.

"Jumpy, Mrs. Tomic." He smiles. "Sorry, I should have coughed or something. I honestly thought you'd see me."

"Sorry, I'm so lost in my head. I just want to make sure these interviews go off without a hitch." I take a deep breath.

"They will. Don't stress it."

I give him a look that says I will absolutely be stressing it because his wife is my idol and I don't want to let her down.

He opens his mouth to say something, but is cut off by the first person video calling in.

We go through three candidates, and all three are misses for me.

"I hate them all. They won't mesh well with the higher-ups, and they want entirely too much money." I sigh and slump back into my chair.

"I agree. I can't believe Sydney lined up Pierre for an interview. He's a slimy snake, and most of the grid fucking hates him," Beck says with disgust.

"We just wanted to look at all the options, and so far, I'm not impressed. And we only have one more interview."

"And the last one is a hail Mary if I've ever seen one," he grumbles.

"Antoinette Bailey is super new to the business, yes, but Sydney's been keeping tabs on her for over a year. She's been killing it in Formula 2, and before that, she was the lead mechanical engineer at a huge aviation company."

"I don't know. Seems a little premature to potentially pull her up. She's just an engineer in Formula 2, right?" he asks.

"And you're just a retired car driver," I counter with an arched eyebrow.

"Point made. Sydney would be proud." He smiles.

My computer rings, effectively cutting off our conversation once again.

"Good afternoon, Antoinette. Thank you for joining us," I say as Beck nods.

"Toni, please, and the pleasure is all mine."

"I'd like to be upfront with you. We're not looking to make a change immediately at Empress, but we recognize that if we're continuing on the path we've started the season on, we'll likely need to make big changes. Hence the reason for this meeting," I tell her.

"I can understand that. I watched the replay yesterday. The inter-driver fighting this early isn't a great sign. Can I ask what position you'd be looking to fill potentially?" she asks, and I admire her straightforward nature. Like me, she doesn't beat around the bush.

"Of course," I say, knowing she's already signed an NDA before this meeting. It was a stipulation in order to even be on the call. "We're looking for a team principal."

"Oh." Her eyes go wide with shock. "And I'm on the call list?"

I give her my professional yet warm smile. "You are, indeed. You've been doing well in Formula 2, and it hasn't gone unnoticed."

"Thank you for that." She nods.

"As you know, Sydney Davis just took over ownership of Empress, and before we undertook a huge shake-up with personnel, we wanted to get a feel of how things were going. As you've observed, they aren't where we wanted to be at the start of the season. We would be looking to potentially ride out the existing principal's contract until summer break, before considering any change. As you know, negotiations take time, and finding a replacement for your current role would take time as well," I explain. "I understand this discussion and the potential position may be a bit of a shock, but can I pose the question to you? Off the top of your head, especially after watching this week's race, what would you say the current problems are and can you offer any solutions?"

"Absolutely," she says with zero hesitation. She goes on to call out problems we've already tagged, as well as a couple Sydney and I hadn't even thought of. She offers more solutions than any of the other candidates combined, and once she takes a pause, I jump in.

"Would you be willing to leave your engineering position to take the team principal position at Empress?"

"I would be honored, honestly. I always love a challenge, and although the learning curve in Formula 2 has been steep, I've set my sights on a more ... substantial position already."

"Well, that's great to hear. I need to take all this information back to Sydney, but do you have any other questions for either of us?"

"How do you feel about firing drivers mid-season?" she asks with a small smirk, and I know instantly she's our new hire.

"Personally, I'm all for it. However, Boss Lady might have a different opinion, but we can chat her up if we decide to move forward." I wink.

We spend a couple of more minutes talking about salary expectations, before we hang up and I turn to Beck.

"She's it."

"I love her," we say simultaneously.

"Glad we're on the same page. I'll talk to Sydney about it when I get home, but if you'll email her your thoughts too, so we have everything together, that would be great," he says, already standing up to head out.

"Will do. Hey, how's she doing?"

"She's okay. Her ankles were really bothering her this morning; that's why I wanted her to stay home."

I nod. Her rheumatoid arthritis has been leaps and bounds better than it was, but it's better to be safe than sorry. Beck and I clearly handled things together well.

"Alright, go pick her up some food on your way home, and I'm going to wrap up a couple of things here before I leave." I'm already turning back to my computer before his words stop me.

"How's he doing? Like, really doing? He won't give me more than a basic response. I've been trying to give him time, but I'm worried."

I sigh. "He's ... better. Working through a lot of things, but his hands are healing well. He should have the bandages off permanently this week, at least until the next surgery."

"That's good to hear. If you, umm, get a chance, will you ask him to call me? Or text me?" Beck, our friend, is one of my favorite people. He stayed in the hospital with me for days after the crash, making sure to not only support Luka but me as well.

"Absolutely." I give him a small smile.

An hour later, I've wrapped up everything I needed to do and am heading home. I decide to stop and get Luka and me some lunch, hoping we can pick back up our fun banter from this morning.

Chapter 21
Luka

Addiction is a strange mistress. There are days I don't think about alcohol at all. Then, there are days where I think of nothing but alcohol. I've officially been sober for forty-nine days, and I'm feeling all the struggles of every one of those days today.

My leg bounces as I stare at the television. Practice Two is on, but I'm not watching it. I had to mute it because the sound was getting to me.

Rage took over, and I almost threw the remote at the television to shut it up, but somehow a smoother head prevailed. I hate that whenever I start to feel good, start to feel like I may be over the hump of shit, days like this happen.

Daisy is at Beck and Sydney's house, watching practice while talking to all their employees as practices finish up, but I declined to join. Everything seems too hard today, like I'm stuck in cement and can't get a handle on anything to pull me out. Now that I think about it, I don't think I've eaten today either.

I run through the mental list my therapist talked about for when things get too overwhelming.

Distraction.

I look around, stand up, and pace the living room. Immediately, I feel like ants are crawling over my skin, so I plop back down on the couch and try something else.

Remember it's only temporary.

My leg starts bouncing again as I repeat the motto, and it doesn't slow down one bit in the ten minutes I keep telling myself it'll go away.

Eat something nutritious and have a fizzy drink.

Heading to the kitchen, I grab some cheese, a beef stick, and a couple of crackers. Might not be ultra healthy, but it'll hopefully take the edge off. I also grab a seltzer and take a sip immediately.

It's a struggle to eat the little meal I made. It's a fight to drink more than half of my drink, but it does take just the hint of an edge off.

Reach out.

I pick up my phone before tossing it back on the couch. I make a loop around the couch before picking it up again and opening my messages.

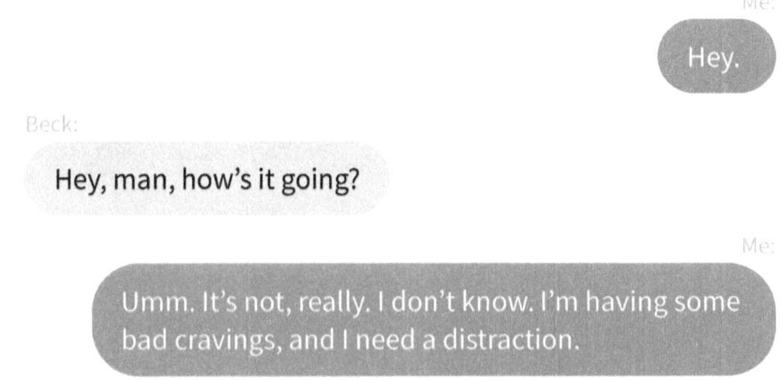

I didn't plan to be this honest, especially to my best friend whom I've essentially shut out since the accident, but desperation does funny things to a man.

Even though I am sad I'm not there to witness it, a small smile graces my face. Daisy is a badass, and it's great to see her shining so brightly in this new role. I just wish I was able to suck up whatever this block is to be able to watch a full race weekend without freaking out.

Beck:

> I can send you a video if you want. Might be a little weird, and I'm pretty sure Daisy would punch me if she figured it out, but I'd do it, man.

That does make me laugh. My chest loosens just enough to let me breathe again.

Me:

> As much as I want that, I'm going to vote no. She will absolutely dick punch you if she catches you taking a weird video of her.

Me:

> How's the season looking? I've been catching things here and there, but it's been … harder than I thought it would be.

Beck:

> Totally understandable. Things are … stressful. Sydney isn't happy with where the team is at, and she's really pissed that they haven't gotten any points yet.

Me:

> Yeah, can't say I blame her.

We talk logistics a little more. Things become easier and easier to talk about when I decide to broach something that scares the shit out of me, but it's something my therapist has been bugging me to at least think about.

Me:

> Hey, do you have contacts in the academy?

Beck:

> Umm, not really, but I'm sure I could find someone who does. Why?

Me:

> I'm … future planning, I guess you could say. F1 Academy feels just far enough away from F1 that I might be able to handle it. Plus, everyone is so fucking excited to just be there every day. It might be a nice change of pace for me.

My disorganized thoughts are latching onto something I've only briefly thought of in passing, but now, it feels imperative that I figure it out.

Beck:

> That's a great idea. I'll look into it and get you in contact with someone.

Me:

> Thanks, man, I appreciate it.

Beck:

> I'm glad you reached out, Luka. Don't be a stranger, okay?

Me:

> I'll try not to be.

I lean back against the couch and ruminate on this impromptu direction. I'm not sure I even realized I wanted to stay within Formula 1, but this is the right move. I feel it in my very shaky bones. Maybe I can find a way to combine my charity work with the academy and try to really make a difference.

The rest of the afternoon is spent thinking of different programs I could create while also looking at the schedule for my next surgery to see what's actually possible.

***

"Hi." Her shy voice kills me every time, knowing I'm the one who made her this way. No bubbly, fun Daisy since I crashed—possibly longer if I think about it—only little peeks here and there.

"Hey, Dais, how'd your day go?"

"Slightly hectic. Slightly exhausting. Slightly exhilarating." She sighs as she sits next to me.

"That's a lot."

"It is. I think a bath is in order tonight."

One of my favorite quirks of hers is the way she takes a bath to clear her head. Whether she's stressed, tired, has too much to work on, or whatever it is, a bath is her cure all.

"I can make that happen. Are you hungry?"

"Nah. Sydney fed me— well, technically, Beck fed her and that overflowed to me, not that I'm complaining. Did you get some dinner?" she asks, tilting her head to look at me.

God, she's so fucking gorgeous. It's been hell to keep my hands to myself, but I didn't feel like either of us were ready to fully recommit to the physical side of things yet.

"I ate." I won't tell her that it was barely an adult-sized Lunchable four hours ago.

"You want to come keep me company while I destress?"

"Always." I stand up and hold out my left hand. The right is healing really nicely, but it's still tender as hell with the new graft.

Leading her to the bathroom, I turn on the water and add bath salts to the tub. I lean against the counter as I watch her undress.

The soft curves of her breasts leading to her waist get me worked up every single time I see them. A flash in my head of her round with my baby shocks me to the core.

And not in a bad way.

No, just the opposite, actually. To know that I made that, created something so fucking permanent with her, almost drops me to my knees. It's not even real, just a glimpse of what could be—what could have been—and now, I can't unsee it.

"You okay?" she asks before she steps into the tub.

"Uh, umm, yeah. I'm good." I clear my throat.

But it's like everything has changed in an instant.

I watch her sink into the cloudy water; she exhales in relief when the hot water hits all the spots that hold her tension.

Suddenly, I can't be on the sidelines watching her or just talking to her. I start to strip. I'm down to my boxer briefs before she notices and scoots forward for me.

Sliding in behind her is like coming home. The closeness, the touch of her soft skin against mine—all of it—is everything I've been starving for.

The stark difference between her alabaster stomach and my angry-red, scarred hands and forearms reminds me that she's the good in our relationship. She always has been. She took pity on a cocky asshole who made too much money, and I loved the attention she gave me.

"You've always been too good for me," I murmur before pressing a kiss to her shoulder.

"Lies. I basically stalked you," she says wistfully.

"I liked it."

"I know you did." She giggles.

My thumb strokes her stomach. "I texted Beck today."

"That's great."

"I was struggling with cravings and I had the practice on, and it was all too much for me," I admit.

"I wish you would have called me. I would have come home."

"I know you would have; that's why I didn't call. You had work to do if that practice was anything to go by. Plus, it ended up being good." My hand spans under her belly button as her hands trail up my thighs.

"Oh yeah?" Her voice is getting a little breathy.

"I asked him about contacts in the F1 Academy." She jolts upright, but I pull her back to me. "I don't know where the idea came from, but the more I thought about it, the more it made sense. I can combine my charity work. Maybe figure out a way to do a fundraiser for Boys and Girls Clubs all over the county. I don't know exactly, but I think this could be good."

"It's phenomenal, Luka. I think it's a great idea, and I'll help you however I can."

"Thank you," I whisper. "I have another surgery in a couple of months, and I'm worried that if I try to get into something or figure out a direction for a job, then I'll have to put it on hold just as soon because of another damn surgery."

"I get that, but if it's something in F1, then no one is going to be an asshole when you need time off to have surgery. Hell, even if it's not in F1, I can't imagine anyone giving you shit for that."

"Maybe. Or what if I'm not good at anything else but driving? What if I can't find something to do long term?" My voice is quiet as I reveal one of my biggest fears.

"Luka, you can do anything you want to do, and I'll help you every step of the way. Whatever makes you happy and content, we'll make happen."

"I love you." My reply is just a horse whisper.

Silence takes over, but it's comfortable for a change. My hand keeps exploring, trailing lower on her stomach before moving to her thighs. I know she feels me reacting against her—it's not like she could miss it—but I'm not pushing for more.

"I'm proud of you for everything you did today. I know it had to be hard." Her soft words permeate my very being, soothing a jagged edge I didn't realize was even there.

"I just want to be good for you, *hercegnőm*." My fingertips trail up her inner thigh. She hesitates only a moment before her thighs fall open against mine. "Am I good for you, Dais?" My fingers barely skim the edge of her pussy as her head leans against my shoulder.

"So good for me. But your hand is still healing."

"I can handle it."

"I'm not jeopardizing it. Hands on my knees," she commands. Her voice may sound soft and sweet, but if she demands, I comply.

My hands land on the outside of her thighs, gripping them tightly to restrain myself. She shifts to slide her legs underneath her, moves my hands closer to her hips, kneels in between my legs, and elevates herself so her ass fits perfectly against my pelvis. She's rubbing against me so damn good that I might come before we get a chance to do anything.

"You're playing with fire," I growl, arching my hips as best as I can.

"Maybe, but you want to be good for me, right? You'll let me play with you, tease you, until I'm ready for more?"

"Holy fuck, Dais. I'll do anything you want me to," I breathe. I have no clue what has brought out this dominance in her, but I want more.

I'm so lost in the pure torture that is Daisy grinding against me that it takes me an extra second to feel her small hand wrap around my cock and brush it against her clit.

Grunting, I grip her hips as hard as I'm able to, wishing I was strong enough to leave my mark. To bruise her so she always remembers who her husband is.

She rises just enough to notch me at her entrance but doesn't go any further. Her fingertips brush against the head of my dick a couple of times, and I realize she's stimulating her clit, trying to get herself off before she fully sinks onto me.

"Fuck, I wish we brought a vibrator in here." My stomach clenches at the thought.

"I didn't…"—she gasps—"didn't think we were going to do this." Her words end on a moan.

I'm holding on for dear life. My balls are so tight that I could come right this second, with my tip barely inside of her.

"Fuck, get there," I growl, hoping she gets there soon.

"Hold on, Luka. Be good for me. Be good and wait for me to…" She moans, and I feel her ripple against me. "Wait for me to come. You know how good it feels when you fill me up mid-orgasm."

My hand starts to cramp and hurt from holding her so tightly, but it barely registers when she throws her head back, calling my name. She drops down with all of her weight as she comes hard against my poor, oversensitive cock.

The feeling of her clenching against me has me gasping for air and holding on with a prayer.

"Don't come yet."

I barely hear her through the whooshing in my ears. "I can't ... I can't hold on."

"You will. You want to be a good boy for me? Then wait. I won't let you come next time if you don't wait."

Without another word, she pulls herself off of me, and the loss is palpable. I ache without her wrapped around me.

Her hips move just enough to where my hands can't hold on anymore, and I feel the water sloshing around us. It's then that I realize I closed my eyes, teeth grinding together so hard that I'm sure to crack a tooth.

But I open my eyes to find myself face to face with my sexy-as-fuck wife.

"I fucking love this side of you," I whisper, unable to contain my need for this new, in-control version of Daisy.

"I think I love it too." She shoves my legs together and straddles me, sinking back onto my cock like she never left.

From this angle, I can look down and see her stretching wide around me. My eyes snap shut because the only thing that's doing is sending me into orgasm way too quickly and jeopardizing my next one.

"I've missed this so much," she says, panting as she really starts to move on me.

"Me too, *hercegnőm*. I miss this closeness," I say, wrapping my arms around her waist and drawing her to me.

I kiss everywhere I can reach, desperate to show her I can be good for her. Impatient to bring her to another orgasm so my muscles can relax as I take my own.

"I miss the connection," she says, kissing my stubbled jaw.

"I miss the way you feel around me." One hand moves to grip her ass and deepen her strokes.

"I miss telling you everything."

"I miss not worrying about the repercussions of everything," I whisper without thought.

"I miss our playfulness. How carefree we were."

"We'll get it back."

"I want to, so badly."

"This is a good start." I pull back to look into her eyes. The same hopefulness I'm feeling is reflecting back to me.

"I've missed you," she says with tears in her eyes.

"You've always had me, even when we were distant. My heart is forever in your hands."

A tear falls as her deep strokes get a little faster. "Come for me, Luka. Be good and come." She gasps as I follow, watching the lone tear trail down her cheek to her jaw before falling and hitting me in the chest.

Right where my heart is.

It sears me like a brand as I pump her full of my cum.

Fuck, I wish she wasn't on birth control. I wish this was the time that took hold.

The thought jolts through my very being. Not because it's scary but because I want it so damn bad.

She nuzzles her head into the crook of my neck as my arms hold her tight.

For all the changes I've made, all the struggles, this moment feels like the turning point. This reconnection is exactly what I needed. It'll be what I keep in the back of my mind when the cravings hit hard, when the loneliness takes over. It'll be what helps me remember that all the hard work means I get to keep this perfect woman in my life.

Chapter 22

Rumors are swirling around Empress Racing ahead of the Miami Grand Prix. Chiefly, will current Team Principal, Gavino, still be with Empress, or are they looking to move in a drastically new direction?

Sources reveal they've been on the hunt since the beginning of the season, so maybe we will see a changing of the guard earlier than expected. It has to be noted that in the last three races, the highest place either driver has placed is fifteenth. Could it be a clash of egos? No answers yet, but there seems to be a turmoil throughout the Empress camp.

There are confirmed reports of Beck and Sydney Davis, as well as Daisy Tomic, in meetings with various crew members throughout the week ahead of this race. Can they turn this season around, or are we just too far in for any changes to matter?

Stay tuned for the latest on Empress, as well as the rest of the grid, ahead of what's shaping up to be a hot Miami Grand Prix race week.

Chapter 23

Daisy

Fucking reporters are going to feel my wrath in exactly three minutes if I have to read another report about Empress sucking ass.

It's not like everyone can't see how terrible we're doing. We aren't oblivious. And the speculation about Sydney, Beck, and me having a million meetings, like all the other team principals and owners aren't doing the exact same thing, is annoying as fuck.

"I'm about to punch out the next reporter who follows me," I tell Sydney as I sling my purse into the visitor's chair in her team-headquarters office behind pit lane. Pacing, I try to calm myself down, but I've never liked being in the media. It was easy to brush off with Luka because he was their main focus, not me.

"They are fucking wolves today." Sydney sighs. "How's everything besides that?"

"Hectic, drama filled. Sawyer is pitching a fit because Malcolm got an upgrade he didn't, but when Cruz tried to tell him calmly that they were testing two different setups and that he also got an upgrade, his toddler-level tantrum wouldn't hear it. I'm shocked Cruz is still in pit lane, honestly."

"We need to make our move," Sydney says, tapping her lips with her pen.

"It's too soon. People will say we haven't given Gavino a real chance."

"Fuck Gavino. He can't reel in Malcolm or Sawyer, and we're drowning. We're about to lose sponsors."

I stop in my tracks and look at Sydney. She looks exhausted, and I feel like shit for just busting in here and making things worse. I didn't realize sponsors were hounding her.

"Shit. Okay. How about I order room service, you and Beck can come to my room, and we can plan how we make this all happen?"

She nods, relief heavy on her face. "Sounds good. I'm done until practice tomorrow, so let's really nail down a plan."

"On it. I'll meet you there in a few."

I'm already texting Luka as I leave the office, warning him that we're about to have company. Sydney and Beck don't know he's here, so I'll be curious how things go down. He wanted to spend more time with me but didn't want to be close to the action, so he relegated himself to our room. It's a huge step for him, and I'm hoping it doesn't lead to ten steps back. Things have been good lately, albeit busy as hell, but I really want to keep it that way.

The walk back to the hotel is quick, but all I can think about is my last therapy session, and how Luka and I really need to talk about our future and how we feel about potentially growing our family. The sex lately has been phenomenal, but it's always in the back of my mind, and I need to just suck it up and face my fears. It's scary. So fucking scary. There's no moving forward until I do, though.

But today is not the day to do that. Today, we need to figure out how to fire and replace our team principal, and hope things go smoothly.

I tap the keycard on the lock. As the green light turns on, I head into our home away from home for the next couple of days.

Luka is sitting on the sofa, wringing his hands together.

"Hey, easy on the hands. They're still new," I try to joke, but it falls flat when I see the anxiety written all over his face. "Hey. It's okay; you're okay. Did you … did you have a drink?" I fucking hate that I feel the need to ask, but I need to know what I'm working with.

"What? No! Jesus, Dais, is that what you think of me?"

"No! No, I just want to make sure you're okay," I say with regret.

He holds my gaze for a minute before all the steam seems to release out of him, his body collapsing back onto the couch.

"I'm sorry. I didn't expect to see anyone besides you, and I just freaked out and jumped to the extreme. I didn't have a drink, though." He pauses before looking up at me. "I thought about it." The guilt and shame are written all over his face, but I have the exact opposite emotions running through me.

I walk over and sit next to him, grabbing his hand and drawing his attention. "Hey. Thinking about it isn't a bad thing. The bigger thing is that you didn't take action. You stopped before you took that step. That's huge, Luka," I implore him to look at it from where I'm sitting.

"No, it's not. When does it fucking stop? When do the thoughts go away?" He grips his overgrown blond hair with his other hand.

"I-I don't know. What has your therapist said?" It reminds me that I need to spend more time learning about his addiction so I can help him. Being slammed at work is a sorry excuse for not supporting him to the fullest.

"He said it may not ever go away, but I can't handle that, Dais." He sounds like he's in physical pain, but I get that it's the emotional turmoil of it all. Lord knows I know how that feels.

"Well, you won't handle it alone. I'm here, your friends are here, and we'll work through it together, okay?" I affirm, hoping it's the right response.

"What if Beck and Sydney are—I don't know—repulsed by me, annoyed that I can't get my shit together? That seven months later, I'm still a shitshow?"

"Hey." I yank his hand a little, making sure he's looking at me. "Step back and revisit what you just said."

He lets out a heavy sigh. "Well, I am still a shitshow."

"We all are, so you aren't alone in that one." I lean back on the couch. "You feel any better?"

"A little. I did order food before I freaked out."

"Thank you for doing that. I appreciate it. Your solitary shitshow will be trumped by a team shitshow as soon as Syd and Beck get here."

"What happened?"

"We're firing Gavino and hiring someone new after Miami." I sigh with exhaustion.

"Oh shit." He sounds almost giddy, and it nearly has me laughing.

"Told you... Shitshow." I smirk at him.

"I can go somewhere else so you guys can figure everything out," he offers, but I'm already shaking my head.

"Stay. We all need to eat, and you may be the fresh eyes we need to see how to fix things since you haven't been in the thick of it all with us."

"I doubt I can fix things." He winces.

Laughter bubbles out of my chest. "You might be right, but we are currently between a rock and a hard place, so we'll take any help."

A knock at the door interrupts anything Luka was going to say.

Opening the door, I usher Beck and Sydney in, but they stop in their tracks, running into each other at the sight of Luka.

"How— Why? Why didn't you tell us?" Sydney turns her accusations on me.

"Bro, it's good to see you," Beck says, going over to him immediately and doing the weird bro-hug thing that I've haven't seen them do in almost two years.

"He wanted to lay low," I whisper to Sydney.

"Understandable. I was just shocked." She nods.

"I know. I was too when he said he wanted to come. But maybe he can help."

"I'm not making him work, Dais. Hell, I won't even make him listen to it. We can go to our room."

"I checked with him. I would have called you if he wasn't okay with it." And I would have, but I did want to see if I could push him out of his reclusive comfort zone a little.

"You don't have to talk about me like I'm not here," Luka calls out to us, my cheeks heating in embarrassment.

"So sorry. I'm just surprised you're here. But it is so great to see you," Sydney says, her words genuine. It always amazes me how she can shift from work Sydney to friend Sydney in a matter of seconds.

"Understandable, and thank you." Luka nods to her.

"So, what's the plan?" Beck asks.

"The plan is we catch up until food gets here because I'm starving and nothing will be productive until we all eat," Sydney says, taking a seat next to Beck. He rubs her back before grabbing one of her hands and massaging her wrist.

Another knock on the door means room service is here, and it takes us less than an hour to demolish the two carts of food Luka ordered.

"Okay, we all agree Toni Bailey is our top candidate, right?" Sydney says from the corner of the sectional, curled up under a blanket.

"By a longgggg mile," I say.

"Yep," Beck adds.

"Wait, who is Toni?" Luka asks.

"She's an engineer for Amaro's team in F2 currently," Sydney says without skipping a beat.

"Your top candidate is a woman who just entered the field? Didn't she just get hired on there not too long ago?" Luka asks in shock.

"And she's proven she can take control and is motivated to pursue bigger things. Everything she touches has turned to gold, and we liked her when we interviewed her. Is your problem that she's a woman or that she's low on experience?" I ask in a condescending tone, channeling my inner Sydney, mostly just to give him shit.

"I don't have a problem with any of it; I'm just trying to understand how that was the best option, I guess." He puts his hands up, and I see Beck and Sydney stare at them from the corner of my eye. I forget that they haven't seen him since the hospital.

"It sounds like you're interested in being included in some of the decisions made at Empress," Sydney says with mirth.

Luka awkwardly chuckles. "Nah. I don't think I'm cut out for all of that. Maybe the academy, but even that feels like a stretch."

"You want to do stuff with the F1 Academy?" Sydney sits up straight.

"Umm. I mean, I was thinking about it. But that's not what we are here to talk about." Luka's cheeks turn a little pink.

Sydney pulls out her phone and types for a minute before dropping it back in her lap and sending me a wink. With that look, I know Luka can have access to anything he wants within the academy, thanks to her.

"Anyway, we can't fire Gavino until immediately after Miami. But we need to make Toni an offer, and she has to accept in order for that to actually be an option," Beck says.

"Okay, I'll call her and see if she can come chat." Sydney shrugs, pulling up her number and putting the phone to her ear.

I turn to Luka with an apologetic look on my face. "Sorry," I whisper. "You can hang out in the bedroom and watch TV if you don't want to stick around for all the business talk."

"I think I want to stay. See how much I can handle." The determination in his eyes is something I didn't even realize I missed. In the seven months since his crash, nothing has piqued his interest, or his willpower when we've talked about his career or the future, like this conversation has. And I'm so fucking proud of him.

"I'll be here every minute."

Toni shows up half an hour later, eager to solidify contracts and sign on the dotted line. Sydney lays out terms, and everything goes incredibly smoothly.

"Okay, I'm going to get this sent over to our lawyers, and they'll draw up the official contract. When it's done, we can do dinner or drinks and sign on the dotted line before celebrating!"

"Thank you so much. I can't wait to start at Empress." Toni stands up and shakes everyone's hands, except Luka's as he doesn't offer, before leaving just as quickly as she came.

"Well, that went well. Now, we can boot Gavino." I smirk.

***

Thirty-six brutal hours after we negotiated the deal with Toni, we're off to celebrate. Practices were so fucking awful that it almost motivated Luka to get out of the hotel room to smack the shit out of Malcolm and Sawyer.

So, I need a drink. But I'm trying to be mindful of Luka as well.

Luka insists on coming, saying being the husband of a hotshot Formula 1 administrator is an important job and he needs to support me. I worry about him being around alcohol, but he called his therapist before we left, and I promised him we could leave if things got overwhelming for him. And Luka promised he wouldn't care if I had a drink, but I'll most likely keep it virgin because I'm not trying to be an asshole.

Now, we're walking hand in hand, far away from the track, going to a fancy tapas restaurant, where hopefully no one will care who we are.

We're the last ones here—no surprise there—and when we reach the table, Toni introduces us to her boyfriend, Brad.

Instantly, I get a bad feeling about him, and Luka tapping my thigh as we sit down tells me he does too.

I look at him, arching my eyebrow and subtly looking over at Brad. Luka discreetly nods back with his eyes comically wide. We may not be the best at silent communication, but we're not the quiet type of people.

I lean forward, close to his ear, as Sydney talks to Brad. "I don't like him," I whisper so only he can hear me.

"Me neither. We'll see how tonight goes."

It takes all of thirty minutes for things to start going downhill.

"I'll have the Porterhouse with all the sides."

"Brad, we're just doing drinks and tapas. I told you that," Toni says in a hushed tone.

"Nah, moneybags is buying, so I'm going all out." He points his thumb to Toni while talking to the waiter.

Sydney and I make eye contact but don't say anything.

Toni is trying to settle him down, but then things go from bad to worse.

"So what, now you're ashamed of me? Like I don't fit into this bullshit world you're pretending to be in? Hell, you've got this disfigured guy in the group." He gestures to Luka, and I almost lose my shit, but Luka grabs my hand as I stand up, stopping me from doing anything. Brad's getting louder with every word he says.

"Brad, that's enough," Toni says, but it's too quiet, too unassuming for him to even notice. And completely different from the badass we know her to be.

"You can't cut it in this world, *Antoinette*. I don't even know why they are hiring you, but I'll take all the perks. I'm going to get to sit in the pit lane for all the races. Maybe teach you guys a thing or two." He gestures to Beck and Luka.

Luka's hand squeezes my thigh with surprising strength, drawing my eyes to him. His jaw is clenched, and there's a fierce fire in his eyes.

Beck looks the exact same, and I know it's taking everything in them not to step in. But it's not our place, no matter how uncomfortable we're feeling right now. If it crosses a line with Toni, I know we'll jump in, though. We can brush him off with no consequence and ban him from pit lane easily enough.

"Sorry, we don't let people just sit in the garage. That's only for sponsors and special occasions," Sydney says with her fake smile that almost has me laughing.

Brad's obnoxious laugh draws the attention of the entire restaurant. "I'm the new team principal's boyfriend. I think you'll find I can do whatever I want."

Holy shit, this guy has a death wish. I can't imagine talking to a billion-dollar company's owner like that and thinking it's okay in any way.

He says something else I can't hear because I'm focusing on the attention around us, but it's apparently bad enough that our waiter comes over.

"Sir, I'm going to have to ask you to keep it down please."

Wrong thing to say to Brad. He shoves his chair back hard as he stands up, going toe to toe with the waiter before a guy twice Brad's size walks up.

"There a problem here?"

"Yes, there is! This asshole is trying to tell me I'm being too loud when I'm just trying to have a good time."

"I was talking to Steve." The burly guy gestures to the poor waiter.

"Do you know who you're talking to? Do you know who's sitting at this table?" Brad says, outraged, pulling all of us into something we absolutely don't want to be a part of.

Shit, I'm going to have to do damage control if someone gets a story, which they undoubtedly will knowing the press.

"Alright, come with me, sir," big bodyguard dude says, hooking his hand around Brad's elbow.

"Don't fucking touch me!"

I cringe at Brad's outrage, but looking over at Toni, I just feel sad for her. I can't imagine having this happen when you're trying to make a good impression on your brand-new bosses. She looks shellshocked, not that I can blame her.

It takes fifteen minutes and a call to the cops for Brad to finally leave. Toni follows him but offers her apologies, one right after the other.

"You think he's going to be an issue?" Beck asks.

"He will be if the media gets a hold of him. They'll tear her apart if they get a whiff of this behavior." I sigh, sinking into my chair.

"I'll give her an hour or two, then give her a call and check in," Sydney says, rubbing her temples with her fingers.

"Well, I'll say he's a fucking asshole, but it was worth coming out of the room to see him get taken out by the cops." Luka smirks.

Laughter sounds around the table, and all I can think about is how proud I am of Luka. He stepped out of his comfort zone and was so damn strong in doing so.

Later that night, curled up in bed, soft words of praise and hope are exchanged between us.

Today, it was "two giant steps forward and zero steps back" kind of day.

Chapter 24

Luka

"So, I'm supposed to fly to London tomorrow, and I'm freaking out," I tell my therapist, Dr. Tate, as I wring my hands together. The smooth, almost plastic-like skin has become a sort of comfort when I'm feeling unsure lately.

"Why are you freaking out?"

"All of this came together so fast. Sydney made one call, and now I'm flying out to go see the F1 Academy in Preston, UK, to see if there's something there I might be able to do. Hell, I don't really know what the plan is; they just booked a flight and said have fun."

"And Daisy isn't going?"

"She isn't. They have the transition for the new team principal, and they need all hands on deck for a few weeks." I sigh.

"And how do you feel about that? About having to take this trip alone?"

I sit back on the couch and contemplate my words. One of his mottos flashes through my head: I can only help to my fullest with honesty.

"I feel ... let down. It's not even her fault. She offered, but I know they are slammed with the new principal, press conferences, and all that shit. But I just... I don't know if I can do it, go to the track and be that close to the action without support."

"There's a little bit of fear there," he observes.

"I guess, yeah."

"Are you fearful that being around the track will elicit emotions associated with your crash? Or are you fearful that you may not be able to stay in Formula 1 in some capacity?"

"The second," I whisper.

"I think that's a healthy fear, but one I believe you need to face. There's a very real possibility that you may feel you won't be able to be a part of the field again, even in a different, lesser role. At this point, I'm not prepared to speculate at a diagnosis of PTSD, but it's not out of the question given the severity of the crash and the impact it's had on your life. You need to prepare for the potential of experiencing flashbacks; you may also experience panic the closer you get to the track. I just want you to be prepared for as many outcomes as possible. If you get there and you can't get near the track, that's okay. If you feel like it's something you want to work toward, we can set up a strategy to make that happen. There are many options and this one experience, this one meeting, doesn't have to dictate how the rest of your life is going to go." His kind but firm tone seeps into my soul. Breathing simplicity into my body and soothing the panic.

"If I panic, what do I do?" I hate how weak my voice is.

"If you panic, you ask if there's a quiet room available to you and take five minutes to do some breathing. To think about the *why* behind the panic. It's easy to just sink into the panic and let it take over, but I really want you to try to calm your body down and try to pinpoint what the trigger was."

I nod, even though he can't see me.

"I truly feel you can do this, Luka. Will it be scary? There is always that possibility, but you've been putting in so much work and have made great progress. I think this is a great step for you."

"Thank you." I clear my throat. "I have to go pack, but thank you for taking my call."

"No thanks needed. If you need me again when you're there, reach out."

"I will. Thanks, Doc." I hang up and toss my phone onto the cushion next to me. Staring at the blank television screen, I try to calm the panic already rising inside of me. This will be a difficult trip, of that I'm certain. But I've also thrown in a little side trip that will hopefully help it all be less overwhelming for me.

Another one of my favorite after-school programs, this one in London, might just be the kind of centering I need.

***

As I'm standing on the empty racetrack in Preston, UK, with nothing but lush greenery surrounding the headquarters, the whole setting seems like a dream. There's this blurred edge in my vision that makes all the greens blend together as my eyes are hyper focused on a painted line in front of me.

I sense her before I hear her.

"How're you doing?" Her soft, caring words drop my shoulders at least two inches, the tension slowly releasing.

"I..." Sighing, I try to find my words. "I'm not sure, honestly. It kind of feels like a dream, like it's not real."

Her hand intertwines with mine, and I finally look over at her.

Hercegnőm. My princess.

"How'd you manage to sneak off?" I ask, glad to turn the attention to her even if it's short lived.

"You don't really think I'd let you get on a track for the first time by yourself, do you? I had to shuffle some things, and I didn't know when I actually could get here so I didn't want to get your hopes up. But I'm glad I made it in time." Her hand squeezes mine as I suck in a breath through my nose.

"Thank you," I croak. "I— This is hard." My whispered words are an admission of weakness, but I don't know how to overcome it.

"I should have been with you this whole time. I'm sorry for that." Her head tilts to the side, landing on my shoulder perfectly. Mine leans onto hers, the crown of her head against my temple giving me the support I was scared to ask for.

"I wanted to ask, but you guys are so busy." It may be hard to say, but it's one of the most honest sentences I've told her in a while.

"Hey." Her hand squeezes mine again. "Never be afraid to ask me to come with you. Never be scared to tell me you need support. None of that is weakness. If you need me, I'll be here."

Silence engulfs us after that. I'm not sure how long we stand on that empty track, but once my hand starts hurting from gripping her hand so hard, I know it's time to move on.

"They're probably waiting for me," I say as I turn to face my wife.

"They'll let you spend as much time out here as you want. You know that." She smiles.

"I know, but I think, for now at least, I'm done."

I'm proud I didn't panic. I'm elated Daisy showed up because I think that made all the difference in the world. But now, it's time to see if this is something I can contribute to long term. The F1 Academy is like a stepping stone. The starting point of many driver's careers and possibly the chance to one day make it into F1. Its beneficiaries are comprised of men and women, aged 18-25, who have the skills but not the opportunity. It opens up our world to people who would otherwise never have a shot. And it's something I want to help nurture, and grow it into something bigger.

"Through here is our video room. We've allotted for growth to accommodate for the development of the academy into the future. Our success already shows us the interest is there, but we need to get the teams on board too," Sandra, the managing director, tells us as we continue the tour. "We have a superb facility, but it's my goal to grow this tenfold. No doubt you've seen our drivers at the handful of races we've been able to attend in the past. I'd like to expand that attendance and aim for the majority of the race schedule, not just a handful, in the next two years. It's important that everyone gets to experience an actual race, but with our sporadic attendance to date, it's less beneficial than we'd like it to be."

"Outside of existing agreements from the committed teams and venue administrators, what do you need to make that happen?" I ask.

"Primarily, sponsorships. We already have some heavy hitters that currently provide the majority of our funding for the facility and staffing, but in order to meet our goals, we obviously need more. We have a substantial waitlist of worthy young candidates eager to demonstrate and build on their skills. Ones we've been scouting and monitoring for a couple of years; we just don't have the capital or the cars to give them that start. And a lot of them will miss their chance altogether, aging out of consideration for any team in F2, F3, or even Formula E. There are too many exceptional drivers who are missing their opportunity with us because of our current limitations."

My mind is firing on all cylinders, pouring over past sponsors of my own, ideas to make the most of what they currently have available here, and what I can see they are going to need. It all starts to formulate into potential solutions in my head, the big lump of gray matter finally getting a decent workout.

"And what about mentors? Do you have people, who have been at the professional elite level, who can give them what they need to ensure their smooth transition up? The goal is to bring them up through the feeder formulae levels, correct?" I ask Sandra as she leads Daisy and me to her office.

"Yes, and you are correct. We currently have engineers who have worked in Formula 2 and Formula E working with some of the teams. However, it is up to the teams when it comes to recruitment. As for the actual academy, we don't have mentors in any current positional role. We have administrators who have been in the system, driven, or been around the sport their whole life, which has already shown proven results with the drivers."

"Okay." I nod, thinking about how I would change their approach to prepare drivers to move more effectively through the ranks.

Conversation continues, though no solid plans or agreements are formulated, and after spending a few hours there, Daisy and I head out with a promise to be there tomorrow to watch some of the drivers' practice.

Daisy starts driving but is heading in the opposite direction of Manchester, where I was planning on staying. If we were closer to London, I would just crash at Beck's place, but a four-hour drive one way isn't really in my plans until after I scope out the academy.

"Where are you going?" I ask.

"Liverpool. There's a Vanstone there," she says as if it's common sense and I should know where all the Vanstone properties are.

Blowing out a stream of air, I tip my head back and stare at the roof of the car.

"What's your first impression?" Daisy asks.

"So many things. My head is already swimming with some of the ideas I have."

"That's good, though, no?"

"It is. How long is the drive?" I ask.

"About an hour." She looks over at me. "Why?"

"I think I'd like to use that hour to get my thoughts in order, and then maybe we can order some food and talk them through?"

"Hell yes! I was listening to an audiobook on the plane, so I'll just pop my headphones in and finish it off."

I reach down for her purse, finding her headphones and handing them to her while I get her phone and find her book app thing to start her audiobook. The blinding smile she gives me in return is like the sunrise on a new day.

Maybe this trip is the sunrise on my new life.

***

"Okay, so they need mentors. Old drivers, retired engineers, and people like that," I tell Daisy before taking a bite of my burger.

"For the teams or the drivers specifically?"

"Both. Mostly the drivers, but if we treat the entire team like it's a development tier in the sport, we can develop the best engineers for the teams as well. Building their skills so we can then embed them within the teams, and then move them up as people leave or retire."

"Oh! I like that. What else have you got?" she says before shoving a bite of chicken into her mouth.

"We need more teams. More drivers. The easiest way to do that is to see which teams currently in the academy want additional cars. You can easily double your driver count just by doing that. Potentially, we can open it up to other teams, depending on how big we want it." I'm on a roll, the excitement about this entire day finally hitting me. "Then, there are the sponsorships. I know how to get sponsorships. I think those they have currently are largely sport focused—I'll have to actually look and see who they've got first—but we expand that reach. Clothing brands, luxury brands, tech... Definitely tech companies."

"Pierce knows a ton of people—hell, Sydney too, I guess. We can get a list of potentials from them."

"Yes! Why didn't I think of them?" I snap my fingers clumsily when she brings the idea up, forgetting about my lack of dexterity.

Frowning at my hand as though it's let me down, I pop a French fry in my mouth before looking over at her. The brightest smile I've seen on her face in far too long hits me dead in the chest. It's that sparkle I thought would never come back.

"What?" I ask.

"I..." She visibly swallows. "I didn't know if I'd ever see you this excited about something again."

"Dais..."

"Sorry." She brushes a tear from under eye, but I grab her hand and bring it to my lips, pressing a kiss to the tear she wiped away.

"Nothing to be sorry for. I didn't think I'd ever be this excited about something race related again. I truly thought I'd be curled up in a ball, crying."

"I have to say it's incredibly sexy to watch the way your mind works with this stuff," she deflects, letting me off the hook and not pushing the more emotional side of things.

"Oh yeah?"

"Oh yeah. I mean, your body has always been nice, but damn, who knew you had this brain in there too?" Her eyes sparkle with her smartass words.

I put my plate onto the side table before grabbing hers and doing the same.

"So, you think I'm only a pretty face?" I growl as I hook my arm around her middle and shift her down to the bed next to me.

"I mean, I did question it once or twice." She giggles.

The rest of the night is spent being playful and talking through my ideas. Coming to the academy is nothing like I thought it would be. It's so much fucking better. Excitement for the future in all facets of my life beams through every cell in my body.

Chapter 25
Tomic Set for a New Venture?

Spotted nine months after his now infamous crash, Tomic appears to be ready to jump back into the fray. Sadly, it doesn't appear we'll see fan favorite, Tomic, back in a Formula 1 car, though. There's no sign of him being in race shape and no indication he ever will be again, but word is he could be shaping the wave of the future within the sport.

Reports say Tomic and his wife, Daisy, assistant to the President of Empress Racing, were touring the F1 Academy headquarters with its managing director, Sandra Haynes, on Tuesday, though with no clear picture of what his role is at this stage.

Many expected Tomic to have a role within Empress Racing post recovery, but has he burned one too many bridges there and is resorting to another option to remain connected to Formula 1? Of course, that's speculation, but we'll be sure to bring you more as soon as we can confirm. For now, we'll hold onto hope that Tomic isn't done with Formula 1 for good.

Chapter 26

Daisy

"I'd like to talk about the pregnancy," my therapist says.

It's like the world closes in on me, and my vision blurs at the edges.

"I understand why you have avoided it before, but I think the key to completely moving forward with Luka is to delve into that event."

"I don't want to," I whisper.

I may be making huge progress, and Luka may be making huge progress, but this is the one topic neither of us have been willing to touch on.

But it seems I've run out of excuses to brush it aside.

"I know you don't, which is why I think we need to."

My leg starts bouncing as I stay quiet.

"I just want to recap what you have already told me, and then we can go from there. Does that sound okay?"

I nod but don't look at her.

"Okay, you have told me you weren't feeling well and as a means to rule things out decided to take a test, which came back positive, and when you told Luka, he didn't react favorably. Upon seeing your doctor to confirm, you found out it was a chemical pregnancy. Is there anything I have missed or is incorrect?" Her tone is caring, not accusatory, just wanting to know the facts.

"No."

"Good. So, let's jump right in. How did you feel when the test was positive?"

I think back to that time in the bathroom at the Australian GP, alone and scared.

"At first, I was freaked out. I had been on birth control; we hadn't even talked about kids, so I wasn't sure how Luka would react. I felt ... out of control, like I was ruining all these plans we hadn't made yet, but somehow, I was still ruining them. Then I sat in the corner of the VIP section, alone, watching my husband race, and all I could picture was a little Luka running around, watching his dad racing. Matching smirks and race suits." I look up with a watery smile. "I wanted it," I whisper.

"And then, what happened when you told Luka?"

"He had just won, and I—" I swallow the lump in my throat as I remember it like it was yesterday. "I couldn't wait to tell him. So, once the podium was over and he was free to leave, we went back to our hotel, and I told him. He…" I trail off as tears slip down my cheeks.

"It's okay."

"He went from celebrating his win, from kissing me and getting"—my cheeks heat—"handsy, to distant in a split second. It was like all the light, all the excitement, drained out of him."

"Did you guys talk about it any more before you went to the doctor?"

"I tried." A sob breaks free, making me so angry that I'm still so emotional about this. "I tried to bring it up once we got back home, but he made some excuse. I don't even remember what it was now."

"And then you got confirmation that it was a chemical pregnancy. Did you have any symptoms that made you suspect something, or was it a complete shock?"

"Complete shock. Like, I had some spotting while I was in Australia, but I didn't think much of it. After talking to the doctor, it was most likely then that everything … happened. Even though the test was positive, if I had tested again in a couple of days, it probably wouldn't have been."

"Talk me through your emotions once you got that diagnosis." She sits back in her chair, placing her notepad on the arm of it and making sure all her focus is on me.

"I felt … alone. I don't know; it's hard to explain. I had never heard of a chemical pregnancy before, so I asked a ton of questions, and it was all very clinical. It didn't really hit me until I was in the car driving home. I had to pull over because I couldn't' see through my tears. I-I don't even remember how long

I sat there crying. Or when I drove home. I know Luka wasn't there when I got home, so I took a bath and just cried."

She nods. "But how did you feel?"

"Sad," I croak as the tears come faster. "I didn't even know I wanted to be pregnant, and then I was and I wasn't before I could even process it. I don't know if I ever saw myself as a mother. Luka and I were supposed to travel the world while he raced. Go do crazy things, be wild and spontaneous together. And then it's like it was all I could see. This little mini version of my husband in our lives, and it wouldn't go away. I knew I wasn't pregnant anymore, but I couldn't shake the vision."

"Did you ever talk to Luka about all of this?"

"No. God no, and I know that's the real problem. He ignored all my attempts, and then his racing was suffering and I felt responsible for it all. I felt like I was ruining his life or, at least, the one he wanted."

"Daisy..."

"I know I wasn't actually doing that, but with his reaction to everything, I genuinely believed he felt that way. I think I still do on some level." It's a hard truth, possibly one of my hardest. My husband resented me and felt like I ruined his last year in racing.

"And do you want to try again? For another baby?"

My heart rate picks up, and I swear I almost hyperventilate, but I try to calm my breathing down and really focus on the question. It's one I've avoided since that doctor's appointment.

"I'm not saying do you want to start trying tomorrow, but in a general sense. Do you think you would like to try and have a baby?"

In my heart of hearts, I know the answer. It's just scary as hell to admit it.

"Yes," I whisper.

"Then I think it's extremely important for you to talk to Luka about all of this. Go back to the beginning and talk it through with him. You both need to air it all out into the open before you can begin to move forward. And if you want to do a couples session in order to accomplish that, my door is always open. But I think holding all of this in and not being open with him about how you felt about it all will only compound. It'll grow and grow, and any resentment that you may feel will only build."

Anxiety courses through me because I know she's right. It's time to face my deepest fears.

***

I've been pacing for hours, just waiting for Luka to come back home. He had a follow-up appointment for his grafts and then physical therapy that he took a rideshare for. His mobility and strength have returned, so I'm not sure why he's not driving yet unless he's too traumatized to drive anymore after his crash. Honestly, I wouldn't blame him if that is the reason.

"Dais! You home? I have thoughts for dinner!" he yells as he walks through the front door and kicks his shoes off. He stops in his tracks when he sees me. "You okay? How was therapy?"

"Umm, it was … it was okay." I internally cringe. It was far from okay.

"You sure?"

"Yeah. Yep. It was fine. What were you thinking for dinner?" *Awesome job, Daisy. Work yourself up for hours, only to cave the second he's home.*

"Oh, I was just thinking about trying that new Mediterranean place that opened on the west side."

"Yeah. Yeah, that sounds good."

"You sure you're okay?"

"Yeah, just trying to get out of the therapy funk."

"I get it. I'm going to go take a shower really quickly because they were mean assholes in PT today and made me sweat my ass off." I nod and follow him to our room. Watching him get undressed flicks a switch in my brain. I've gone from hyper-determined to talk about the pregnancy, to wanting to avoid it at all costs, and he just gave me the perfect distraction to do so.

He walks to the bathroom, butt naked, and turns the water on in the shower. He waits for it to steam up as I strip out of my clothes and join him, just as he gets under the hot water.

"Well, hello." He smirks.

"Hi." My hand runs from his abs to his chest. The light dusting of hair is dripping with water.

"I take it we're postponing dinner?"

"Not for long if I have anything to say about it." I step back, pulling him with me. The back of my knees hit the bench we have in the shower.

"Oh ho, someone is cocky." His smirk is deadly, and I want nothing more than to wipe it off of his face.

My hands drag down his chest, scratching him with my nails as I move to his stomach and the V leading to a very prominent erection. Yeah, he's not sad over the turn of events at all.

"Daisy..."

"Shh." My hand wraps around his dick, sliding down gently before squeezing tighter. His intake of breath only fuels my exploits.

Pumping my hand up and down, I spread my legs and scoot to the edge of the bench before bending down to kiss the tip. There are perks sometimes to being pint-sized.

My lips wrap around his tip, licking all around, before I move back and lookup at him.

"You're a tease," he growls.

"I am." I smirk before bending over again and licking him along the vein that juts out on his underside. His hips jerk, making me lick it again.

His hand slides into my hair, gently cupping the back of my head, as I continue to tease him. As his grip slowly tightens, I know he's on edge. The tighter his fist, the less control he has, and I love every second of it.

My tongue circles around the head, waiting until his hips arch forward and his hand in my hair is almost to the point of pain, before I slide down him with my mouth, taking him as far as I can go right off the bat. I've always had to work up to deep throating him, and that hasn't changed.

A strangled groan sounds from him. My hands wrap around his ass, gripping it hard and guiding his hips.

Deeper and deeper I take him until I know, on the next one, I will take him all the way. Breathing in through my nose, I slowly slide down his length until my nose hits his pelvis. I swallow around him, making him emit a garbled groan.

I keep him there as long as I can. Until it feels like all the oxygen has been sucked out of the room and I can barely breathe. Jerking back, I pop off of him and gasp for air, but I don't wait long to get back to it, only long enough to regulate my breathing again.

"Jesus, Dais. What did I do to earn this?" he moans as his other hand runs up and down his abs before moving up to his nipple and pinching it.

I fucking love how open he is with what he likes and what turns him on. And playing with his nipples is one of my favorite things. I shift one of my hands, batting his away and circling my fingertips before pinching it hard. He moans so loud and braces himself against the shower wall as his knees give way a little.

"Daisy," he gasps. "I'm so fucking close."

I bob up and down a few times, spit trailing down my chin, before I take a deep breath and take him to the back of the throat again. The mix of my throat closing around him and me pinching his nipples gets him off at lightning speed. He comes down my throat, curling his entire body around me as he jerks to the rhythm of his cum spurting into my mouth.

I manage to slide off of him, but he keeps his body wrapped around mine as he struggles to draw in air.

"Did you just suck my soul through my dick?" He gasps, but all I can do is giggle as I wipe the trail of spilt cum off my chin and neck.

I cup water in my hands and splash my face once Luka moves back, but that's all I get to do before he says, "My turn," and picks me up from the bench to stand on the tiled floor as he sits where I just was.

My eyes widen because I didn't think he would reciprocate. I mean, I've blown him many times with nothing in return, so I just assumed. But as he picks up my right leg, hoisting it up and over his shoulder, I know things are different now.

Just like they should have been today. You shouldn't be having sex of any kind after what happened in therapy.

My inner, logical bitch rears her ugly head, side-swiping my mind until fingertips grazing my clit startle me back to Luka.

"Where's your head at?"

It's like he knew that was the exact right question to ask. Too bad I'm still on my track of avoidance.

"I don't know, but make me give you my attention." It's me begging, but he hears it as a command, and I won't tell him otherwise.

His hand cups my pussy, putting pressure on my clit and making me pulse with need.

Bracing myself with both hands on the shower wall in front of me, I close my eyes, and decide to remove all thoughts from my head and just *feel*. I want to feel his every touch, every graze of his lips along my body.

The nip of his teeth on my thigh. The soothing lick afterward.

I sink into the sensations he's flooding me with.

His muscular hand, different in texture but no less strong than it was before the accident, wraps around my hip, snaking around my ass as his fingers find my opening. It's a layer of stability I'm desperate for.

He dips a finger inside of me at the same time his lips trail a path to the crease where my thigh meets my hip. It's a matter of seconds before he nips there, then licks my clit, making me gasp and tip my head back.

"Oh God." I moan as his finger pumps inside of me and his tongue runs lazy circles around my clit. It's only a matter of time before I go off like a bomb, but I'm desperate to keep the pleasure going, to draw it out.

Because when I finally come, I have to go back to reality, and I'm not ready for that yet.

A nip at my clit has me so close to the edge, and my hand reaches back instinctively, grabbing the hand wrapped around me and stopping his movements.

He pulls back. "You're going to come for me, *hercegnőm*. You don't get to direct me today."

As much as I love my newfound dominant side, and I do, hearing Luka take charge sends a thrill through me. *Fuck, I missed this side of him.*

I loosen my hold on his hand, and he returns it, using two fingers instead of one as his lips suck my clit hard.

I come as a shock hits my body. A careening cry reverberates through me, echoing off of the tiles as I grip his hair in my hand for support.

It feels like I've blacked out, and by the time I come to, Luka's arms are wrapped around me and I'm curled up in his lap.

"Hi," he says as I lean back.

"Hi."

"That was fun." He chuckles.

I laugh with him, but it's hollow. Now that there isn't the distraction of an orgasm, guilt is creeping in.

My therapist is right; I've avoided the topic for too long, and this just shows how important it is for me to suck it up and talk to Luka. I'm an asshole for using sex as a way to get out of the hard conversation.

But one more night won't hurt.

Chapter 27

Luka

'I'm just getting out of the therapy funk.'

That's what she said, and I believed her. I didn't think anything of it to be honest, but now? Now, I'm second-guessing everything. Which means she could have used sex to push aside the real problem, which is hard to swallow, although I'm not entirely sure why at the moment.

Dinner was delicious, but I could tell Daisy was in her head. I was too chickenshit to ask about it because it most likely means I need to do some hard thinking. Figure out some hard truths I'm not ready to face yet. I wish we could just throw everything out onto the table and be done with it, but that's not how humans are. That's not how our brains work. Things are scary. Talking about things you're unsure of, fearful of, isn't usually something people run willingly toward.

Now, it's three in the morning, and I haven't slept a wink because whatever went on in her therapy session was a big deal. In my mind, that can only mean one thing: the pregnancy.

Fuck, I still have such a hard time even thinking the word. The craving to drink hits me so hard that it almost has me standing up and heading to the kitchen, even though I know there's nothing to drink there.

Instead, I grab my phone.

Me:

How's it going, man?

Beck:

It's going. Everything okay?

Me:

Yeah, totally. Why do you ask?

Beck:

Because it's, like, 3am there, and I would think sleep is more important than texting me.

Me:

Shit, I'm sorry. Forget about me. Sorry for bugging you so early.

Beck:

You're fine. We're up and out of town. What's up?

I hesitate. I'm not sure why I impulsively texted Beck, but now I'm wondering what to say.

Me:

I'm scheduled to be in Preston for a couple of weeks leading up to Silverstone. Seeing if I can help the Academy at all.

Beck:

That's great, man. Super exciting. It's a good thing, right?

Me:

It is. But Daisy has to work, so we'll be apart for a couple of weeks, and I don't think that's necessarily the best option for where we're at right now.

Beck:

> I won't pretend to be privy to your relationship, but there are ways to get time together. Hell, I know Sydney won't care if she works from Preston. They have offices; she can borrow one, I'm sure.

Me:

> Yeah, yeah, you're right.

Beck:

> You didn't ask, but if you want my advice, here it is. If you love her, do whatever it takes to make sure she knows it. Do the hard stuff, talk about the shit that sucks if it means you get to be together. You only have one life, and if you're lucky, you find the person who makes that life worth living. Don't waste it away because you're scared.

I lie in silence. Beck's words permeate a layer of my thick skull that no one has to date.

Me:

> Thanks, man. I'll talk to you later.

"Hey, you okay?" Daisy's sleep-roughened voice pulls me from my introspection.

"Um, I'm not sure." I roll over to face her. "Today, what did you talk about at your therapy appointment?" I know it's unfair to ask her, but I just have an itch that it's about the pregnancy.

"Luka..."

"Just tell me ... please," I whisper.

"She made me talk about the pregnancy." I can already hear the knot in her throat clogging her words.

"What did she say?"

"That we needed to talk about it." Light glistens off of the lone tear that falls from her eye.

"I think…" I take a deep breath. "I think we do too."

"Luka—"

"*Hercegnőm*, we need to do this. We've both avoided it for long enough." Mostly me. I know that, and pushing her to talk about it likely means I'm an asshole, but Beck is right. For us to survive this, we need to finally have this last big hard conversation in order to move forward.

Her eyes shift between mine. "It's still so hard," she whispers. "It makes me so damn sad."

"What part makes you sad?" I don't want to assume anything in this conversation.

"The loss. Being alone during all of it. Not understanding your reaction then and after at the time."

"I'm sorry I wasn't there for any of it. I … I didn't know how to handle it. I think just hearing you were pregnant shocked me to my core, and I couldn't understand it. That wasn't an excuse to leave you to handle everything on your own." Guilt sits heavy on my chest. It's something I've tried to work on in therapy, but hearing how Daisy was actually feeling during that time is hard as hell.

"A big thing we've talked about in therapy is how I never really grieved any of it. I just got the shock of a positive test, told you, then went to the doctor and it was all over. But then, you were having a hard time driving, and I just … didn't *feel* any of it. I kept telling myself the pregnancy wasn't actually viable. There was nothing to be sad about because it couldn't grow into anything more. At least, that's what my doctor said. But it felt real." She hiccups.

"Do you want to hear something shitty? And it won't help any of this?" She nods, so I continue, "I looked up what a chemical pregnancy was three months ago. Before that, I didn't know or … care." I cringe. "No, it's not that I didn't care; I think I just didn't want to face it. Like, if I learned about it, it made it real. It made me have to face my feelings on it."

"And what are your feelings on it?"

"I feel like I'd be a shitty dad. I didn't have a role model growing up. There's no one to look to for an example of what a good dad should look like. I feel like I would fail, and because I would fail, I would fuck up my kid. I never wanted that. I never wanted to be responsible for making someone that miserable or setting them up for failure. And then I started drinking, and I knew I was nothing but bad news for a kid." Pain at the truth of my words stabs my body like a million knife cuts. The burns on my hands hurt less than this.

"But the drinking was a result of not dealing with it, and then your struggles in the car," she says.

"Technically, yes. But now, I'll always be an ... alcoholic. I'll always carry that label." I've only called myself that a handful of times, and each time I do, shame fills my body at how far I've fallen.

"But—""No, *hercegnőm*. I did it to myself, and it's the truth." I didn't realize that she may have trouble coming to terms with being married to an alcoholic, but maybe I should have.

"So, me getting pregnant scared you more than anything else?" she asks softly.

"It was terrifying. And every time I got into my car to drive, my mind would wander. I would see all these outcomes, all these ways I could mess up a kid. The loss of focus is what ultimately made my season shitty, not the pregnancy." I don't want her to feel like anything that happened is her fault. Because seeing her this upset, and hearing how she never got the opportunity to grieve the loss, is one hundred percent on me. It'll be something I have to live with for the rest of my life.

The need to pay any price to get her to see no blame lies on her is all I can think about.

I reach my mangled hand out and brush away the tears with my thumb. "I'm sorry it's taken us this long to talk about it. I'm sorry it's been building for so long," I whisper.

"I just... Do you just not want to have a baby at all, or just not with me?" Her voice is so broken that if I was standing, I would fall to my knees in front of her.

"Oh, Daisy," I murmur, pulling her to me. Maybe if I don't have to see her reaction this all will be easier to say because I feel like I'm fucking everything up more. "You're the only one I want a baby with. You're the only one I could ever see myself creating a family with. It's you, or it doesn't happen for me." Her shoulders shake as I continue. "I think... I'm not saying yes, mostly because I know I have more I need to work through before I would feel confident that I wouldn't mess them up, but I think, eventually... Yeah, I do want to have a baby with you. You... God, Dais, you would be the best mother, and I just don't want the be the thing that holds you back from that." I feel those words in the depth of my soul. There's no doubt in my mind that she would be the best mother; it's just the question of whether I could bring anything to the table. Could I get over all of my issues, all of my faults, to make sure we bring a baby into the best world possible?

The answer is unknown at the moment.

"You wouldn't ruin it," she says through her sobs. "Look at all the charity work you do that no one knows about. How can't you see you're already so damn good at this?"

"I might, though, Dais. I really might, and that's not a position I want to put you in."

She cries in my arms for a long while. I feel a few traitorous tears on my own cheeks, but maybe this is the release we both need.

After a long while, I broach what I should have almost two years ago now. "How can I help you grieve, *hercegnőm*?" My whispered words are met with more sobs. Sobs meant for the time all those months ago, when I should have been there for her. When I should have swallowed my fear, my pride, and been the husband I was supposed to be for her.

Chapter 28

Daisy

"It still hurts so bad," I gasp through my tears. "Did I do something wrong? Did I cause it?" Questions that circle my head to this day yet ones that don't have an answer. Even my doctor said that chemical pregnancies are more common than anyone thinks, but it's likely that most go undetected because it gets mistaken for a period or a fluke. If you didn't take the test early, you'd never even know it happened. The knowledge doesn't make it any easier.

"No, no, you didn't. I was reading about how there's no real reasoning, that it's just something that happens and it's not on you. There's nothing you could have done to save the pregnancy."

The same words my doctor told me somehow feel more truthful from Luka. Like I can finally believe them. It wasn't my fault that I lost the baby.

I think, on some level, I'll always feel some sort of responsibility for it all, but being able to let all the emotions out in Luka's arms is releasing some of it. Even if it is over a year and a half later.

I'm not sure how long I lie there crying, but once the tears finally stop, it's like a rebirth. A new Daisy came up from the ashes and is ready to move forward. Does that mean we don't have a shit ton of things to work through? Absolutely not, but I'm less weighed down by guilt and shame than I was a couple of hours ago.

Pressing my forehead to his, I inhale deeply. "I think I needed that." The smallest smile graces my lips, but it's the haunted look in Luka's eyes that stops me. "Talk to me," I whisper.

"What if I can't give you what you want? What if, even if I put in the work, I'm not father material? What if I fail?"

My hand cups his cheek as his fingers dig into my side at the pain in his words.

"If you put in the work, then you won't fail. You accomplish anything you put your mind to, and that hasn't changed in the last couple of years. Look at how well you're doing staying sober," I offer.

"I wanted a drink so fucking bad tonight. I texted Beck instead," he confesses.

"See? You're so fucking strong. If you want something, you make it happen."

He runs his fingertips along my cheek, down my throat to my collar bone, finally ending on my heart.

"I want to keep this." He taps my heart.

"You never lost it," I whisper as more tears fill my eyes.

His fingers trace a pattern on my chest for a long minute before he looks back at me. "I want to get to a place where I'm not terrified of bringing a baby into this world. I know..." He sighs. "I know it's going to take time, and I don't want you to have to wait for me to figure out my shit."

"What are you saying?" My brow furrows.

"If a family is something you want soon, I'm not sure I can give it to you. If you need an out, you have it."

I react. I don't think.

Both of my hands land on his chest and shove him to the edge of the bed as I scramble out of bed.

"Is that what you want?" I'm bordering on yelling.

"No! God no! I want you! And a family, but shit, you've waited through enough of my bullshit, Dais. I don't want to be what holds you back from living the life you should have." There's so much raw pain in his voice that I instantly deflate.

"Everything is so hard. Does it ever get easy again?" I ask as I pace the bedroom.

"I think our version of easy was just having fun and not talking about the bigger things. It probably contributed to us getting to this point, honestly." He sits on the edge of the bed and snags my hand as I pass him. "It's going to take work, but I'm in this for the long haul. You're it for me, *hercegnőm*. Whatever it takes to keep you, to make you happy and create a life you can be proud of, I'll do. It just might take me some time to make that happen."

"What about a life you can be proud of?" I wrap my hands around his neck as he looks up at me.

"I'm getting there... I think." The uncertainty in his eyes is a dagger to the heart.

Here we are, talking about things we've needed to talk about for a long while. And although he's put in so much work, I forget that he's in this sort of limbo with his career and future.

"We'll get there together," I tell him as I kneel between his legs. "We'll figure this all out together, and then maybe when the time is right, we can worry about growing our family."

"The time will never be right, Dais, but that doesn't mean I don't want it. I just want to make sure we're bringing them into the best version of our world." He presses a kiss to my temple.

We stay like that until my legs go numb. Even then, I don't want to break the moment.

It feels monumental. Both of us committing to a future together, to working through the hard shit together instead of bottling it all up.

Today is the day we truly can move forward.

***

I must have fallen back asleep because the beeping of my phone startles me awake. Grabbing it, I rub my eyes so I can focus and find an email from Sydney about the upcoming Grand Prix in Barcelona, but am interrupted by Luka coming through the bedroom door.

Coffee and a paper bag fill his hands, and I know without seeing the label that it's from my favorite bagel shop.

"Gimmie." I make the grabby hands motion, making him smile.

"Alright, I'm coming, bagel monster. Chill." He leans forward, tucking the coffee and food behind his back, and puckers up for a kiss.

I press a kiss to his lips, intending it to be chaste, but he feels so good. And after our middle-of-the-night confessions, it's like everything has changed and this kiss solidifies that it all actually happened. That we're going to be okay. I finally believe that. They aren't just empty words that I'm desperate to believe. I trust myself more, and more importantly, I trust Luka implicitly.

He pulls back slightly before pressing another kiss to my lips, but he doesn't push for more.

"Eat. I want to ask you something." He hands the food and coffee to me and kicks off his shoes, joining me back in bed.

"What's up?" I say after I chug half of my iced latte.

"So, I'm supposed to be in Preston for a couple of weeks leading up to the Silverstone race, and I want to ask you to come with me. I know you're busy with Toni and getting her up to speed, and I understand if it's not possible—"

I shut him up with a kiss. "Of course I'll come. I'll call Sandra and see if she has an office I can borrow when I need to get some work done, but I would love to come and help in whatever way I can."

His shoulders drop with a release of tension, and I realize just how stressed he was about going to Preston alone.

"Hey." I put my coffee down. "I'll always figure out a way to come with you. If you don't want me there, that's fine too, but don't be afraid to ask me. Sydney doesn't care where I work from most of the time, as long as I get my shit done."

When we first got together, I travelled everywhere with him. Hell, I'm not sure he ever asked; it was just a given, this connection between us. So, having him ask me, like there was a chance I would say no, shows how far we've drifted apart in the last two years.

"Thank you," he mutters. It's then that I see his nervousness.

I don't want to draw attention to it, but I can tell he's anxious about this F1 Academy venture. I can't believe I didn't see it earlier, but it makes perfect sense. This is his first big step to coming back into the racing world. It was one thing to do a tour but another one entirely to actively consult and work with them.

We eat our breakfast in the quiet light of the early morning while I plan something special to ease his trepidation with this new endeavor.

Now, more than ever, we need to celebrate each other's victories and support each other's struggles. We're a team, and that's never been clearer.

Chapter 29

Luka

When I enter the meeting room at the F1 Academy headquarters, it's filled with not only drivers but various other staff as well. It is standing room only, and Daisy heads to the back corner of the bustling space in a quiet show of support.

"Hi. I clear my throat. "Umm, hello. You all sure you're in the right room?" I smirk as they all laugh. "No, but honestly, thank you all for being here. Firstly, I'd like to thank you for welcoming me on board of your team, and in tandem with your managing director, my aim is to help provide you with the necessary experience you all need to continue to improve, and hopefully find a way to provide the resources that you need to accomplish that. I think everyone in this room can agree that our primary goal is the growth of the academy. To increase the number of teams, drivers, and support staff. Personally, I would love to see it as a stepping stone to continue on to Formula 3 and 2, and ultimately Formula 1. So, my goal is to help all of you get there. I'll be present until after the Silverstone race, and then I'll be back periodically to help with consulting, establishing mentorships—which I believe is something that can further our goals—as well as obtaining potential sponsorships." I look around the room at all the wide-eyed, excited people, and that feeling I used to get before races, the high of it all, starts to build in my chest.

"Any questions?"

A hundred hands pop up, and I take my time answering as many questions as I can. Everyone keeps it professional—there are no personal questions asked—and it makes me think that this was the exact move I was supposed to make in my career. Every single person in this room is here to grow because they love the sport. They aren't here to gossip and get close to the bigger drivers; no, they are here because of their obsession with racing and their drive to make a career out of it.

They come up with insightful questions that I have zero real answers for at this point, but I'll endeavor to find if it keeps this level of excitement humming. The meeting takes up more time than Sandra, Daisy, or I were expecting, but it's breathed fresh life into me. Something to get excited about once again in the world of racing.

The next day, I'm out on the track with a couple of teams for their practice, and Daisy is inside working, when I meet someone that I have a hunch is going places.

"So, tell me how long you've been driving," I ask Remi Bouchard, a twenty-three-year-old driving for Amara Racing.

She's older than most of the drivers in the academy, but I think that drives her to be better.

"All my life, it feels like. Mostly karting, like many of us, but Sandra scouted me at one of my races and, as they say, the rest is history." She smiles as we walk the pit lane.

"And what's your end goal in the sport?"

"I want to be the first female to drive Formula 1." She says it with such confidence that it reads as fact. It's not that she wants to be; it's that she will be.

"Lofty goal, but I like it. When do you hit the track?" I ask.

"In about fifteen minutes."

"Perfect. I'll hang out and watch some of your laps."

We stop in front of the Amara garage, and I watch her engage with every single person in the garage. A simple greeting by name, a question about their family, or something about her upcoming laps—she talks to every person. It's easy to see she's well liked. Everyone is happy to talk to her, to help her with whatever she needs, and increased buzz of excitement when she hops into the car to do some laps tells me they all want that success for her.

After watching a few laps, I'm even more impressed. With thoughts of how to improve a few things, as well as the thrill of watching Remi, I head off to find

Sandra to game plan.

"Hey, I was just coming to find you," she says as she meets me just inside the lobby of their main building.

"Same." I smile.

"Come to my office. Let's chat."

I follow her up the grand staircase and into her office that overlooks the track.

"I don't think I'd ever leave if I had this view," I say in awe.

"Some days, I don't, much to my husband's chagrin. So, what are your initial thoughts?"

"Right off the bat, I want to find a way to double the number of drivers. Ten is great, but we need more. I know Sydney over at Empress would love to get a team going with two drivers in the upcoming season." There are perks to being friends with the new president of Empress, even if I have ruined my chance of ever racing again— if that was ever in the cards for me anyway after the crash.

"That's incredible. Obviously, I want that as well. It's just been like pulling teeth to get teams to commit. They haven't wanted to devote the resources to it, even though it would help feed directly into their teams."

"Which brings me to my next thought: sponsorships. We need a ton more. If we want to get more teams on board, they need to see there's money here. It's shitty, but it's the only way they'll want to be a part of it. The other thing is attention. We need more attention on this whole setup. There are talented female drivers here, and currently, we aren't capitalizing on the marketing of that. Women make up roughly fifty percent of the world population, and they are begging for diversity, for representation in this sport, and you've got it here on a silver platter. Yet you aren't getting the eyes on it you need."

She nods as she pulls out a notepad and starts jotting down something.

"First step is television rights. In order to be seen, you need broadcasting rights. There are enough streaming services out there, so we should be able to find one that'll see the potential. From there, we run with it and push for more. Maybe a vlog straight from the academy website with behind-the-scenes stuff: race preparation, how they got here, their camaraderie, that kind of thing."

As we continue to talk, I get more and more ideas. Before I know it, there's a knock at Sandra's door. Stopping mid-sentence, I find Daisy standing in the doorway.

"Sorry to interrupt, but it's past dinner and you both haven't eaten all day." She cringes, holding up a huge bag of takeout. "I can just drop this off and head out."

"God no, stay! Please," Sandra says, standing up and heading to the little four-seater table she has on the other side of her office.

"You guys have been busy." Daisy gestures to Sandra's desk, which is covered with paper. Plans for expansion, immediate plans and future plans—we've covered it all.

"I think your man here has found his calling," Sandra says as she starts unloading all the containers of food.

"Oh yeah? That's good to hear. He likes to pretend he's just a dumb jock, but inside that thick head of his, there's a smart cookie." Daisy smiles over at me.

Sandra laughs, but I'm overwhelmed with everything that's happened in the last few hours. My thoughts spewed out like a never-ending waterfall, I couldn't stop, and I kept building on the ideas I'd already had. Everything in my head was making sense, like it was finally firing properly and I had found what I was supposed to do. My purpose.

Dinner is a more mellow affair; we don't talk about work. Instead, I learn that Sandra's husband is a vintner and spends half the year in Italy. She offers us a couple of her favorite wines, and we take them with the plan to regift them at a later date. Daisy promises later that night to keep them at her office so I don't have any temptation. What's wild is that I didn't even think about drinking them. Not even an itch to smell the cork.

Today has been a masterclass of possibilities for my future. It all felt seamless, and the excitement flooding through my veins just confirms I'm making the right move signing on as a consultant at the academy.

***

The Silverstone GP is upon us, and I'm watching on like a proud parent.

Over the last two and a half weeks, I've gotten to know the drivers, the teams, and offered even more thoughts and ideas to Sandra on how to make the academy grow exponentially. I didn't really think about how the race would make me feel. I'm nervous that once it starts up, I'll panic, but I have a contingency plan for that, just in case.

There's one driver within the program that I just clicked with: one Margret Bouchard—or Remi, as she likes to be called.

She's a fucking powerhouse and destined for great things in the sport. She takes no shit and has the skill to back it up. Kind of like me back in the day. But she's also one of the nicest people I've ever met.

"What are your thoughts on her?" Daisy asks from my side as we watch her race on the monitors.

As I follow her progress around the track, I reply, "If she isn't already on your radar, she should be. It's a big leap from the academy to F1, but I think investing in her and seeing if she can climb the ranks in the next couple of years would be worth it."

"Sydney has a meeting with her tomorrow." She smirks over at me.

"No shit?" Pure excitement for Remi hit my veins. She's worked hard for this, and I hope it pans out for her. I would love to be able to follow her career, offer advice when I can, and be a fan of hers.

"Yeah. If it isn't obvious, Sydney's really hitting the feminine energy hard with Empress. Women in key roles where it's never been the case before." Daisy shrugs. "It's not out of the realm of possibilities to be the first team to have a female F1 driver."

"Holy shit, that would be..." I shake my head. "Fucking amazing."

"Right?!" she squeals as her cool exterior deteriorates into her bubbly excitement. "Gah, I want a woman driver on the team so badly, just so I can say, 'Fuck you boys! We're better!'" she yells at the ceiling. Luckily, it's so damn loud in here that she doesn't pull attention.

I missed the bubbly, loud Daisy. It's infectious and makes me realize I haven't seen this Daisy in months. She's slowly coming back to herself after everything we've been through. I just hope she can see I'm getting there as well.

We turn back to the race for a couple of minutes. The format of this race is essentially the same as F1. They do less laps, which irritates me, but they collect points just the same, and there will ultimately be a "winner" of the season, but it doesn't mean they make money or move up—something I'm hoping to change while I'm signed on.

"You're cute when you're mad at the man." I bite my lip to keep from smiling.

She pumps her golden curls with an exaggerated motion. "Someone needs to be."

The race is over before I'm ready, and Remi wins in spades. Daisy and I scream our heads off for her, congratulating her once she's parked in winner's lane and supporting her on the podium.

Later that night, Daisy and I stumble into our hotel suite—courtesy of Mr. Pierce Vanstone himself—after an evening of food, laughs, and outrageous plans with Sandra and her husband, Enzo.

"God, that was fun." Daisy sighs as she collapses back onto the bed.

"It really was. Thank you for being here for the last couple of weeks. It meant a lot to me," I tell her softly as I sit next to her.

She turns her bright smile toward me. "You know I would do anything for you, right?"

"I don't know what I did to deserve that, but I'll be the greedy asshole who takes it. And same, *hercegnőm*. Whatever you need, whatever I can do to make you happy, just tell me and I'll make it happen."

"Well, lucky for you, I happen to have a plan for this very special occasion, Mr. F1 Academy Consultant." Her eyebrows raise twice with mischievousness.

"Oh yeah?"

"Oh yeah." She sits up and swings her legs off the bed. Walking to her suitcase, she grabs something before heading to the bathroom.

When she comes out, I'm instantly hard and grateful to have such an incredible woman by my side. Because Daisy in maroon, strappy lingerie might just be the best fucking way to celebrate a new job.

"I feel like I didn't do anything to merit such a sight," I tell her as I lean back on my elbows.

"Sometimes, we just need to appreciate the good days." She smirks with a cocky edge to it, and it looks maddeningly like mine used to. She looks sexy as hell.

Her fingertips skate from my knee as she gets closer to the inside of my thigh. She grazes the very obvious outline of my dick before landing on the button of my jeans, popping it with the flick of her fingers. I suck in a breath of exhilaration.

Dominant Daisy is a force of nature. One I have no reason to test because I'd happily drown in her control. All five-foot-nothing, bubbly, blonde-haired sprite ready to steal my soul out to sea, and I'd happily let her take it.

I watch as she shimmies my jeans down, leaving my boxer briefs on for now before climbing back on top of me. There are deep maroon straps covering her nipples and crossing over her midsection that I can't look away from.

"How the fuck did you get into that thing?" I murmur, unable to keep my hands to myself, sliding a finger under one of the straps.

Swinging a leg over, she turns so I can see the back. A thong framing her perfect ass cheeks is all I see until she says, "It clips in the back. Super easy." Then she spins back around, straddling me once more.

"All I heard is it's easy to take off."

"I think I'll keep it on, actually." She shifts, her hands landing flat on my hips before sliding underneath my shirt, drawing it up with her as she does. I lift just enough that she can get it over my shoulders before falling back and trying to slide my arms out, but the fabric tightens.

"I want to try something," Daisy whispers as she leans down over me. She does something to the shirt, twisting it before testing it. I quickly realize she's managed to restrain me.

"Please continue trying things." I moan. Precum seeping through my boxer briefs has my hips arching to get closer to her.

Her eyes light up at my words, and that's when I know I'm in trouble.

She slides her body down so that she's sitting right on top of my cock, and shifts back and forth, giving us both friction even though we still have clothes on.

"Shit," I curse at how good this already feels. My toes curl when her nails scratch down my torso, and I grunt when she pinches my nipple. "Keep that up, and I'll come in my underwear."

"Tempting." Raising up on her knees, she pulls them down enough to free my over-eager cock. "Maybe I'll just be the one who comes in their underwear."

She drops back down on my now bare dick but doesn't me actually sink into her. The heat of her is overwhelming. Her hips tilt back and forth, and I can tell she's hitting her clit perfectly on the ridge along my underside. My head pounds back against the bed as I cling to every ounce of strength I have to not come yet.

"Daisy..." Do I sound as desperate as I feel? Because, fuck, I'm losing it quickly.

"Do it, Luka." Her voice breathy as she anchors herself to my chest.

"Get there," I growl.

The dam breaks, and her muscles clench throughout her entire body, and I fucking wish I was feeling that around my cock.

Without missing a beat, she trembles as she lifts just enough to take hold of me, slide her excuse for panties to the side, and put me exactly where I've been begging to be. I pull my knees up as she slides down, her orgasm still sending shockwaves through her wet-as-fuck pussy. She leans back against my legs, sinking into the feel of me inside of her, and it gives me a minute to get ahold of my shit.

Arms still tied above my head, I get to watch as the most gorgeous sight I'll ever see slides up and down me. Wet with her orgasm, her pussy glistens in the moonlight streaming in, before I watch her stretch around me again.

"Holy shit, *hercegnőm*. You are a sight." Arching my hips, I sink in deeper when her hips press against mine.

The pace isn't hurried—quite the opposite, actually—and yet I'm as close as I would be if I was pounding her hard from behind.

She leans forward enough for her hands to reach my nipples, and I know the second before she pinches them that I'm done for.

I come instantly. The slight hint of pain mixed with the image seared into my head is too much.

"God, that was sexy." Daisy sighs as she rotates her hips. She reaches up and deftly unties my bond.

I waste no time. One hand goes straight to her clit, the other to her breast, and I play her body like a damn instrument. Luckily, once she's orgasmed if we keep stimulation high, she goes off like a cannon again pretty easily. My dick doesn't deflate as I combine my ministrations with gentle thrusts of my hips. Her moans ratchet up, her head tipping back on a groan, and I know I have her.

And when she comes around my already spent cock? Pure heaven. I'm overstimulated in the best kind of way, and I think about how it's my turn to do something for her while we're in London.

Chapter 30
Daisy

A date in London.

I gave him hot sex in lingerie, and he's giving me a date in London. What a way to celebrate everything that's been happening lately.

The tides have finally turned. Things are looking up, and I couldn't be happier.

"Where are we going?"

"Out," he clips as he drags me along the sidewalk.

"Out where?"

"You'll see."

"Cryptic," I mumble, but the smile never leaves my face. I'm so damn excited to go out with my husband that nothing will bring me down.

I'm not even paying attention to where we are until he abruptly stops. That's when I look around and realize where our date is taking place.

"Really?" I ask, emotions getting the better of me.

"We haven't been back since our first official date. Felt like the right time." The corners of his lips tip up in a small smile.

I turn back to the little French restaurant we had our first date at. Nostalgia floats over my body. All the happy memories of us dating, running around like we didn't have a care in the world. Traveling all over the world like it would never end.

"This is perfect." I rise up on my toes and press a kiss to the corner of his mouth before dragging him into the restaurant.

"Mr. and Mrs. Tomic!" The owner, whom we met on our first date, calls to us as we walk in.

"Hugo, it's Daisy, please. How are you? It's been too long." I give him a hug, impressed as hell that he remembers us.

"Oh, we're doing just fine. Come, I've set up a table for you."

I look back at Luka, who's just smiling at me, and pull him along to the table we had our first date at. The perfect view of the London streets sits before us, and I feel settled for the first time in over a year.

"This is— Gah, I don't even know. It's so perfect, Luka." A wistful sigh escapes me as I lean back.

"You deserve perfect."

I don't get to linger on his words before Hugo is back and taking our order. I wave off a bottle of wine quickly, and then we're left on our own once more.

"Nothing is perfect. You know that right?" I ask.

Luka shrugs but doesn't answer.

"Do you feel like you need to be perfect? Do I make you feel like that's what I need?"

"No, but it doesn't mean you deserve less. You should have perfect. You should have everything you want in life, *hercegnőm*."

"And you think I don't feel like I have that? That I don't feel like I have everything I want?" I didn't expect our conversation to go in this direction, but I'll take it.

He sighs, picking up his water and taking a sip before he sets it down again. "I think, sometimes, I'm not the best option for you. I worry that I can't overcome all my"—he gestures around himself—"issues."

"You're doing a damn good job of overcoming a lot right now; don't discount that. What are you worried about? Kids?" I ask.

"I mean, yeah. My childhood was filled with nothing but pressure. The demand that I do better. It was only my dad, and it's not like he ever showed emotions. How do I not turn into that when that's all I've known?"

Hugo quietly places our food down in front of us, but I don't take a bite yet.

"Well, my family is too big and always in everyone's business; that's not something I hope for our future either, you know."

"Your family is the best. They're so supportive," he says softly.

"They are, but they don't come without their faults. Let me ask you a question. When you go to all the after-school clubs, do you put a lot of pressure on the kids? Do you hound them to do better in whatever it is you're doing that day?" I've been in touch with Mary, and have learned more about her programs and what Luka does at the Boys and Girls Club. He doesn't see how damn good he is with them, but I hope he will.

"Of course not!" He sounds offended, but he's making my point easily.

"Exactly. You don't even think about doing what your father did to you to them. So, what makes you think you'd do it to your own child?"

"Genetics? I don't know, but it's possible, Dais. I want to have a family with you, but it's scary as hell. What if I fuck it up?"

"Well, I'm sure we'll both fuck it up. Who goes into parenting knowing it all? We have to step back from this idea that'll we'll be perfect at anything. Fucking it up is part of the process; it's how you bounce back from the fuck-up that means more. You still have no clue how good you are with kids, do you?"

He shrugs, but I can see his mind working overtime.

"You remember that award you got?" He nods. "Do you think they give awards like that to people who suck with kids?"

He scoffs but chuckles. "No, I suppose not."

"Exactly. Look, if we have a baby, it's a learning experience for both of us. We have to lean on each other when we're unsure or struggling, which I'm assuming we both will at some point. Multiple points, probably," I add.

He looks me straight in the eyes like he's debating something. "You're a smart woman. How'd you end up with a deadbeat like me?" He smirks.

"Well, I stalked you just a little bit, so am I really that smart?" I grin back.

The serious nature of the conversation is put on the backburner in an instant. I love that about him, though. We can be serious, but we don't get stuck in it if we don't want to be. He's always been so flexible with his life, and I never realized how much I missed and loved that quality until this past year.

We continue eating until our plates are clean and Hugo waves off the bill.

"Where to now?" I ask once we walk out into the cool evening air.

"Want to go for a walk?" he asks, intertwining our hands.

"Absolutely." We make it a couple of blocks, both taking in the feel that's distinctly London in the fall.

"Surgery is in a couple of months," he says.

"You ready?"

"Yeah. Dr. Branch said it's likely the last one unless something crazy happens, so I'm ready to finally be done and put it all behind me."

"Me too. I didn't realize, when they were talking about skin grafts, that meant multiple surgeries spread out over a year. It's time to be done with the accident." And I mean it. We've both put in so much work to be past this dark spot in our lives and our marriage that I'm ready to look toward the future.

"Luka! Luka!" A young voice calls from our left.

Luka freezes, but I squeeze his hand in support.

"Oh my gosh, I thought that was you, and my best friend said it wasn't, but it is! Oh my gosh. Can I have your autograph?" The kid, who can't be more than twelve, pats his pockets and miraculously finds a sharpie. He takes his hat off—a Legacy hat of all things—and hands them both to Luka.

Luka looks shell-shocked but takes the proffered items and asks what the kid's name is.

"Joey."

I watch as my husband signs his name on something other than medical papers for the first time in over a year, and somehow, that's the thing that gets me.

He hands the items back and asks if the kid wants a picture. I offer to take it, and I watch as Luka strategically places his hands so you can't see them, but he gives the same cocky smile he's known for.

Once the kid is beaming and racing off to God knows where, Luka turns back to me. "Sorry."

"Don't be sorry. You used to get bombarded any time we went out. I'm used to it; it's just been a minute." I rejoin our hands and continue our walk.

"It's different, being able to go places and not be noticed as much. It never bothered me, but not having the media attention so focused on me is actually super freeing," he says, swinging our hands.

"I think you still have media attention; they just back off and speculate instead of jumping straight into your face now." I've seen the articles, and I hate every single one of them.

"You might be right about that, but I can avoid those at least."

"Very true." *I wish I could avoid them.*

We make our way down the street. Shops and restaurants bustle with activity. It's almost soothing, this normalcy I don't think we've ever had in our relationship.

"I think ... I think I want us to really consider taking out your IUD." He says it like he's saying it might rain.

I stop in my tracks, pulling his arm as he continues to walk. "What?"

"I think we should seriously start trying for a baby."

"Yeah?" I'm afraid to let my excitement show. Ever since my talk with my therapist, when I realized I did want to try for a baby, it's been on my mind constantly. But I never wanted to pressure Luka, especially not with so much going on.

He pulls me to him, wrapping his arms around me. "Yeah, *hercegnőm*. I mean, it doesn't mean things will happen immediately. But maybe after Circuit of the Americas?"

"I'll make an appointment."

He leans down to kiss me. It's a promise, this kiss. A promise that we'll grow together. That things are finally on the up and up. And that this is the first step to creating a family together.

Chapter 31

Tomic's New Role, And a Disappointing Start for the New Team Principal at Empress

It's been an eventful few weeks in Formula One, and everyone is surprised by the development of ex-driver, Luka Tomic, taking on a consultant job over at the F1 Academy. He's not known for his coddling, so this is a surprising move. It is not known what exactly his role as consultant will look like, but he was at the headquarters for an extended time before the race at Silverstone.

Sandra Haynes's statement acknowledged his new role and said the entire group was happy to have him on the team. She didn't give details on what exactly he would be handling, but the world of Formula One will be watching to see the kind of impact the notorious hothead brings to the table.

That brings us to Empress Racing and their dismal showing at Silverstone. Sawyer Joseph and Malcolm Acheson placed sixteenth and nineteenth respectively, not doing any favors for the new team principal.

Empress President, Sydney Davis, said it was a "disappointment" in the post-race press conference. Stating, "We need to do better. The hunger isn't there, and it shows in every race." We're hard-pressed to disagree with her statement. Toni Bailey, in just her fifth grand prix with the team, was noticeably frustrated toward the end of the race. Her press conference was filled with clipped words and not much information for a plan going forward. It makes us wonder what the future holds for the new owner and the team in general. We would expect major changes over the remaining races and into the offseason.

Chapter 32

Luka

"You seem lighter. Happier, even," my therapist says a few minutes into our session.

"I honestly feel it. Things with the academy have been going extremely well. I've already secured some sponsorships for the drivers, so they're actually making money. Things with Daisy are ... so fucking good. We're talking about possibly getting her IUD removed." We've been loosely talking about it, but every time we have sex, all I can picture is her growing our baby.

"Wow, that's quite a huge step for you guys. And you're okay with this?"

"I am. I mean, I'm sure it'll freak me out a little bit if it actually happens, just because it makes it real. We wouldn't just be talking about it. But I am sure I want a family with Dais."

"I encourage you to keep talking to her when things get overwhelming. If you get freaked out, talk to her or call me. I want to make sure you don't go backwards or relapse."

I scoff. "I haven't thought about drinking in weeks. I feel good about that at least. But I will promise to talk to you both if I get too in my head about it all. We've been talking a lot about our childhoods, and that's helped us both, I think, to understand where each other's heads are at."

"That's a great idea. I'm glad you're talking about the past as that's been something you've avoided." He smiles.

"Is this where I tell you you're the almighty therapist and know-it-all? That you were right about talking about it all?" I laugh.

"No, although it is nice to hear once in a while." He joins me in laughter before clearing his throat. "Update me on your hands. How's PT? Do you have anything on the schedule?"

I sigh. "PT sucks, but my mobility is almost at a hundred percent, and my strength is almost there too. I have what we're hoping is my last skin graft two weeks before the COTA race." My breath stalls in my lungs.

"What just happened there?" he asks.

"Circuit of the Americas. I haven't been back on that track since I..." I gulp for air. "Since I crashed," I whisper.

"And you're having a skin graft just before that. That's a lot to handle in a short amount of time."

I decide to just talk it all out instead of attempting to figure out the right way to say things. "I think I've been pushing going back to COTA to the back of my head. If I'm honest, I didn't know if I would actually go, even though Daisy will be going."

"Understandable. It's safer to plan to not go than to think about what going actually means."

"Exactly. I am scared I'm going to panic. I'm not so much worried about relapsing but more so having a full-on panic attack when there are cameras around. I won't have a private moment to go on the track."

"But you'll have Daisy, and Beck will be there, I'm sure. All of your friends will be there to support you. And if you need a minute without cameras, I think the people around you will make that happen."

"Should they have to focus on me, though? I feel like I've been the focus of everyone's worry for so long, and it's been a year—a full year—since the crash. When does it stop? When do people stop looking at me like I'm a ticking time bomb?"

"I understand it probably feels that way, but I'd think they're just worried about you and want to do what they can to help you move past that incredibly traumatic event. I'm not saying it doesn't feel like you're in a fishbowl from your side of things, but perhaps they just want the best for you."

"I know." I sigh and slump back. "It's just strange that it's already been a year. It feels like I blinked, and we're already a year out. Yes, I've done so much in that time, but it's almost like I haven't done anything."

"You've gotten a new job. You've quit drinking. You've repaired things with Daisy. You've learned how to be open and how to communicate. You've decided to start a family in the future. Why are you discounting all of that?"

I take in his list of my accomplishments. I'm not sure I've ever sat back and thought about everything that's happened in the last year like that, and it's eye-opening to say the least. But the self-doubt is always present in my head.

"What if that's not enough?"

"What would make it not enough? Your work life is thriving. Your home life is thriving. You've put in the work to better yourself and are making huge strides toward your future. What about that isn't enough? I'm genuinely asking," he says.

"I'm not a Formula 1 driver anymore. I don't make that kind of money anymore. Is the life I'm providing my wife and future kid going to be good enough?"

"Replay that sentence in your head."

I do as he demands and hear how ridiculous it is, but it doesn't mean it's less of a worry for me.

"I get it, but I want to make sure Daisy has the best life."

"How about you let her decide what 'the best life' looks like. I know it's a point of pride, but how you live your life is a team decision with your wife."

I nod, really taking in his words.

I keep thinking about them the entire ride home, and that's when I realize I haven't gotten behind the wheel of a car in almost a year. Daisy and rideshares have been my go-to, never driving myself. Something so simple, really, but it's a hurdle that I haven't been able to even think about.

Walking through our door, I find Daisy at the dining room table, flipping through some paperwork.

"You want to go for a drive?" I ask.

"Where are we going?" she asks absentmindedly.

"Daisy." I wait until she looks up at me. "Let's go for a drive." I hold up the keys I grabbed and show her what I mean.

"You're driving?" She stares at me. "You're driving!" She jumps up with shock on her face.

"I think it's time to try. In a couple of weeks, I'll be all bandaged up and won't be able to." I chuckle to hide my insecurity.

"I mean, yes, obviously I would love to go for a drive, but don't feel like you have to do this."

"If I don't do it now, when will I? It's been almost a year, Dais," I say quietly.

"And you can wait another year if that's what you need. No one is pressuring you." She makes her way over to me.

"I want to try."

She grabs the hand not holding the keys and squeezes gently. "Then let's go for a drive. We can switch out whenever if you need to."

We make our way to the garage, and I climb into the sporty little number I picked up to have here after Daisy and I got married. One that's sat idle for over a year.

Opening the garage door, I turn the car on and put it in reverse, and then freeze. The sound of the engine, the feel of the vibrations in my hands on the wheel, has my grip so tight that my knuckles are pure white. The tight, glossy skin on my hands is stretched to the point where it almost hurts, but I push through.

Slowly, so fucking slowly, I let my foot off the brake. We creep out of the garage at a snail's pace, but my grip doesn't loosen. The panic doesn't subside.

Once daylight streams in through the windshield, I press on the brakes hard, stopping us in the driveway.

"Talk to me," Daisy says from the passenger seat.

"The vibrations in the wheel. It's not like a flashback but more like muscle memory? My whole chest feels tight." Even to my own ears, my stilted words don't inspire the confidence that I can actually do this.

"Okay. Let's do some breathing." She takes control, and I'm beyond grateful.

After a few rounds of breathing exercises, my chest starts to loosen its tight grip on my body.

With my foot still on the brake, I peel my hands off the steering wheel and flex them. They ache, but I just keep telling myself it means I'm alive. The panic tells me I survived.

Daisy's hand softly rests on my thigh, a silent show of support that does more than I could ever find the words to tell her.

I let my foot off the brake once more; the movement is smoother this time. I manage to get us out onto the street and put the car in drive before I have to flex my hands again.

It's painfully slow, but within fifteen minutes, I've found a sort of groove.

"Where are we headed?" Daisy asks.

"I have no clue." My voice sounds like I've been screaming at a concert. It's scratchy and faint, but I don't have the wherewithal to care about it.

A few minutes later, I pull up to a parking area along the river. Four steadying breaths help me come to the realization that I just drove for the first time in almost a year. It was scary—it was *terrifying*, actually—but I did it. One of the hardest things I feel like I've ever had to do, as dramatic as that sounds.

"Let's go sit," I tell Daisy as I climb out of the car.

We find a quiet spot that's hidden from the busier section and sit down.

"I'm so proud of you," Daisy chokes out. I look over and see the tears falling down her face, but it's the smile—the big, bright one I love so much—that releases the last of my tension.

"Why did it take me so long to do that?" I ask.

"Because you went through something that rocked your world, completely changed the trajectory of your life, and it all boiled down to driving. I think anyone would feel the same if they went through what you did."

"I wasn't focused," I murmur. "That day. I wasn't focused on driving. I was mad, angry that my season was shit. I was mad at you for getting pregnant, as unfair as that is. I think I blamed you for how shitty my season was going, even though you had nothing to do with it. COTA had always been one of the easier races for me. The track isn't complicated, and I put my brain in neutral. I still don't remember crashing. But I've watched the video so many times. I jerked the wheel. There was no one around, and I jerked the wheel. It wasn't intentional, but my head wasn't in the race, and that's one of the most dangerous things a driver can do. I put myself at risk, knowingly."

Admitting I shouldn't have been driving is hard. I didn't even realize that's where my head would go today, but I'm glad it did. Owning up to the fact that I most likely could have prevented the accident sucks, but I need to take responsibility.

In order to fully move forward and be prepared to be at COTA again, I need to face everything that happened.

Broken sobs sound from Daisy. Hearing that your husband didn't care enough about his life to not put himself at risk can't be easy. It's like I'm hurting her all over again, making her relive the crash. Except, this time, she knows I could have—should have—prevented it. She has every right to be furious with me.

Pulling her to my side, I hold her as her painful cries fizzle out.

"I'm sorry," she whimpers, and my heart breaks in two.

"Dais, *hercegnőm*, no. You have nothing to be sorry for. *I'm* sorry that I didn't just talk to you. That I put myself at risk instead of growing the fuck up and just figuring my shit out. It was so fucking selfish."

She shoves against my side, sitting up, and shoves me once more. "Don't ever do that shit again. We have to grow old together. We have to make babies. We have so much life to live. Don't ever put yourself at risk like that again. I won't survive it."

"I won't. I promise." I pull her to me.

We spend the next hour soaking in the afternoon sun before we decide to head back home. The drive back is a million times easier, and I even stop to pick us up some food. The dam has broken on this roadblock, one of the last hurdles I had to conquer.

Only a couple more weeks until the final one.

Chapter 33
Daisy

Back in the hospital. Hopefully for the last time.

Dr. Branch said it shouldn't be as long as there are no surprises, which leaves entirely too much open to chance for my liking.

One year ago, almost to the day, I was sitting in the waiting room down the hall, hysterical. It feels like yesterday and just a blip in my memory at the same time. So much has happened in a year, and yet we're back here, waiting for another surgery.

"Dais, it'll be fine," Luka says from the pre-op bed.

Nodding in a daze, I know it will be, but there's always that fear. The what-ifs that could happen.

"Come here, *hercegnőm*," he says softly.

Standing up, I walk over to his bedside, my nerves on edge. He grabs my hand and pulls me onto the small bed with him. There, curled up against his side, I can finally breathe.

"It'll be over before you know it," Luka murmurs against my temple.

"It's your pinkie; it's complicated," I counter.

"But we have the most badass doctor, and he'll do it like it's nothing and then we're done."

"I know. I just hate being back here."

"I'll admit the timing isn't great. Probably should have thought about that when I scheduled this shit."

"It needed to get done. I don't think there is a good time for it, honestly."

His hand strokes my arm. Turning my head, I press a kiss to his chest, right over his heart, through the scratchy hospital gown.

"Just ... make it through this, okay?" I murmur against his heart.

"Always." A kiss is pressed to the crown of my head. We get another two minutes of peace before a knock sounds at the door.

I scramble out of the bed and hear the nurse chuckle behind me. "You're fine. I just have the pre-op paperwork to go over."

Sitting in the chair, I listen to the litany of questions. The anesthetist comes in and does the same before the doctor arrives.

"Last one, hopefully," he says cheerfully.

"Only if you don't fuck it up." Luka smirks with nothing but mirth on his face.

"Luka ... you can't say that," I sigh.

"Nah, he's good. It's been a long year, and I know you're ready for this to be done. I foresee this going well. The pinkie is technically going to be the most difficult repair yet, and recovery will once again be lengthy, but you've been doing all the right things with PT and aftercare, so I think you'll do just fine. Any questions?" He looks at both of us.

I shake my head and turn to Luka.

"Can you promise this is the last one?"

My heart hurts for my husband. He's been through so much, and the physical healing has been dragged out for over year. It would be hard on anyone, let alone someone who's had to do so much mental healing as well.

"I never promise that. However, I will say I can't see a scenario where you would need another graft. Your hands have taken well to the ones you currently have, and you aren't doing anything that would jeopardize the viability of any of the grafts. Does that work?" He gives him a look that says he knows the pain Luka is in, the struggle to keep undergoing these surgeries while trying to move on.

Luka nods, reaching out for my hand. I clasp his in mine as the last of the administrative shit gets taken care of. Before I know it, they're getting ready to wheel him back to surgery.

"I love you. I'll see you when you wake up, okay?" I tell him before kissing him.

"I love you too. So damn much, Daisy. We're almost done."

One last kiss, and they wheel him out of the room. I'm not sure how long I stand there, looking at the door, but when nurses come to clean out the room, I know I've overstayed my welcome.

"So sorry. I'm heading to the waiting room now." I pick up all of our stuff.

"No worries. Take your time." The kind nurse smiles at me.

Walking into the same waiting room I was in when they brought him here after the accident brings back a flood of memories. The panic and fear—*God*, it was terrifying not knowing how bad things were. None of us knew what recovery would look like, what treatment for burns looked like. It was all a guessing game. A very traumatic one at that.

Me:

> Will being in the waiting room of the hospital ever not be fucking awful?

Ruby:

> Probably not.

Heather:

> A little tact, Rubes. Jeez.

Ruby:

> What? It's the truth. Why lie about it? Daisy doesn't want shit sugarcoated.

Heather:

> Doesn't mean you have to be so blunt about it.

Ah, sibling fights. The best way to get me out of my head.

Autumn:

> Gotta be honest; you both kind of suck at this whole make-Daisy-feel-better thing.

I smirk at her response. She may be the baby of the family, but she pulls no punches.

> **Me:**
> Honestly, this argument is doing wonders as a distraction. Please continue.

Ruby:
See, Daisy loves it.

Heather:
She didn't say she loved it; she said it was a distraction. That's not the same.

Autumn:
Honestly, I don't know why I attempt to get in the middle of you two. It's not like either of you listen.

Ruby:
Well, this is about Daisy and not you, Autumn.

Autumn:
Damn, who pissed in your Cheerios today? Don't be a dick to me because you're pissed off at the world in general.

> **Me:**
> And now we're done. While this was nice and all, I don't think listening to the three of you bicker is really going to help me out right now.

Autumn:
That's on me. I'm sorry.

Ruby:
Me too. I just wanted to irritate Heather.

Heather:

What did I do?? We literally just went out to dinner last night, and you were fine!

Ruby:

I mean, when do we go more than one day without an argument? You know I love to needle.

Autumn:

I can't with you two. Is this your love language? Being dumbass siblings who make no sense?

Ruby:

Aww, someone feels left out. Don't worry; tomorrow, it's your turn.

Me:

You know, sometimes I miss the crazy. It's far too quiet here without the three of you arguing all day, every day.

Heather:

Let's not pretend you don't start half the shit, Dais. You're the impulsive one here; your hands aren't clean.

Me:

I like how you turned that into me somehow committing a crime. Don't be jealous that I travel the world.

Ruby:

If I remember correctly, you said you were going to bring us on trips occasionally... When's that happening again?

Well damn, she's got me there.

I concede. What if I offer VIP tickets to the Austin race? It's not exactly traveling the world, but it's a mini vacation … rooms at the Vanstone … hot race car drivers … some hot engineers…

I'M IN.

Sign me up.

Ugh … way to twist my arm.

Consider it done. Details will be in your emails shortly.

At least that gives me something to work on while Luka is under the knife.

Anyone heard from Adam recently?

Nothing. I think he's undercover this time, so we may be in the dark for a while.

Mom said he's going quiet for a while, so I think you're right.

I know he's in New York and will be for at least a few months.

Autumn knows more. They're the closest, but she never tells us anything, sworn to secrecy and all that.

Four hours later, I have rooms set up at our Austin location and VIP tickets reserved because Sydney is awesome and didn't even bat an eye when I asked. The COTA race is turning into a large affair since I invited Mary and the kids from the Boys and Girls Club too. Apparently, Sydney didn't know I had a huge family and was *very* interested in meeting them. Meaning, she wants to see if I'm just wild and slightly a mess on my own or if it's a familial trait. Spoiler: it's a family trait.

"Daisy?" Dr. Branch calls from the doorway.

"Hey! Hi!" I jump up, shocked the surgery is already over.

"Surgery went great." He smiles. "Pinkie looks great, zero complications. He'll probably be pretty ornery at PT for this one because the skin is so tight, but once he gets through that, he's done. This was the last one, Daisy," he adds softly.

Big, fat tears roll down my cheeks. He's been with us since they brought Luka in, and it's both a relief and the end of an era. One I'm not sad to leave, to be honest, but I'll miss Dr. Branch.

"I—" I swallow and blink to clear the tears. "I can never thank you enough for what you've done for our family. Our door is always open for tickets to races and stays at the Vanstone. Please take us up on it. It's not nearly enough to repay you for all you've done this past year."

"The two of you have had a hard year, but the support and love you both have makes my job well and truly worth it. Luka will have a fully functional life moving forward, and that's all I can really ask for." His smile is genuine.

"Can I be awkward and snag a hug? I feel like this is the last time we'll see you, even though we'll have follow-ups."

"Of course. It's been a pleasure to get you know you both." It's a quick hug but no less supportive. This man has seen both Luka and me at our worst, and has felt like a lifeline back to normalcy as he worked on Luka's hands.

Once he heads back, I slump back into the chair, relief heavy in my veins.

We made it through surgery. Next, we're going back to Circuit of the Americas.

Chapter 34
Luka

The Empress garage is a strange place to be when you aren't a driver. I've never been here in any other capacity.

Daisy is currently running a couple of things by Sydney and Beck while I shuffle idly in the corner, trying desperately to not let the panic get to me.

Flashes of everything leading up to the crash pop into my head periodically, and it's making it so hard to separate today from a year ago. I know this is the right thing to do, and I knew it would be hard, but this is more of a struggle than I was prepared for.

"Luka." Daisy's concerned voice pulls me out of a vision of me walking around my car, getting ready to jump in for the race.

"What's up?" I croak.

"We can go back to the hotel. You don't need to do this."

"I do need to do this." Luckily, it's Thursday, and the only thing on the agenda is press conferences with the drivers. It's giving me some space to figure out how to go out onto the actual track. There are still too many people here for my liking, but it's something I have to deal with. Should I have come here when it was completely empty months ago? Probably, but I wasn't ready then.

Am I ready now?

Who the fuck knows, but we're about to find out.

"Media will be in a press conference in about thirty minutes. It'll be the best chance to get on the track without attention."

It's what I asked for, but it makes me feel weak. Like I can't handle something as simple as coming back to a track I've been on many times before, just because I'm hung up on the crash.

But I'm not sure I can handle it, and I am weak.

"Can you just … come get me when it's time?" I ask shakily.

"You want me to stay with you?" Daisy asks, clearly unsure how to approach this.

"No. I'm just going to go in the back." I pivot quickly and go around the corner to where the cool down room is. Am I intentionally pushing away Daisy yet again? I'm not sure if I'm clear-headed enough to say one way or the other, but I'm not leaning on her like I should be. Like my therapist and I talked about doing.

"Hey, man, you need some company?" Beck walks in and shuts the door quietly behind him.

"I don't know if I can go on the track, and it's so fucking stupid." Anger shoots through me. At myself, at everyone making a big deal of this, and I can't shut it off.

"It's not stupid. You had one of the worst crashes in modern Formula 1; you're allowed to never come back here."

"But if I can't overcome this, how can I move forward with anything? How can I boast all this bullshit healing if I can't even walk onto a fucking track? I've been to Silverstone; this isn't different." I'm borderline yelling.

"This is wildly different. And this one thing doesn't negate everything you've done and worked on in the past year. I've watched you go from a closed-off asshole to a loving husband who is trying like hell to make a life you both can be happy in. A man who put in the work instead of saying 'fuck it' and moving to some faraway land to forever be a recluse. You've done the hard stuff, Luka. Don't let this derail you."

"It already is." My throat is scratchy. I hear his words, but I don't actually *hear* him. I don't take in what he's saying, and it just shows how far off I really am.

"Do you want me to sneak you out there with no one around?"

"I want you to stop trying," I yell and finally look up at him.

I see a flash of hurt, then resolve. "I can do that." He turns to walk back out the door before stopping. "We all just want the best for you, Luka. And maybe forcing yourself to go out onto that track isn't what's best."

The door shuts with a resounding click. Shame fills me, but I also can't bring myself out of it enough to go apologize. The determination to see this through is all I'm focused on.

I stare at my bandaged hand. I have to keep it covered because the sun is terrible for grafts, but it's also a reminder of why I need to step onto that godforsaken track. I need to overcome this. I need to just be done with this shit.

"Hey. Coast is mostly clear." Daisy's voice is small and worried.

"Great. Let's do this." The false confidence doesn't pull one over on her, but she doesn't stop me.

I walk on unsteady feet through the garage onto the pit lane and head toward the exit. My breathing is picking up, but so far, I think I can do this. I feel Daisy, Beck, and Sydney follow behind me, but I don't focus on them. I wrap around the barrier separating out the pit lane from the track and step onto the track for the first time. Frozen, I look down at the deep, dark, black nothingness of the road. So unassuming, yet it changed my life in an instant.

No, you did that all by yourself.

Looking up, I make a sharp left and start walking on the edge of the pit lane back toward Turn Thirteen. A shortcut through some grass and smaller side walkways, and past the tower, leads directly to where I crashed.

"Luka!" Daisy calls out behind me, but I ignore her. I'm a man on a mission, and no one can stop me.

The fast clip of my walk has sweat beading on my brow. It's October in Austin; it's naturally still hot, but this isn't from exertion. It's from stress and panic.

I'm not sure how long it takes me to walk to Turn Thirteen, but once I'm there, it's like I can still see my car. The pictures of the crash that will forever be on the internet flash through my head. The safety crew dragging my lifeless body out of the burning remnants. Daisy sprinting out of the garage. I may not remember it, but it's forever found online. It's something I can't ever forget, no matter how much I want to.

My legs collapse underneath me, dropping me to my knees as my bandaged hand catches my weight. The pain to my knees and hand don't register. Sounds don't register. It's like I'm in a vortex of water. My ears feel plugged; I can hear the whooshing of the water, but I can't get out.

I gasp for air, and the heat hits me hard. Engulfed in flames, I can't feel anything but the extreme heat.

Hands grab at my shoulders and shake me, but they can't pull me out of this weird water-fire combination. There's no way to escape.

"LUKA!" A loud, booming voice jolts me out of the flashback, and I look up from the track to see Daisy sobbing as Sydney holds her, with tears streaming down her face too. Beck stands above me with fear on his face.

"We need to get you up. Can you stand?" His voice is raspy like he has been yelling for a while.

My mouth opens a couple of times before I give up trying to say anything and shake my head. I feel paralyzed. My muscles won't cooperate when I try to move them.

"Shit," Beck curses and turns around as he pulls out his phone. He talks to someone for a brief moment before looking at Sydney. "Can you take her back to the garage or—shit, better yet—the hotel?"

"No!" Daisy screams, and if we hadn't drawn attention, that would have done it.

Attention, fuck.

"Help," I gasp out and plead with Beck to get me out of here with only a look.

"It's coming. I promise we'll get you out of here," he says before kneeling down next to me. "Do I need to call someone? Your therapist? Hospital? Do we need to take you to the hospital?" he asks gently, but it's like a knife to the gut.

I failed. Miserably.

Weak.

A headcase.

Good for nothing.

Before my words of self-deprecation can go any further, a van comes careening around the corner and stops just in front of us.

Felix and Nate jump out to help Beck get me up and into it while the women watch on. Once I'm in, Daisy sits next to me on the bench, gripping my hand like she's afraid to lose me. I realize, as I look at our hands, that mine is shaking so hard it's tapping against the leather chair. My teeth click together, and it dawns on me that my entire body is shaking that hard.

The body is so stupid. When it's in fight-or-flight mode, it doesn't do something cool; no, it fucking shakes like an earthquake.

"Can you handle getting him to the room?" Beck's voice sounds from somewhere behind me.

I'm assuming someone says "yes" as the van door is shut before I truly understand what just happened.

The drive to the hotel is over in a blink. Daisy whispers words of positivity, but I can't really hear her.

Nate helps me step out of the van, and we're met with a wheelchair that adds insult to injury, spiking my anger at this entire situation. But mostly at myself.

Daisy and Nate talk for a minute, before they wheel me into the hotel and up to our room. Once there, Daisy goes to the little coffee area and makes some tea.

I'm not sure why her making tea sets me off, but it sends me over the edge.

I grab a lamp off the table and throw it as hard as my fucked-up body will let me at the wall opposite Daisy. I may be pissed at myself, but I would never put her in jeopardy. I vaguely hear her gasp in shock.

Seeing the lamp burst into pieces loosens the tension throughout my body just enough to take the edge off. So, I throw whatever I can find within reach: the remote, a glass we left on the table this morning. Nothing is off limits.

The tears start as I lose control, if I ever had it to begin with. Painful screams come from my chest as I throw things at the wall and watch them shatter. Once I'm breathing heavily and exhausted, I look around at the damage. The room is a mess, which I'll pay for, but the catharsis of it all is something I desperately needed. To be in control for a couple of minutes.

As I slump onto the couch, Daisy rushes over and holds me to her chest. It's shaky with her own fight against the sobs.

We cry for hours. Knocks at our door go unanswered. Phones ringing and vibrating go unanswered.

Sometime later that night—or a couple of hours later, who knows—I fall asleep in my woman's arms, realizing how truly undeserving I am of her.

Chapter 35

Tomic's Breakdown Overshadows What Could be One of the Best Races of the Season

Empress Racing finally had a great showing in Practices One and Two, but sadly, they aren't the focus of this weekend's United States Grand Prix.

On Thursday, Luka Tomic was seen in the Empress garage with his wife, Daisy Tomic, and Empress President, Sydney Davis, and her husband, former Formula 1 driver and last year's champion, Beck Davis. During the normal press conferences on race week, Tomic was seen leaving the garage and heading out to the track.

For those who don't remember, a year ago on this very track, Tomic had a crash that derailed his career. Randomly crashing into the wall left him with severe burns on his hands after the car had gone up in flames.

Tomic has been notoriously quiet since the accident, so it was a surprise to see him at this particular race.

Once on the track, Tomic was seen walking to the turn he crashed on. According to eyewitnesses, Tomic appeared to collapse to the ground. Within minutes, he and his wife were whisked away from the scene while Beck and Sydney Davis, as well as Felix Karlsson, were left doing damage control.

Another source also says there was damage done to the Tomic's hotel room sometime over the last day as well.

It begs the question: why was Tomic even at Circuit of the Americas? His presence has derailed the focus off this year's race and turned the attention to what is clearly a man still dealing with the events of last year.

We have nothing but well wishes for the Tomic family and hope they are able to move forward from this. We'll continue to bring you the latest from the United States Grand Prix and any updates on the situation with Luka Tomic.

Chapter 36
Daisy

Fucking asshole pundits.

My fingertips swipe under my eyes, catching the tears falling, as I continue to look at the articles flooding in.

I'm still at a loss. I'd like to say that I have a plan, that I can help Luka and know exactly what to do to get him back on the right path, but I've got nothing.

Yesterday... His reaction to everything tore my heart out. His reaction on the track was nothing short of devastating to witness, and I can't even imagine how he felt. But then we came back to our room and ... it was *awful*. Never has Luka been violent in any way. I'd already called Pierce and Sydney, and down to the front desk to let them know about the damages, but an employee already blabbing to the media just adds more salt to the wound.

And we're supposed to be trying for a baby. My stupid, traitorous brain decides now is the best time to turn the tables and make this about me. However valid the thought, it shouldn't be my focus. It *isn't* my focus, but things were going so well, and now ... it's like we've traveled back in time to a year ago. I made a decision to trust him not all that long ago, trust in his ability to be aware of what he needs and what he can handle, and now, all of that is up in the air.

Turning to look at Luka, so pale and gaunt from the strain of everything, I have no idea what to do next. It's Friday night; he's been sleeping for almost a full day, and tomorrow I have the Boys and Girls Club coming to qualifiers, as well as my sisters.

What a clusterfuck. I should have known things weren't going to go as planned. It was stupid to make this huge plan and invite all these people when I didn't know how Luka would react.

And then I have to think about how much to actually tell Luka. Do I tell him about everyone showing up? Do I tell him about the articles and how his private moment was anything but? No, I can't do that to him. He's going to wake up and struggle enough without adding fuel to the fire.

I don't know what to do. Tears well in my eyes again as the paralysis to make a decision about what happens next feels too overwhelming. My phone vibrates in my hands.

Sydney:

Don't look at your phone except for my texts.

Me:

Too late.

Sydney:

Shit. I already called the GM and gave him an earful. He's finding whomever leaked the information, and they'll be fired as soon as we know.

Me:

You shouldn't fire anyone.

Sydney:

Umm, yes, we should. We're a luxury brand that deals with famous people on the daily. Our discretion and non-disclosure policy are *why* people stay with us. This was a gross violation, and we're not standing for it.

Me:

Luka destroyed half the room, Syd. Call it even.

Sydney:

Daisy… I'm not worried about the room. I'm worried about you.

Me:

I'll be fine.

Even through a text, I can hear the despondency in my voice. I'm not fine.

Sydney:

> Can I send food? Booze? Chocolate? Bath bombs? Please let me do something. I know that's selfish, but I need to help.

Me:

> No alcohol.

My response is immediate, but the last thing I want to do is give Luka access to alcohol after all of this. Maybe that can be the one positive, that he came out of this sober.

Me:

> I wouldn't say no to some bath bombs, though.

Sydney:

> Consider it done. We're all here for you, for whatever you need.

Me:

> Thank you.

Less than ten minutes later, a soft knock on the door followed by the door opening and closing means Sydney worked her magic, as per usual.

Getting out of bed proves difficult. I move a centimeter at a time, not wanting to wake up my husband. By the time I make my way out to the living room, it's been almost ten minutes, but it kept Luka asleep.

In the basket, there are handful of bath bombs, but there's also the fancy chocolate that's my favorite and some of my favorite snacks. A note tucked in the middle draws my attention.

We love you both. Please, please don't hesitate to ask if you need something. I'll make anything happen.

Love, S & B

Have the tears actually stopped? Water droplets on the note say they haven't. If ever there was a time for clarity, this is it. Grabbing a bath bomb, I sneak back into our room and into the huge bathroom, shutting the door behind me. Hopefully, the running water doesn't wake him up, but if it does, so be it.

Stripping out of my oversized T-shirt and panties, I toss the ball in and watch it fizz up. Aromatic steam rises from the water, inviting me in to lose myself in my thoughts.

The water envelopes me in heat as I sink down into it, hissing at abrupt change in temperature.

Okay, so what do I know?

Luka had a … breakdown? We'll call it a breakdown, even though that feels grossly understated.

I have two groups of people here this weekend, who came to support me and Luka at this race.

I need to figure out a way to tell them what's going on, although if they've read any F1 news, they'll already know.

And I need to keep Luka safe until we can figure out the next steps.

Taking a deep breath, I sink under the water.

Maybe I should call his therapist? I know he won't talk to me but, shit, how else do I help my husband?

Then I need to, at a minimum, text my sisters and update them. Probably shut my phone off after I do because I know they'll bombard me with questions.

And then there's the Boys and Girls Club. Shit, the kids are going to be so disappointed they can't see Luka.

The flash of sparkle from my wedding ring catches my eye.

In sickness and health.

For better or for worse.

We made those vows, and I stand by them. I promised myself to Luka through it all on our wedding day. I twist it around my finger, sliding it back and forth before shoving it firmly back on my finger.

Nothing has changed. Through all of this, I'll be by his side, helping him as much as I can—as much as he'll let me. That doesn't change tomorrow, and it won't change a decade from now.

My lungs start to hurt in the way that means I need air. Gasping as I surge up, I sluice the water off of my face and hair before leaning back.

"Brought your chocolate in," Luka rasps, scaring the shit out of me.

My hand goes to my chest in shock as the air I just worked hard to bring in escapes my lungs. "Oh my God, you scared me," I pant, catching my breath.

"Sorry." He clears his throat. "I heard the water and knew you came into here to think"

"I... Uh, how are you?" I ask.

He nods, looking at the floor. "Not great. I feel like I've been run over by a semi."

"Go back to bed, then. I didn't mean to wake you up." My voice cracks.

The worst part about this conversation is that I don't know how to have it. I don't know if something I say will set him off; I don't know what to say to make things better. I'm walking on eggshells, and it's like we're right back to a year ago when I walked out on him. Except, this time, I'm not going anywhere. He needs me more than ever; I know that. It's just so hard. Everything feels so goddamn hard all the time.

He holds out the chocolate to me, already unwrapped, and I take it gingerly.

"There's snacks. Help yourself or order some room service; I know you're probably hungry."

"Thanks." He nods but doesn't move. "I'm sorry, *hercegnőm*. I thought I was better." His voice, so broken, has the tears start to flow freely again.

"Nothing to be sorry about. Healing isn't linear. You're going to have bumps in the road; we just pushed things too fast, I think." A diplomatic answer. The right response, but it rings hollow.

When he's not too broken and beaten down, I'll tell him how badly he scared me. How heartbreaking it was to watch him self-destruct emotionally. How fucking scared I am that things just won't work out for us.

But that day is not today. Today, I push it all down and help him move forward.

Clearing my throat, I figure out what I have to do. "I need to go down to the track for qualifiers. My sisters and another group I invited are there, and I need to make sure they are all set up. Are you going to be okay here by yourself? I can have Nate or someone come stay with you while I'm gone." I need a break. I need fresh air away from Luka in order to see more clearly.

"I don't need a babysitter." His abrupt tone change makes me close my eyes. "Sorry, shit. This sucks so fucking bad. I'm sorry. Go work. I'll be fine here. I'm sorry for making things so complicated."

"Luka ... that's not what I meant."

"I know, but it doesn't make it less true. Go work. I'll be fine."

It's a lie we both choose to believe in this moment. Because facing the truth, *dealing* with the truth of not being fine, not being better, is harder to handle. It's realizing that a year of work on both of our ends just wasn't enough today.

***

"Oh my God, we've been seeing it everywhere. Are you okay?" Heather rushes over to me when she sees me. Luckily, Sydney brought them all into our building behind the pit wall, so I didn't have to face the media or people in general.

They all rush me with a hug before continuing their line of questioning.

"Is Luka okay?" Autumn asks.

"Of course he isn't! You saw the pictures!" Ruby butts in.

I haven't been able to bring myself to look at the pictures, and Ruby saying that means I won't be doing so if I can help it.

"He's ... fine." I sigh. "He's as good as he can be, honestly, which isn't great but ... it's to be expected."

"Shit. I'm sorry. What can we do?" Heather asks.

"Just hang out and have fun this weekend. I'll see about dinner tonight, but you might be on your own." I cringe at ditching them when I haven't seen them in months.

"Don't worry about us. Seriously, we're self-sufficient and will be totally fine. We're just worried about you," Autumn says.

"Thank you. In a few minutes, I need to go meet a group I invited here and break the news that Luka won't be hanging out with them."

"Well, sit for a couple of minutes at least." Ruby pulls out a chair and forces me to sit down.

We talk about everything and nothing, and I'm grateful that they are here for what's turning out to be a terrible weekend.

Next, it's time to talk to Mary from the Boys and Girls Club.

They are all up in the VIP area above the pits, and it takes me a minute to work my way up there. I try to avoid any cameras, but I know it's a lost cause. Once I'm finally up there, I beeline it toward the group of kids pressed face-first against the glass wall.

"Good afternoon, lovely friends," I say with what I hope is a cheerful smile on my face. I look around and find Mary walking up to me with a sad smile.

"Thanks so much for inviting the kids. It's all they've been talking about since I told them." She gives me a small hug. "How's he doing?" she whispers in my ear before she steps back.

"Umm... He's ... working through it." I hate not having a better answer, but this is the best I can do.

"And you? How are you doing?" Mary is the sweetest woman in existence. When I called her to see if they wanted to come to the race as my treat, she instantly said yes. We became fast friends when I started learning more about what they do and why Luka loves going there so much. I see why he connects so much with her.

"I'm..." My eyes fill with tears, but I lock them down with a tight smile. Tilting my head, I give her a knowing look, and she nods in reply.

"That's okay, dear. Don't you worry about us. We are good here, and you don't need to worry about anything," Mary says.

"Who's worrying?" A voice I shouldn't be hearing calls from behind me.

"Luka!" the kids all yell at once.

I stand stock-still, confused as to what I'm seeing here.

Luka should not be here. He shouldn't be where there are cameras. He should be sleeping. Talking to his therapist or literally doing anything except standing in front of me.

Chapter 37

Luka

I was going fucking crazy sitting in that room like an insolent child.

Seeing Daisy so fucked up over my meltdown was too much. Should I have called my therapist? Probably, but I didn't.

I went to the bar.

And that first drink was so fucking good.

It calmed my body and my mind. Eased it out of the never-ending pit of despair. The second drink was just as good, but I knew if I planned to go out in the world, I needed to stop there. Popping gum in my mouth, I went on a mission.

My first stop was to Sydney, who answered my questions about where Daisy was cautiously. I could tell she was confused, but I didn't pay her much mind. I was on a mission to find my wife.

But what I ended up finding was so much better.

"Who's worrying?" I ask with a smile as I walk up to Daisy and Mary above the pits.

I give Mary, who looks unsure but happy, a hug as all the kids yell my name.

"This is a surprise! I didn't know I was going to have special visitors today," I tell them with my signature smirk.

I feel Daisy's stare before she seems to snap out of it. "Can I talk to you for a second?"

"Of course. We'll be right back, Mary." I smile before following Daisy at a fast clip. She may only be five feet tall, but the woman moves when she really wants to.

"What the fuck is happening right now?" she whispers once we're in a little side room.

"I'm visiting the Boys and Girls Club because Sydney said you invited them out," I say like it's obvious.

"What ... what the actual fuck, Luka?" she hisses.

"Look..." I sigh. "I didn't want to be couped up in the room anymore. I was going a little cabin crazy. I feel mostly better. I called my therapist." White lies, that's all these are. "I wanted to hang out like I was supposed to."

Her eyes shift between mine. "Are you okay?"

"I'm better." And that's not a complete lie. Mostly because I have just enough alcohol in my system to forget about yesterday for a minute.

"Are you—" She walks up to me and sniffs. "Are you fucking serious right now?"

"What?" My insurance of gum is apparently not paying off like I wanted it to.

"I knew I shouldn't have left you alone."

"I'm not a fucking child, Daisy."

"Then don't fucking act like one. I'm out of here. Do not fuck up those kids' day. I'm sending Sydney to keep an eye on you." The hurt in her eyes barely registers.

"I can handle the kids."

"I'm going home. Your bag will be on the doorstep." Her soft words don't convey the bomb of the words she just spoke.

"What?"

"I'm kicking you out. I can't do this again. I can't. I trusted you." She shakes her head, tears falling from her cheeks. "I can't watch you do this to yourself. After everything we've been through. After an entire year of fighting for us. You just blew it all up in thirty minutes. I hope it helped. I really do. Once you sober up, I hope you got what you needed out of those couple of drinks," she whispers before walking off.

Confusion hits me first as I watch her leave. I mean, I know drinking is bad. I know I worked hard to get sober. I know it's a crutch for me, but were two drinks really that awful if it made me feel slightly human for a second? After what happened on the track, I needed something to dull the pain. Does everything need to be so fucking hard all the time?

Answers don't come. Sydney does, though. She keeps a guarded eye on me the rest of the day before sending me back to the hotel, alone. I guess it wasn't an empty threat from Daisy. A couple of hours later, a knock sounds at the door of the cleaned-up hotel room. The alcohol is long gone from my system, in its place a pounding headache and depression.

"What?" I yank the door open to find Nate, Beck's longtime friend and trainer.

"I was told to bring this to you." His words are clipped and angry.

I have a feeling everyone's wrath is currently on me. "Thanks."

I take it from his hands, pull it to the side, and open my mouth to ask—what, I'm not sure—but it doesn't matter anyway because he's already walking away.

Shutting the door, I eye the suitcase.

Daisy kicked me out.

I relapsed.

Fuck, I relapsed.

I walk over to the couch, where I left my phone, like I'm a zombie. I'm not sure how I even dial the number I do, but I'm grateful I figured it out.

"Luka?" my therapist answers.

"I fucked up." My words are weak. "I had two drinks." My voice cracks.

"Okay, start at the beginning."

I tell him as much as I remember about going onto the track, about that night crying in Daisy's arms, and then feeling like everything was against me. How out of control everything felt. So, I rebelled. And it was fucking stupid.

"What worries me the most is that this was a true test for you. We discussed it before you went to the track, and you promised that you would call me or lean on Daisy if you felt like you were going to relapse, and you didn't. I think it might be a good idea to get you into an actual program, to learn coping mechanisms and really understand the depth of this disease. There are some great day programs that I can send your way, but I think understanding *why* you did this instead of leaning into all the work you've done over the past year is ultimately what will help you."

"Did I lose Daisy?" I ask feebly.

"I don't have an answer for you. But I think it's telling that she's kicked you out as soon as she realized you were drinking. You betrayed her trust, and she acted accordingly. I've no doubt she's thinking about how the two of you can move forward if you remain stagnant. If you can't stay sober. You were talking about having a family, and I'm sure that's very much at large in her head." His words cut to the quick, and as hard as it is to hear, I listen. "I think it's going to take a lot of work to regain her trust after this."

"I know," I whisper. I do know; I just wish I had taken more than two minutes to think about my actions. A fork in the road, and I chose the worst path.

"I'm glad you called me, though. That's a huge first step, and I'll be here for our sessions and you can always call me if you need anything." There's no judgment in the entire conversation, and I'm so grateful for that.

We hang up after discussing logistics of a day program, and I sit on the edge of the bed, trying to figure out the next step.

Looking down at my hand, I peel back the bandage I put there this morning. As much as my panic attack on the track hurt, I didn't do any real damage to my new graft, thank God. But I'm keeping it wrapped and protected while I'm still in … limbo.

Another fucking knock on my door has me angrily walking to the door. Opening it with force, I'm unprepared for the right hook Beck throws my way, which lands me on my ass on the ground in hot second.

"Shit." I gasp, touching my fingers to my tender cheek.

"That's for breaking Daisy's heart," he growls, fists clenched at his side.

"I deserve far more than that."

"Yes, you do." He walks over me, slamming the door behind him.

I clamber to my feet, careful to not put a ton of weight on my hand, and follow him to the living area.

"I'm sorry," I say as I sit next to him.

"Don't tell me sorry. Tell me how you're going to fix this. You have a drinking problem? How the fuck did none of us know? Why didn't you talk to anyone?" There's still a shit-ton of anger in his voice, but it's the hurt in his eyes that makes me stand down.

"At first, it was my way to cope. Everything hurt less with the booze; my mind didn't go in a million circles. It was a break from it all."

"And then you couldn't stop," he surmises.

"And then I couldn't stop. I was distant from Daisy. Didn't concern myself with how this entire situation affected her. She was pregnant ... at the beginning of the season."

"Fuck."

"Miscarried, a chemical pregnancy. I didn't know how to feel about it. It messed me up, and I didn't think about how it affected her. I focused on racing ... and drinking. Then she left me for a little bit, not too long after the crash. We ... reconciled. Things were going so fucking good." I'm not sure why I'm telling him all of this, but now that I've started, I can't stop. "We were so fucking good, Beck. Talking about trying for another baby after this race, and it all felt so fucking perfect. We were us again."

"Luka..."

"And then I fucked everything up again. It's like I'm scared to have the good things. Scared to have it all."

Because if I have it all, what's left? What's the challenge? What's the next big step? Does having it all mean I get complacent?

Talk about a revelation at the wrong time.

"Can I say something that probably makes me an asshole?" he asks.

I nod for him to continue.

"When you and Daisy got together, it was so fucking easy for you two. You got together, made time for each other, and got married. Everything was so effortless. Sydney and I were battling back and forth for almost four years before things calmed down enough to call them easy. And that wasn't because of our chemistry. We were made to be together, but circumstances meant we had to work our asses off for it. You and Daisy never went through that hard period. This is your hard time. This is the point in your lives together where you have to fight tooth and nail to be together.”

"How did you make it work?" I know a lot of what happened between the two of them, but not the details like this.

"I never gave up. She's my soulmate, and she was struggling. I never gave up, and she never gave me a reason to do so. Daisy has been by your side during the most horrific thing you could have ever gone through. She stood by your side while you turned to alcohol as a short-term solution. She stood by your side as you collapsed on the track out there because it was so fucking hard. And you repaid her by taking a goddamned drink."

I look down at the floor, my good hand pinching my thigh so hard it hurts.

"Daisy is a better person than I am. She has a heart of gold and does everything for everyone all the time. She never bats an eye. The *first* person who should be making her a priority is you." He stands up, gripping my shoulder. "I'm always here if you need me, but you need to truly figure things out before you drag that woman into this shit again."

I hear the door shut, and then I'm alone.

Never in my life, except when I was a kid, have I felt this alone. I've always had friends, women, or whatever. I've had Daisy for the past few years, Beck for longer.

And now, they're all gone because of my actions.

Chapter 38
Daisy

Numb.

I think that's the best way to describe the way I'm feeling.

It's been a week since COTA, and I've done nothing but stay couped up in the house. The only thing I've stayed on top of is work. Sydney told me to take some time off, but fuck, what would I even do? Allow my head to focus on what's happening with me and Luka more than I already am? No, thanks. I'll drown myself in work instead.

But now it's Friday, and the weekend is looming like a dark cloud in my mind.

The worst part is that I just want to call Luka and make sure he's okay. I've picked up the phone a million times, and yet I can't bring myself to hit call. For once, I want—no, *need*—to focus on me and not bring whatever Luka's doing or not doing into the fray. Trying to make sure I'm okay with ... everything while taking care of Luka just splits the focus.

And I really need to focus on myself.

My doorbell rings, and my heart starts pounding. *Is it Luka?* I rush to the door, pulling it open to find my sisters and Sydney dressed in pajamas, holding endless bags of food.

"Surprise!" Ruby yells.

Sydney cringes. "You were expecting Luka."

Apparently, my face isn't good at hiding how I'm feeling currently. Good to know.

"It's— I wasn't— What are you doing here?" I ask.

"We figured this weekend would suck, so we didn't want you to be alone. We decided a girls' weekend is in order. So, sleepover time!" She gestures to all the women standing on my front step.

Everything I've been avoiding. All the emotions, the pain, and the loneliness hit me at once, and I break out into an ugly cry.

"Oh shit." Autumn rushes in to hug me.

Multiple arms wrap around me as I release a week's worth of emotions.

I have no concept of how long we stand there, but once I realize we're still standing out on the entryway, I pull back and usher everyone in.

"You guys didn't need to come back here again," I tell my sisters as we move to my kitchen to organize the food.

"Umm, yes, we did." Ruby furrows her eyebrows.

"What Rubes means is that of course we had to come and make sure you were okay. We got in touch with Sydney to check on you because we didn't want to bombard you, and then she says all you were doing was working, so we had to come up. Sydney was more than happy to organize things to get us here," Heather says. "Thank you, by the way." She nods to Sydney.

"Working isn't a bad thing," I mumble.

"It is when you just kicked your husband out of the house." Sydney arches an eyebrow at me.

"So, the plan is we eat our weight in food, watch shitty television or 2000s rom coms, and if you want to talk about things, we're here. If not, that's cool too. But at least you have company." Autumn shrugs then grabs a bag of Jolly Ranchers. I watch as she rips open the bag, spilling half the contents onto the island before popping a red one into her mouth.

"It's like we're back in high school," I mutter, shaking my head.

"Yep. So, pick what we're watching and change into your pajamas." Ruby smiles.

Twenty minutes later, we're all snuggled into my sectional, watching *Sweet Home Alabama*.

As the movie rolls, I start thinking about Luka and what our future holds. I'm not ready to think about a life without him, but I know I need to be prepared for that because there's a real possibility that he won't stay sober. That he won't be who I need in a partner. It just hurts to even consider. Our vows mean something, but only if he isn't actively choosing to self-destruct and throw everything away.

When the most iconic line in the movie comes on the screen, I'm sobbing before I can stop myself.

"Why"—hiccup—"is he so damn"—hiccup—"sweet to her? Men aren't like this!" I yell at the TV as Josh Lucas's character proves he was always supposed to be with Reese Whitherspoon's.

"Ooookay, that might be enough of the rom coms," Ruby says, reaching for the remote.

"NO! No. I'm okay." I wipe the tears off my face before clearing my throat. "I'm okay. Let's finish it." But I'm not okay. I'm so very, very far from okay, and I don't know how to verbalize it.

The movie ends, and I'm still trying to subtly wipe tears away, but it doesn't go unnoticed.

"Okay. I think we should talk." Heather shifts so her leg is underneath her as she faces me.

"I don't want to," I whine.

"We know, but holding in all your emotions and feelings surrounding what's going on isn't going to help," Sydney says sympathetically.

Four sets of eyes stare at me and make me break, damn them.

"What if kicking him out was the wrong thing to do and it only makes him worse? What if he needs me to support him, even though he needs his ass kicked too? What if I die alone because I wanted to be stubborn and *right* and not a good wife?" I drone on.

"Well, I was worried that the bubbly, slightly dramatic Daisy we all know and love was gone, but there you are!" Sydney says with a small smile.

"It's not dramatic if he kills himself in the process." I glare.

"Beck has been talking to him, and he's focused. I wouldn't say he's doing well, but he's focused, and that's a positive," Sydney says, dropping the playfulness.

"Can I also point out that, during all of that, your focus was on Luka and how he was doing and feeling?" Autumn says. "What about how you're feeling?"

"I'm..." *How am I feeling?* "Is it bad to say I have no idea? I'm sad, so fucking sad all the time, and if I dwell on it too much, it feels so all-consuming."

Four heads nod but don't say anything. They all know I'll fill in the silence because that's just who I am.

"What if things don't get better? Does that mean I have to take drastic steps to leave him? I don't want to leave him. Hell, I barely wanted to kick him out, but it felt like the only option at the time." I sigh, my thumb rotating my engagement ring on my finger as a sort of fidget.

"I'm going out on a limb here and saying that you've been hiding a lot of what's been going on with you two because a lot of this is a huge surprise to us," Heather says gently. "That's not a bad thing, but we're all here all weekend, so how about you fill us in and we can go from there. Maybe we can help you get some clarity or, at the very least, talking everything out will help get the pressure off of your shoulders."

And so, I do. I spill every sordid detail. Everything I've kept bottled up for almost two years. I tell them about the pregnancy and Luka's reaction to it. His drinking and everything that happened—both good and bad—after his crash. Finally, I tell them about Luka breaking his sobriety last weekend and how much it broke my trust in him.

"No one would tell you that you did the wrong thing by kicking him out. Maybe he needs something this drastic to kick his ass in gear," Ruby says.

"But what if it does the opposite?" I ask.

"I'm going to be super blunt, so don't hate me," Sydney pipes in. "Luka fucked up in a big way. Sure, his panic attack on the track was awful to witness and I'm sure doubly as awful to experience, but you never left his side until you absolutely had to. If I know you, you also offered to have someone stay with him because you knew the whole weekend was a giant trigger for him. This entire time—hell, for almost two years—you've solely put your focus on him. How is this affecting him? How will he handle it? Are you doing enough?" She pauses to make sure I'm really listening.

I nod for her to continue.

"What about how everything has affected you? The outspoken, vivacious

Daisy you are has been pushed to the side. In its place is an overly cautious, hidden version that I think is hindering how you move forward. It's like you're always on eggshells, even if it's not around Luka."

I let her words sink in and realize she's right. I haven't been myself in a long time. I mean, there's been moments and days, but nothing consistent. I'm not sure how I get back to her, but maybe that's the key in all of this. I've been so blinded by everything Luka went through that I've never stopped to process how I've changed because of it. In therapy, I've talked about it, but we'd mostly focus on what I wanted from my future. She didn't know past Daisy, so she couldn't compare the me now to who I was pre-miscarriage and pre-crash. Sure, people evolve, but what if I'm evolving backwards? What if my evolution is hindering both of us, not just me?

"I want her back," I whisper.

That Daisy would take no shit and stop second-guessing herself. That Daisy would bend over backwards for her loved ones but also know when it's time to stop because she's losing herself and being used as a door mat. Luka's been so focused on him, which he should be, but how could I truly help him if I'm not in a place where I can help myself? Pushing things down for so long has clearly created something akin to a volcano for both of us, spewing our damage all over our lives but never having the wherewithal to attempt to clean it up.

"Then we'll help you however we can," Autumn responds.

"Can we put on something not romantic and jump back into this tomorrow when I can organize my thoughts more?" I ask weakly.

"Hell yes, we can! How about that new reality show about those social media people?" Ruby asks, jumping up and down in her spot on the couch.

I chuckle. "Sounds perfect, actually."

The rest of the night, we eat junk food and talk shit about the show, and it heals something in me I didn't realize was broken. I think I've been in a Daisy and Luka centered world for too long, and I missed hanging out with the girls. Missed friendship. When we break apart to go to bed, I decide to take a bath, the one thing that's stayed a constant and the only thing that helps me think clearly.

Sinking deep into the heated water, I let my mind wander.

Sydney was right; my normal outgoing nature has been on the backburner for months. With the grief of the miscarriage less prominent, have I really let myself relax and be who I used to be? Am I walking on eggshells with everyone, not just Luka? If I look back, I would say yes. It wasn't a conscious decision, but it's there nonetheless.

Then, there's the sheer stress of it all. It's like I'm constantly in fight or flight, and that can't be healthy. Lord knows I sleep like shit right now.

Surging up for air, I think about how all the stress has affected me. Emotionally, it's exhausting. I'm so tired at night, but I've tried to not let it show. Physically, I've gained weight, and although I'm putting on a brave face for everyone outwardly, I'm so damn depressed underneath.

I thought going to therapy and getting Luka help would be enough. I thought buckling down and working would help.

But Luka still took that drink.

Leaning my head back, I look at the ceiling. I remember the time not so long ago that he came in here with me. I remember the way he felt against my back. The intimacy of it all. I wonder if we'll ever get back there. I wonder if we can grow together instead of apart.

My fingertips trail against the skin on my stomach, reminiscing and hoping. My thoughts turn to when my last period was, and I can't remember. The stress of ... everything has had a profound effect on the body, and this is probably just one in a long line of symptoms that arise when you're under this much strain.

It doesn't make me want a baby any less. I took out the IUD early for a reason. I wanted to give my body time to adjust before we officially started trying, but now that's on hold too.

This week was supposed to be it. From here on out, it was the start of a new chapter in our lives.

Instead, we've taken a million steps back, and I'm not sure where it leads to or if we can find our way back together. I want to, though.

What I do know is I told Luka I wouldn't give up on him, and I don't plan to. This time apart just means I need to figure out this shit before I lose myself again. And Luka needs time to find himself again too.

But I'm not giving up.

Chapter 39

Luka

Three weeks.

Three weeks of intensive treatment, soul searching, and missing Daisy so damn much it feels like I can barely breathe some days.

But today, I'm officially discharged from my outpatient treatment program.

Beck waits for me in the lobby, shaking my hand and clapping my back once I walk out. "Proud of you."

"Thanks. I've learned a lot, and I feel better." And I do. I feel healthier and, more importantly, stronger mentally. Now, I just need to find a way to show Daisy that.

"Are we celebrating your graduation?" He smirks over at me.

"Actually, I was wondering if you could take me home." I clear my throat.

"To the rental it is." He sighs.

"No, actually. Home, to..." It hurts to say. "Daisy's house."

He stares at me for a minute before nodding and putting the car in drive without further question.

I'm not expecting much, but it's been too long since I've seen her, and I need her to know that I'm all in. This is the start of rebuilding her trust in me, and I know I won't get another chance.

Silently, we drive to the house. My mind is running a million miles an hour, but I've practiced this. I've talked about this moment to death with my therapist and my substance abuse counselor, but it doesn't make it any easier.

Beck parks on the street, and I freeze up.

"I can take you back—"

"No. I just need a second." *I can do this.* I *have* to do this.

Breathing in and exhaling, I open the car door, waving to Beck as I get out and walk up to the front door.

Knocking on the door, I count the seconds until I hear the locks disengage.

A tentative Daisy greets me, but all I feel is relief. She's the reason I worked so hard the past three weeks. The reason I took extra classes, took extra sessions with my therapist. It's why I waited the full three weeks to see her. I needed to be ready. I needed to be all in and committed to earning her back.

"Hi." Her soft voice is a balm to my soul.

"Hi. I hope it's okay that I'm here."

"Of course. You want to come in?" She holds the door open.

"I would love that." I step inside the house I haven't lived in for almost a month. It's like stepping back in time. Everything is the same—it smells the same—but it's somehow different.

I take a seat on the couch and watch as Daisy sits in the chair across from me. It's a little stab to the heart, but I have to remember that nothing will happen overnight. I need time to fix the damage I've caused.

Clearing my throat, I jump off the cliff. "I wanted to stop by and apologize. For so many things, but first and foremost is for putting you in that situation at COTA. My first time back on that track shouldn't have been at a race, and it was stupid of me to think I could cope with that extra pressure. And, more importantly, I'm so damn sorry for having those drinks. It was a lapse in judgment, but I had put in enough work to know better. It was..." I sigh. "The worst mistake of my life."

I look up and see her nodding with barely concealed tears in her eyes. "I appreciate the apology," she squeaks out.

"I know this is a reach, and I will understand and respect your decision, but let me explain before you decline." I wait for her nod before continuing. "I'd really love to take you out on a date. There's a lot that I want to talk about and tell you about, but I don't want to overwhelm you with all of it. I think dating, if you're amenable, can help us get to know each other again and help me tell you everything I need to. I want to regain your trust, and I know it will take time, so I thought dating might be a way I can convince you that I am committed to you and to doing this right." I'm rambling, but I just want this so fucking bad. I need her to say yes.

"You want to date? Like, multiple dates?" she asks, wringing her hands together, so unsure of herself.

"I would love multiple dates, but I would be grateful if we can start with one."

She really looks at me then. Her eyes trail from mine down to my arms and hands that have healed up well enough, down my body then back up. I feel healthier, so maybe she can see it too.

"I think I can do a date," she says softly, and I almost jump up and yell in excitement.

"On another topic, would it be okay if I take one of the cars? I love Beck and all, but having him as my personal Uber driver is getting a little old." I smirk, but it's not my cocky one.

"Oh yeah, of course! It's your car. Please take it." She jumps up and heads to the kitchen to grab the keys, I assume. Quickly returning, she places them in my hand, standing there a second longer than needed before stepping back.

"It's good to see you. You look ... happy," she says quietly.

"Not yet, but hopefully soon." I look up at her, so she knows what I mean. I may look better, but I won't be happy until I have this woman, *my wife*, back in my arms.

I stand up, stretching my hands because I didn't realize I was clenching them most of this time.

"Does Friday night work for you?" It's Tuesday, which gives her time to process what I'm asking at least.

"Friday should be great. Am I meeting you there? Or..."

"I'll be picking you up. Six o'clock on the dot." I smile. "See you then, *hercegnőm*."

Her eyes dilate at my usage of her nickname, but I don't wait around for more. I head to the garage and grab my car, leaving a piece of my soul in the house until Friday.

Chapter 40

Daisy

I'm panicking. Full-on hyperventilating in my closet.

My phone rings with a Facetime call and I answer it, propping it up on the dresser as I go back to pacing the room.

"Woah, I figured you'd be freaking out, but this is more than I thought," Sydney says through the phone speaker.

"What if I don't hold strong? What if I cave at the first pretty promise he makes?"

"What if he puts in real effort and doesn't push you too hard? What if he's truly trying his hardest and doing his best to show he is?" she counters.

"Screw you and your level-headedness," I grumble. Her laughter sparks a smile from me, but I'm still so nervous.

"Why are you really freaking out?"

"I'm scared that he'll say all the right things. We'll go on all these dates, I'll forgive him, and then what happens in two years? Ten? Does he relapse again? I know that's not fair to ask, but how can I trust this?" I whisper, sitting on the bed.

"It's a possibility. We don't know the future; we can't begin to guess if he'll stay sober or relapse, but I think what you can do is look at his actions, his words, and see if it's enough to take the chance. There's always a chance of bad things. A car crash, a life-threatening disease, substance abuse... They're all things that can happen to anyone. But you have to ask yourself if you're willing to take the chance. Is your marriage enough? If he shows that he's serious and that he's putting in the work, is loving him enough for you?"

My heart screams yes, but my head is more cautious.

"You don't need to decide now. Go out with him tonight and see how it goes. I'm here if you need to talk things out, but just go in open-minded tonight and try to give him the benefit of the doubt."

"What has Beck told you?" I ask with a smirk.

She sighs. "All I know is that Luka has busted his ass the last month. I'm not saying it'll be enough for you, but I'm saying feel it out first."

"I think I can do that."

"Good. Now, change into that little black dress you never wear and have fun! Call me if you need anything." She hangs up without preamble.

Looking down at my simple orange T-shirt dress, I decide to listen to Sydney's advice.

Twenty minutes later, the doorbell rings.

Slipping on my chunky heels, I make my way to the door, opening it without thought.

"Damn," Luka curses at the same time my eyes go wide.

He's in slacks and a black button-down rolled up at the sleeves. I think the last time I saw him dressed up was when he won the Driver's Championship and went to Paris to collect his trophy. The bigger shock is that he's willingly showing his hands and forearms. It seems the last month did him a lot of good.

"Umm, you look ... good. R-really good," I stammer.

"Ditto, Daisy. Holy hell. You ready? If we stay at the house any longer, we won't be leaving, and that's not really my plan right now." He blows out a breath.

His earnestness is unexpected. My lips roll inward to stop my smile from forming.

"I think so. Judging by your attire, I think I'm dressed okay, yeah?" I ask to double check.

"Perfect. You're dressed perfectly. You could wear a paper sack and be gorgeous."

Well damn... How am I supposed to keep level-headed with this new, extra sweet version of Luka beside me?

"Alright, Romeo, let's go." I grab his hand and drag him out to his car. This

Luka is dangerous, and I need to be cautious.

The drive to our destination feels very much like a first date. We catch up with little things that have been happening in the last month. I tell him about how Empress is doing, and he tells me he hasn't been watching any of the races.

It's nothing of consequence, but it lets me know that he really has been working on things. Watching the races used to be his form of self-punishment. A way to keep himself paralyzed in grief over the loss of his career. I didn't realize it at the time, but since COTA, I've been doing a lot of reminiscing to think what I could have done differently to help him.

I look around, and confusion hits me. "Where are we going?"

"Give it a minute," Luka says with a smile.

The minute I see the iconic sign, I start laughing.

"I think we're overdressed for this." I chuckle.

"Nah, this is a classy date. Gotta make sure you're dressed up for mini golf."

Peter Pan Mini Golf is an Austin icon. One I've never gotten the chance to experience.

I can't lie; I'm excited as hell. I mentioned coming here once, and Luka shut it down, saying he didn't want to get accosted by fans while trying to play.

He's not only okay with that now, apparently, but showing off his burn scars in the same breath.

I wordlessly follow his lead after he helps me out of his low car. We get our balls and clubs before joining the queue to play mini golf.

"Thank you for this," I tell him when we're waiting for our turn at the first hole.

"I'm sorry I never did it before. I thought mini golf was lame and didn't want to do it. That was a bullshit reason for not doing something you wanted to. I'm trying to make up for a lot of my shortcomings." A self-deprecating smile replaces his usual smirk.

I tap my ball, and it goes halfway down the green. Stepping aside, I let Luka take his shot, and he makes it significantly farther than I do.

"You want to talk about it?" I ask, not sure if I should even broach the subject.

"Right to the thick of it, huh? I guess I deserve that."

"We don't have to. I just feel … awkward, and I hate it." I sigh as I walk up to my ball.

"No, you're right. I, umm… Well, Beck punched me."

"What?" I gasp.

"It was necessary. In the hotel after COTA when you left, he stopped by and decked me. Knocked some sense into me too, so that was helpful. I called my therapist pretty quickly after that, and he suggested an intensive program for my drinking. It took three weeks, and combined with more sessions with my therapist, it really helped me understand some things. I wanted to tell you more, but I didn't want to dig into anything before my program was over. That's why I texted you a vague timeline at the beginning, so you hopefully worried about me less." He hits his ball and gets it in the hole.

I absentmindedly hit my ball, missing the hole completely, but I don't care right now.

"I'm … really glad you took those steps, Luka." I'm not sure what someone is supposed to say in situations like these, but this is as good as I can come up with.

"Me too. It helped me see how selfish I've been for most of our relationship. My racing, my career, took precedence over everything else in either of our lives, including our marriage. And that wasn't…" He sighs. "It shouldn't have been that way."

"It wasn't like I was an unwilling participant. I never felt like I was missing out on things prior to … everything happening," I tell him.

"But how long would that have been sustainable?" he asks as we walk to the next hole.

"Well, we'll never know because that's not what happened in our lives." There's no use in dwelling. I've learned that much, at least. The what-ifs don't do anyone any good.

"Very true. So, while I was working on all of that, I talked with Mary a lot about creating a new program for the Girls and Boys Club. COTA is so close; there's a ton of opportunity there if we can get the funding."

"That's a wonderful idea," I tell him as we wait our turn on the next hole.

"I also apologized and explained everything to Mary. It wasn't fair to expose those kids to more shit, and it certainly wasn't okay for me to act like nothing happened."

He's saying all the right things, and it worries me. I know I need to get over that if we're going to really make this work, but as a first date goes, I'm cautiously optimistic.

"Thanks for coming out with me tonight," he says shyly, reaching for my hand but only allowing our pinkies to touch. It's a question more than anything.

I move my hand to gently intertwine our fingers, and we stay that way until it's our turn to putt again.

We're on the last hole, and I feel like after the heavy talk at the beginning of our round things have gotten a lot less serious. We've been catching each other up on Sydney and Beck, who decided to tackle each of us but that meant not hearing from the other friend while doing so.

Once our balls are eaten up on the last hole, I turn to him. "This was really fun. Thank you for bringing me here."

"Thank you for hearing me out. I'm sorry I didn't bring you here earlier. I have something else planned if you're open to more." He's hesitant but hopeful; I can see it written all over his face.

"Sure. Let's do it." *Stay optimistic.* That's all I have to do right now: stay optimistic and let him lead where things are going. Let him show me who he is now as a person.

"Are you good to walk a couple of blocks in those heels?" he asks, looking down with concern.

"Oh please. You've seen me sprint in stilettos; these are nothing." I scoff.

"Yeah, I have." The salacious, reminiscent look on his face makes me laugh.

We walk hand in hand through the park next to Peter Pan Mini Golf and weave our way through the various things they've got going on. We make it to the river, where there's an entire picnic set up.

"And how did you manage this one, Mr. Tomic?" I ask as I sit down on the plush blanket.

"Had a little help from some friends." He looks up and winks, drawing my attention to the couple walking away in the distance.

Sydney and Beckett. What a little hoe for not telling me she knew exactly what was happening tonight.

"You're winning people over quite quickly." I say it playfully, but as soon as the words register, my smile drops. "That's not what I meant."

"It is what you meant, and all I can say is that I'm trying. All I can do is apologize for my past behavior and show them that I'm really trying to change things. You included, but I don't expect things to be easy, Dais. I know I have a lot to show you." His eyes bleed earnestness.

They make me want to say "fuck it" so badly, but I can't. I don't trust him yet. And as fun as this night has been, I don't truly believe he's in a good place yet.

He hands out the food and drinks that were dropped off, and we settle in.

"I…" I sigh. "This is hard. I'm not sure what to trust, and you're saying all the right things." Honesty. I need to stick with honesty. It did us good for a while there, so we need to go back to that.

"I think this is what the movies and books call a grovel. I have a lot of things to earn with you, and I don't expect it to happen overnight. I know I need to work my ass off to earn your trust, Dais, and I'm going to. However long it takes you to trust me again is how long it will take. I'm willing to wait a hundred years, so long as I get to call you my wife and have you by my side every single day."

"Luka…" It's more than I can handle right now.

"I know. I know it's too much, but I don't want you to have any doubt about where I stand. I love you. You're it for me, and I promise I will do anything to make you happy. And I'll keep reminding you of that every chance I get."

"Okay," I whisper, completely overwhelmed.

The rest of the date is spent talking about the Formula 1 project with the Girls and Boys Club. We talk logistics, possible people to bring into the fray, and how to fund it. I make a huge point to pull the conversation away from anything us related. Everything he's said tonight has been too much for me to deal with all at once. He's like a completely different person, and I'm not sure how to handle that.

After he drops me off, I walk to the bedroom like a zombie. Plopping down on the bed, I don't even feel the tears until they're dripping off my chin. Tonight was intense and, in some ways, I don't believe the things he said were true. It's like I can't separate this Luka from the one a month ago—hell, a year ago. So, I release all the pent-up emotions tonight brought up.

The fear that we'll never be the same.

The worry that this amazing change within Luka is only temporary.

And the hope. The scariest one of all.

I let myself hope that this is all real.

Chapter 41

Tomic Seen Around the Austin Area, with Rumored Estranged Wife, Daisy Tomic

It's been quiet on the Luka Tomic front for a while, but he's recently been seen with his rumored estranged wife around town. After the United States Grand Prix, radio silence had everyone wondering if the breakdown at the race prompted the former racer to undergo some form of specialized treatment. Only whispers have been heard but nothing concrete in confirmation.

It seems whatever did happen during those few weeks is over, and the couple has been seen canoodling by the river.

We reached out to both Luka and Daisy Tomic, but they each declined to comment. We'll be on the lookout for more sightings as the Formula One season draws to a close.

Chapter 42

Luka

Date number two.

If it's possible, I'm even more nervous than I was for the first date. Maybe that's because my plan is to do a lot more talking, and there will be a lot less distraction.

The Formula 1 season just finished, and Empress Racing has had a horrendous season. Beck and Sydney are taking it hard, and I know that means Daisy is too. So, I decided to cook.

I've never cooked before in my life.

Currently, I'm running around the kitchen in my rental, attempting to keep things from burning when the doorbell rings. I offered to pick up Daisy, but she declined.

Tossing the kitchen towel onto the counter, I rush to the door out of breath.

"Hi." Daisy jolts back as soon as I open the door.

"Hi. Come in. I need to check the food." My words rush out as I turn around, leaving the door open for her to come in.

"Wait, you're cooking?" she asks incredulously as she walks into the war zone that is the kitchen.

"Attempting to. Although now, I think it was a terrible idea." I shove my hand into an oven mitt and pull out the salmon from the oven.

The rice on the stove bubbles over, and I toss the pan I just pulled out of the oven onto the counter and pull the pot off the stove.

"Shit," I mumble.

Looking around the kitchen, it's a fucking disaster. I take a deep breath so I don't lose my shit and turn to apologize to Daisy.

Except she's laughing. No, not just laughing; she's laughing so hard she's crying.

Awesome fucking impression, dickhead. Now, she'll never think you've got your shit together.

"Oh my God, this is the best thing I've seen in so long," she says through her laughter.

"What?" I'm sure I misheard her.

She brushes her fingers under her eyes and wipes them on her jeans. "I can't believe you tried to cook. Do you remember that time you tried to make pre-made cookies from the refrigerator?"

"No."

"You made a sheet-pan cookie basically and burned it to a crisp. All the cookies melted together, and I couldn't figure out how you even did that. They were prepackaged! They aren't supposed to do that." She shakes her head with a smile.

"I think I mentally blocked that out. But could you ... uh ... help me figure out how to not ruin dinner?" I cringe. "Please," I add.

"On it." She rolls up the sleeves of her sweater and walks over to the sink to wash her hands.

What a fucking failure. I had one job: to make an awesome meal for my wife to show her I'm different, that I'm better. I thought salmon and rice would be simple. Pop some shit in the oven, and toss some water and box rice onto the stove. What could go wrong?

A lot, apparently.

She pokes the salmon before putting it back in the oven and lowering the temperature. The rice, she peeks under the lid before pushing it to the back of the stove with the lid on.

"You did pretty good!" She turns around with a smile. It drops off her face in an instant when she sees mine. "What's wrong?"

"I can't even cook you dinner. What a fucking disaster," I mumble. "No wonder the fucking tabloids are talking so much shit."

"Hey." She walks up to me and grabs my hands. "First off, fuck the tabloids.

You know they're total bullshit, and I don't know why you're reading them. Second, the fact that you even tried to cook dinner for me is so damn sweet."

"But I'm trying to be good for you, better to you, and I'm failing." That self-deprecation is back with a vengeance, and I hate it. I'm almost whining, and that's not how I want Daisy to see me.

"Okay, so let me tell you a little secret. I'm so happy that you're working to better yourself. But I'm also so fucking happy to see you are still the Luka I fell in love with. I love that you suck at cooking. That you almost burned down your rental because you thought that was the way to my heart. Seeing that there are pieces of the man I feel in love with in the first place is ... so damn good. You've been so good, so *perfect,* that it made me wonder if that Luka was gone forever." She squeezes my hands, and I melt.

"So, I didn't fuck up?" God, I sound like a child begging for praise from their parent.

"I mean, you didn't fuck up dinner and you didn't fuck up things with me." Her eyes shift between mine. "I don't want to lose the you that I married," she whispers.

"I just..." Sighing, I try to find the words to explain. "I want to be the perfect husband for you, and I feel like if I don't get things perfect, I'll lose you."

"Can we make a deal?" she asks, and I nod in return. "Neither of us are perfect, so let's not try to be. Let's just try to be ourselves, okay?"

"But—"

"Working through our ... problems doesn't mean I need you to be perfect, Luka. It just means I want to be able to trust you again."

It's like the puzzle pieces click in my brain. I've been trying so damn hard to be perfect, and that's not what she wants or needs. I just need to prove to her that she can trust me. That I won't relapse again.

"Holy shit, I'm stupid," I mutter.

"No, you aren't." She lets go of my hands and checks on the salmon again before pulling it out. "You just thought that being perfect would solve all the problems. It's that dumb jock brain of yours." She looks over her shoulder with a wink. "It's so used to being phenomenal at everything it touches that you think perfection is the answer to all the things."

"Are you making a joke, Mrs. Tomic?" I smirk. "Saying I'm just a dumb jock?" I grab her hand and spin her to me once she's put the salmon down.

"If the shoe fits." Her smile is so bright. It's the one I fell in love with. The one that had me so gone for this woman within weeks.

My eyes shift between hers. "I really want to kiss you," I whisper, not wanting to break this moment we're having.

"Then do it," she whispers back.

Tentatively, I slide my hand along her jaw to cup the back of her neck. Bending down a little, I bring my lips to hers in a barely there kiss. It's an electric field. Weeks. It's been weeks since I kissed her last, and I somehow forgot the power she holds over me.

My brain stops thinking. I don't think about how to gain her trust. I don't think about fucking up dinner.

I sink into her.

The wild blonde curls, the sassy attitude I can see slowly coming back after everything I've put her through. *I missed her, missed this, so fucking much.*

She pulls back, wrapping her hand around my wrist to keep my hand where it is. "As much as I loved that, I think it's time to eat." Her words are barely over a whisper, but they break the spell.

I remember I don't get to kiss her any time I want. It's something still to be earned, but I'm going to fight like hell to get it back.

"Of course." I clear my throat before turning to grab plates and utensils.

Dinner is an innocuous thing, but it's more normalcy than we've had in months. We talk like everything hasn't been falling apart around us. We joke like my drinking hasn't almost destroyed us. And we kiss. A corner of the mouth here, a peck there. All little touches that add up to something much bigger.

We wash the dishes together, me drying after she scrubs them clean.

"This is all very domesticated. I don't think we ever washed dishes before this," I joke.

"Well, I did, but our housekeeper definitely took care of a lot." She smiles.

Looking down, there's the realization that I would change so much if I could go back in time. There's so much I would have focused on instead of just racing.

A wet sponge hits the side of my face, jolting my head up in shock. "Did you just throw a gross kitchen sponge at me?" I ask, appalled.

"It was a brand-new one, and yes, I did. You were in your head, so I got you out of it." She's awfully proud of herself.

I arch an eyebrow at her, and she does it right back. It's a dare, one I'll gladly take.

"Luka... Don't," she warns.

"Don't what, *hercegnőm*?" I reach my hand closer to the sink. The water is still running, and I act, splashing my hand through the running water. It lands directly on Daisy. Her sweater is drenched in an instant, and her squeal is music to my ears.

"LUKA!" she screams and starts running, but I give chase.

She runs down the hallway, but all the doors are shut, and she's stuck before she can get a door open. I cage her in, my heart pounding in my chest.

"I told you I'd always chase you, Dais. That I'd always come for you." A conversation from so long ago now means more than anything.

Nodding, she lets out a shaky breath.

"I won't ever stop chasing you," I murmur as I run my nose along her jaw. "I won't ever stop trying to earn back your trust."

Unsteady hands wrap around my forearms that are caging her in. "Luka..."

"Don't give up on me," I whisper.

"Never."

And the dam breaks.

Chapter 43
Daisy

What am I doing?

One minute I'm telling myself to stay strong, the next I'm caged in by my husband, ready to drop to my knees for him.

"Tell me to stop," he whispers in my ear, making goosebumps pop up along my arms.

I hesitate for only a moment before shaking my head.

I want this. I want *him.*

"Say the words, Daisy," he growls, making me whimper.

"Don't stop." I barely get the words out before the door gives way and he's hauling me up in his arms. I squeak at the shock of it all, but before I know it, I'm tossed on the bed and watching Luka flex his hands like a caged animal.

"I— This…" He shakes his head. "I don't know if I can control myself." The pained words only fuel my need for more.

"Then don't." Sitting up, I strip out of my drenched sweater, tossing it on the floor at his feet as he watches my every move. Next is my bra, slowly sliding down my arms. I throw it right at his chest.

"Hercegnőm…"

"Don't stop, Luka," I whisper, unbuttoning my jeans.

He moves so fast it shocks me. His hands take over, yanking my jeans off roughly before running over every inch of skin he can touch.

I reach for his collar, trying desperately to get his shirt off so I can feel him too. He doesn't help me, though; no, he lets me struggle until I finally get it over his head and chuck it at the floor like it personally wronged me.

"I've missed you so fucking much," he murmurs against the skin of my stomach. "I've done so much wrong."

Tears well in my eyes at his words.

"I want to give you everything." He kisses up my ribcage. "Anything you want, I want to be the one to give it to you." His tongue traces the underside of my breast. "I'll never jeopardize this again."

My hands glide into his overgrown blond hair, gripping it tight and keeping him locked to me.

"I'll do anything, Dais." He nips at my nipple before soothing it with a kiss.

My back arches with need, desperate for more.

"For better or for worse." He trails kisses along my collarbone. "You and me forever." He hovers over me, eye to eye, as he says those last words, and I believe him.

I finally believe him and, more importantly, I *trust* him.

It's been almost two months since COTA. Two long months without my soulmate. And here he is, laying bare for me.

"Forever," I choke out.

He descends on me like I just turned his dreams into reality. This kiss is one of new beginnings, of acceptance and true love.

It takes my breath away.

I claw at his shoulders and back, begging for him to be closer. I need him to infiltrate every molecule in my body, and even then, it doesn't feel like it will be close enough.

He shoves between us and fumbles a little before he shifts back and unbuttons his jeans clumsily. My hands move to push them over his ass, but we're both too frantic, too hurried for anything to go smoothly.

Finally, he sighs, shifting off the bed completely, but smiles at my whimper.

"I'm coming back, I promise. Nothing could keep you from me." He finally gets his jeans off and wastes no time kicking off his boxer briefs too. My hands move to my panties when I realize they're still on, but he shakes his head. "I know we both love when you take control, but not today, *hercegnőm*. Today, I worship you. I show you exactly what you mean to me." His hands slide up my legs. "You just have to lie there and let me do it. Let me love you." His voice is hoarse with emotion.

I couldn't talk for anything right now. My throat is so tight, keeping the tears at bay. Nodding, I reach for him, silently begging him to come back to me.

He doesn't listen to my urging, though. Instead, he spends forever kissing every inch of skin, not leaving an inch untouched by his lips after taking my panties off.

I pound on the bed, kick my feet, and grip the sheets—anything to stop from taking over. I'm so desperate for more, so wet and needy that I'm making a mess of the sheets, but he doesn't care. He's on a mission, and nothing I do will interrupt him.

He finally makes his way to my face. Placing the softest kisses everywhere, he runs his nose back and forth over mine before pulling back just enough for us to look at each other.

"You are my whole world. I love you so damn much, Daisy." The tears in his eyes are like permission for mine to fall.

He tenderly brushes the hair from my face, kissing each tear that falls before pressing a kiss to my lips.

His hand moves to my leg trapped underneath us, and shoves it up and open. My hips arch up, feeling the tip of him against me, making me moan with need.

"Luka, please." I gasp as I pull away from kissing him.

"Shh." He touches me everywhere. Fingertips brushing my leg and his full palm in a hard grip on my ass make me ache for him to be inside of me.

When I finally feel his hips moving, he naturally notches against me, and on the next small thrust of his hips, he sinks into me.

"Shit. Shit, shit, shit," he chants, arching his head back, the veins in his neck prominent with the strain. His hands grip my hips hard, sure to bruise later, and it only turns me on more.

I plant my feet and thrust my hips up as much as I can to get more friction, but he shoves them back down with a growl.

"No. You aren't leading this."

I'm fighting against him, but he proves that his mind isn't the only thing he's been working on the last two months. No, he's stronger than he has been since before the accident.

"Daisy, I swear to God... I want this to last, but if you keep fucking wiggling, I'm going to come like it's my first time," he groans as I wiggle again.

It breaks the overwhelming emotions in me enough to make me giggle.

"Nope. Not that either. Shit," he curses.

I hold back my laughter this time, pulling him down to kiss me instead.

"Love me," I whisper against his lips with a smile, and that's exactly what he does.

Somehow, his thrusts are both deep and soft at the same time. His hips rolling against me, hitting my clit with every stroke, send me spiraling.

"Fuck, Dais. I feel you clenching tight against me." He bites the side of my breast. "You're going to make me come so fucking hard inside of you."

"Oh my God," I breathe out.

"You like that? You want me to come so deep inside of you that it'll stick? To feel me fill you up and keep it there?"

I have no clue where this Luka has come from, but I'm sure as hell not complaining.

"Please," I moan.

His thrusts get faster, hips driving harder and harder into me. "And when I slide out of you, instead of cleaning you up, I'm going to push all of my cum back inside of you. Keep my hand there all night so you still feel it in the morning."

Our heavy panting mixes with the sexiest dirty talk I've ever heard from him. I don't even care if we haven't talked about how we move forward with getting pregnant; in my head, all this talk means it's a green light.

Before I can catch my breath, my orgasm crests over the peak. A silent scream is all I have the energy for, but I pull his hips to mine to keep me full as I come.

"Daisy." Luka gasps as he follows me right over the edge.

We lie, motionless, holding each other so tightly as we catch our breath. Eventually, my grip loosens and I trail my nails down his back.

"Mmm," he moans, pressing a kiss to my cheek but not pulling back.

"I—" Words don't come.

"You are my everything, Daisy. Never forget that. I'll never stop fighting for you. For us."

My eye close at his words, knowing the fight is over.

We've done enough fighting, enough struggling. That's not to say there won't be more. But for now? For now, it's over.

"I love you," I murmur. "Come home please."

"Dais—"

"As nice as this house is, come home, Luka. I need you in my bed every night."

He leans back just enough to look in my eyes. He has to see the truth in them.

I believe you.

I trust you.

I want you now and forever.

"Just in your bed?" he asks cheekily, but there's a vulnerability just below the surface that I see.

"No." I shake my head with a smile. "I need you, Luka."

***

We move him back home that night.

And have round two.

And three ... until the early hours in the morning.

Chapter 44

Luka

It's Christmas. I didn't think it was possible to have a happy holiday this year, yet here we are.

Daisy is in a Christmas onesie with buttons on the ass like we're in the early 1900s, but all it does it make me want to pop them and bend her over the couch.

"Keep looking at me like that, and I won't be making cookies," she scolds from the kitchen.

"I mean, I'll take sex over cookies."

"No! I mean, yes but no! I need to make these cookies. The girls are coming over later, and I want to get this all done so we can actually enjoy the company and not have a shit-ton to do."

By the girls, she means her sisters—a last-minute plan but something she really wanted, and I wasn't about to say no. My last impression with them wasn't a great one, so I'm hoping to make up for it this time.

"How can I help?" I stand and join her in the kitchen, wrapping my arms around her waist and pulling her back to me.

"Mmm. We can mix dough like this, right?" She leans back against me.

"We can do whatever you want, Dais." And I mean that with every ounce of my being. I will make whatever she wants happen, no matter how big or small.

"I'm sad that I have to go back to work after this week. It's been nice just being home for so long." She sighs against my shoulder.

"Well, good news for you... If you're travelling I'm coming with you." I kiss her temple.

"Luka..."

"I have a plan. Tomorrow, I'm going to go to COTA and get over this fear of the track. However long it takes, I'm going to sit my ass out there and figure it out."

"Yeah?" She turns her head more to look at me as I nod in response. "Then I shall sit my happy ass on the track with you."

That night almost three months ago changed us both. I think trust will always be a hard thing, but she doesn't doubt me and always asks if she has concerns or questions now. We've vowed to be completely honest with everything, and it's helped a lot.

"Thank you," I whisper.

"Okay, time to finish these cookies." She runs her hands together and gets back to work.

I stay wrapped around her, making her take twice as long to make the cookies, but she doesn't complain.

"So, I have a present for you before everyone gets here," I tell her after she puts the cookies in the oven.

"Well, that's very interesting. So do I." She smiles.

We stare at each other before racing to the tree and grabbing our presents. I hold mine above my head first, and she curses at losing.

"Come sit." I grab her hand and lead her to the couch with me. We exchange presents, and I make her open mine first.

She opens up the envelope and reads over it. I see her mind working overtime before her eyes skim it again.

"Luka..."

"I fucked things up, and I felt like renewing our vows was important in order to move forward. I don't want doubts or second-guessing. I want you to know that I choose you every single day, every hour, every second."

"I really love it," she says through tears.

"Aww, Dais, I didn't want to make you cry." Lord knows the woman's cried enough. I pull her into my lap and hold her.

"It's just so thoughtful and perfect, and I'm just..." She reaches over and grabs her present, handing it to me. "Open," she squeaks.

Confusion at why she doesn't want to talk and instead have me open the present swirls in my head. I gingerly unwrap it, and it only grows stronger.

"A pregnancy test," I say dumbly, looking at it from all angles. It's a brand-new one, judging by the shrink wrap still on it.

"I'm not sure, and my period hasn't been exactly regular, but I didn't want to do it without you."

It's right this minute that I realize she was going to take her IUD out around COTA and probably still did. Logic leads me to believe she never did anything to cover herself, and we've had a lot of sex since then with zero regard for protection.

Holy shit, I hope she's pregnant.

A flash of Daisy pregnant morphs to a mini Daisy running around the halls of this house, and it feels like my heart triples in size.

I was ready when we talked about it before my meltdown, as I affectionately call it now, but I can picture it all now. And I want it so badly.

"Take it," I say on a broken whisper.

"Now?"

"Fuck yes! I need to know, like, yesterday if you're pregnant."

"Like, in a bad way?" she meekly asks.

That's when I turn my focus onto Daisy. "No, Dais, in the best fucking way. I just don't want to start monologuing if it's not positive yet."

Her eyebrow arches up. "Got some poetic thoughts in that jock brain of yours?"

"So poetic. You're not ready." I kiss her forehead. "Seriously, go take it." I tap her ass and follow her to the bathroom.

"Dear God, please don't watch me pee." She sighs.

"Umm, I mean, I'm not going to literally watch you pee, but I'm staying here. You don't get to find out before me."

"I love you so much." She gives me her dreamy eyes before straightening up. "Now, turn around."

"Daisy. I literally lick your pussy as my day job. I think I'm good."

"Jesus, and we're talking about bringing a kid into this nonsense," she mutters.

"Take the damn test and stop stalling." Am I antsy? A million percent yes, but I'm desperately trying to not let it show for Daisy.

I grab the instructions as she pees on the little stick thing and am trying to make sense of what all the lines mean.

"Okay, we have to wait three to five minutes." I pull out my phone and set a timer. "And we can't read it after that because it won't be accurate."

"Luka."

"And maybe we should get one of the ones that actually say 'pregnant' and 'not pregnant'."

"Luka," Daisy says, pulling the piece of paper out of my hands and wrapping her arms around my neck. "Just be with me."

She's nervous, I realize.

"Hey, whatever the result, it's okay. We'll be okay."

"What if it's positive but I have another miscarriage?" she whispers.

"If—and that's a big if—that happens, then we'll work through it together. We'll figure out the next steps and move forward. I'll be here every step of the way, no matter what happens, okay?"

Her eyes shift between mine as she takes a steadying breath.

Nodding, she opens her mouth to say something, but my timer goes off.

"We don't have to look. We can throw this one away and wait. We can do whatever you want to do, *hercegnőm*."

"We're not throwing it away, you crazy man. I'm just ... scared. I don't know if I want it to be positive or negative."

"Is your only worry about it being positive the risk of miscarriage?" I ask because I genuinely don't want to add any pressure if this isn't something she truly wants.

"Yeah. I don't want to go through that again." Her eyes glisten with unshed tears as I pull her in for a hug.

"It's your call, Dais. I'm not going to force you to look."

"You look. And I'll look at your reaction."

No pressure there.

"Okay. You ready?" She nods, and I shift to pick up the test.

My eyes immediately widen at the two dark pink lines.

"Fuck, it's negative, isn't it?" She sighs and tries to step back.

"Daisy…" I breathe out, barely able to say it. "No, it's positive."

"What?"

"It's positive. You're pregnant." I can't take my eyes off the test. Everything feels surreal, like it's happening to someone else and I'm just watching it all from a distance.

"Oh my God," she whispers, drawing my attention. "Oh my God."

"Hey, talk to me. Good or bad?" I honestly can't tell.

"Good." Tears start to fall. "So damn good. Oh my God, I wanted it so badly." She laughs as she grabs it out of my hand.

Once I know she's okay, I let the news sink in.

It's Christmas Day. We're renewing our vows, and Daisy is pregnant. *Holy shit, talk about the perfect day.*

I don't think; I wrap my arms around her, burying my head in her neck, and spin her around in a circle before everything catches up to me and I'm bawling into her neck. My shoulders shake with the force of it as I hold her close to me.

We stand in our bathroom, crying over a positive test, for a long time.

She pulls back eventually. "Are you sure you're okay with this?"

"So much more than okay. I've wanted this for so damn long," I whisper.

"What?"

"It just hit me out of nowhere. One minute, I pictured you pregnant and that's all I could think about even if the timing was terrible at the time. I just…" I shake my head with a smile on my face. "I just want a mini Daisy running around, causing terror. Wild blonde curls that I have zero clue how to tame, but I'll learn. I'll practice."

"Please stop." She chuckles through tears. "I'm already pregnant; there's no need to make me want it more."

I cup her cheeks and kiss her hard.

Holding her, I pull back so she can see me. "On a serious note, I will absolutely step up my therapy. I don't ever want you to feel like I'm at risk of relapsing, especially with the little one on the way. When I freak out, I'll talk to you and put in the work to be here one hundred percent for both of you."

"I know you will. I haven't doubted you since we started dating again." She puts her hands on top of mine. "We're having a baby," she whispers with a smile so damn big that I swear it lights up the universe.

"We are." My smile might match hers.

"Holy shit, I'm so scared and happy."

"Let's just take it one day at a time. I know after everything this isn't going to be easy, but if we take it day by day, we can handle it." And I mean it. She's not alone in this like last time. I'll be at every appointment. I'll rub her feet every single day. I'll learn to cook. Well, maybe not that one. Can't burn down the house before we bring the kid home.

"What's going through your mind?" she asks.

"That I'll do everything to take care of you, but in my head, I said I would learn to cook, but that feels like a terrible idea."

"Worst idea ever. You'd burn down the house." She gives me a watery laugh.

"Well, at least we're on the same page about that." I smirk.

"Can we not tell the girls? I just want to... I want to confirm things and enjoy it just between the two of us for a while."

"Absolutely. I will try extremely hard to keep my hands to myself and not ravage you, as well as constantly touch your stomach." I nod earnestly before moving my hand to said stomach.

My kid is growing in here.

The thought is wild. I'm in awe that this is real. I did this. I put a baby inside my wife.

"You're thinking caveman thoughts, aren't you?" Daisy asks out of nowhere.

"No," I say instantly. "Yes ... kind of."

She sighs in faux exasperation.

"I can't help it. I did this." My thumb strokes her stomach.

"I mean, you needed my egg to make that happen, but sure, go ahead and take all the credit."

"Oh, I will. I used to race fast cars. Now, I just have fast—"

"For the love of our marriage, do not say what I think you're about to say."

She covers my mouth.

"I love you," I mumble against her hand before kissing it.

"I love you too." She tosses the test on the counter and snuggles into my arms.

Four hours later, our house is infiltrated by the Morrison women, sans their brother. It's loud and hectic, and so fucking perfect.

I probably don't do a good job of hiding the sheer happiness I'm feeling, but I don't care.

This has been the hardest two years of my life, and in a matter of a couple of months, I've figured out what's important to me, gotten my wife back, and we're starting a family. I had no idea it was possible to be this lucky in life, but here I am. And I'll never take it for granted again.

Chapter 45

Daisy

Mid-January was the earliest appointment I could get. I've spent the last three weeks alternating between deliriously happy and scared shitless every single day.

"Hey, you ready to go?" Luka walks up and stops in front of me.

"No. Yes. No." And I should probably call my therapist and see if she can squeeze me in this week with the way I'm spiraling.

"Totally get that. How do I help? Do you want to go get that lemonade you're obsessed with? Do you want me to shut up?" He looks panicked, and his words are just enough to make me take a breath and calm myself down a little.

"I do not want you to shut up, although I withhold the right to change my mind if you start getting weird about things ... like the ultrasound thing at the doctor's office."

"Why would I get weird about an ultrasound thing?" He arches an eyebrow more out of curiosity.

"You'll see. But I reserve the right." I point at him.

"Absolutely, *hercegnőm*." He nods exaggeratedly.

"And maybe a lemonade after." I pout.

"Done."

One more inhale and exhale. "Okay, let's do this."

"I'll be there the whole time," Luka says as he directs me to the garage.

"I know."

"And you can ... squeeze my hand, punch me, or whatever you need to do in the office."

"I'm not in labor." I roll my eyes, but as I'm getting into the car, I see him wringing his hands together, waiting for me to get in.

He's just as freaked out as me.

"Hey," I say softly, making him look at me. "What can I do for you?"

"Oh, Dais, nothing. I'm more nervous for you, I think. I have no doubt everything's going to be fine when we check it out, but I just want to make sure you're okay."

"How are you so sure?"

"Umm, let's see." He holds his hand out and starts holding up fingers as he names things. "You're craving lemonade all fucking day. You're hornier than I've ever known you to be, and that's saying something. You've been..." He hesitates. "Crying at those dog commercials when you make me watch that dumb reality TV show."

"Hey! Those dogs are so sad! Who doesn't cry at them?"

"Yep, you are absolutely right." He nods with a smirk.

I sigh. "Fine. There are signs, but that doesn't mean anything."

"How many more tests have you taken?" he asks, calling me out.

"Too many. Fine. Just get in the car, and let's do this."

"I'm not discounting how you're feeling, Dais. I just want to support you. But there's also no doubt in my mind that my baby is growing strong as fuck in there."

"Oh my God, you're ridiculous."

"I am, but it did take your mind off of things for a minute." He leans in and kisses me. "I love you. I'll be here for whatever happens. And I'm really fucking excited to see our baby."

Tears well up in my eyes, but I blink them away. Luka is not about to use that as another example. I can't let him be right more than once a day; his head wouldn't fit into the garage.

He gets into the car and reaches for my hand immediately.

***

"Okay, so here's the sac, and it's looking really good. It's hard to see, but there's your baby." The doctor circles a blob on the screen.

I blink, afraid to accept that this is real.

Luka and I are silent as we wait for the other shoe to drop.

"I'm just going to turn on the sound and get that heartbeat."

The whooshing followed by the staccato of the fast heartbeat hit me dead in the chest, and I cover my mouth as a sob breaks free. Luka squeezes the hand he's holding, and I look over at him. Tears fall freely down his face, and he looks this incredible mixture of elated and in awe.

"That's our baby. We made that," he whispers, making me cry harder.

"Congratulations to you both." The doctor smiles at us. "According to the measurements, you're looking to be around eight weeks, and things are looking right on track."

"And nothing is wrong? There's no sign that things could … happen again?" Luka asks as he swipes at his face.

"While I can't say for sure because sometimes tragic things just happen, things are looking wonderful. Right around twelve weeks is when you're out of the highest risk zone, and then at twenty-four weeks is our larger gauge at overall viability. Although, with advancements, there are some incredible accounts of preemies growing big and strong before that." She smiles. "That's not something I want you to worry about, although I know you most likely will with your history. But what I want you to focus on is enjoying this pregnancy as much as you can."

I nod, still sobbing my brains out as Luka thanks her profusely. She gives me time to get dressed again and returns with a bunch of paperwork.

"This will be overwhelming because there's a lot of stuff, but this packet basically has a list of everything we're looking at for each appointment and the testing we'll be doing. There's also information about classes and hospital tours. Those aren't something you need to jump on immediately, but nearing the end of your second trimester, I would line some things up. Do either of you have any questions for me?"

Luka and I shake our heads, and we walk out of our appointment on a high like I've never felt before. We wordlessly walk down to the car, and then we both just sit there.

I break the silence first. "Holy shit, there's a baby in there," I murmur.

Luka pulls out the strip of ultrasound pictures. "I think they look more like you."

Laughter bubbles out of me, but I love him for keeping things lighter.

"Yeah, it's uncanny. That blob definitely screams me."

"How dare you call our baby a blob!" He gasps in faux outrage. "But seriously, did you see that probe? Be honest; I'm bigger, right?" He smirks, making me giggle more.

"You're so dumb. I'm not even justifying that with a response. I told you not to get weird about it."

"That's a hell yes."

"Seriously, though, thank you," I tell him.

He reaches over and intertwines our hands. "Never thank me for that, *hercegnőm*. I'm here for you and the babes for all the things. And honestly? That was the most overwhelming, amazingly fucking cool thing I've ever witnessed in my life."

"Same. Can you believe this is real?" I ask.

"No, but I'm so damn glad it is." He puts the car in reverse. "You ready for some lemonade?"

"Hell yes, I am."

Lemonade in hand, we drive around the city, talking about all of our hopes and dreams for this kiddo. It's wild to think that, two years ago, life was falling apart around me. I was drowning, and I couldn't find air.

"What are we going to name her?" he asks as we start to make our way home.

"What makes you so sure it's a girl?" I suck the last of my lemonade through the straw, sad it's gone.

"Just a hunch. I've had visions of a tiny Daisy running around our house for weeks."

"You want to make a bet?" I ask, knowing he won't be able to resist.

"Is the sky blue?"

"Okay, if it's a boy, I get ... a two-week vacation to Greece."

He scoffs. "Child's play. If it's a girl, we open up a foundation to fund a whole bunch of shit for kids in need."

"Well, shit. I hope it's a girl."

Epilogue

Luka

You know what's great about your wife still technically working under the Vanstone umbrella? When you decide to do a vow renewal, you get your pick of any resort you want on a very short time frame.

It's the last weekend in February, and man, it was an ask for all of our friends to be here so close to the Formula 1 season starting. But they showed up in spades. I suppose a quick weekend in Costa Rica before the season starts is good enough motivation.

I look out upon the gorgeous area Sydney set up for us. We told her not to stress it, but just like with our first wedding, she disregarded that wish.

"She outdoes herself every time." Daisy walks up and wraps her arms around my middle.

"How are you feeling?" I ask.

"Ugh. Okay. I thought the nausea was supposed to be over. Maybe flying somewhere was a stupid idea." Her forehead rests against my back.

"Did you take some of that stuff the doctor prescribed?" I can never remember the name of it, but it kicks her nausea quick.

"I just did. I have, like, fifteen minutes for it to kick in before I need to get dressed."

Spinning around, I wrap my arms around her but catch a glimpse of some sexy-as-hell peach lingerie. "Well, what do we have here, Mrs. Tomic?"

"I was trying to be sexy." She pouts.

She has no idea that she's effortlessly sexy, even more so with the small bump that practically popped out overnight before we left to come here.

"Oh, mama, you don't even need to try." I put my finger under her chin, drawing her eyes up to mine. "I get to marry you again today, and you have my baby in your belly. There is literally nothing sexier than that; I promise you."

Her eyes fill with tears, and she starts waving her hands in front of them. "Fucking hormones. You have to be chill on the romantic shit. I'm crying at the drop of a hat lately."

"I think that might pose an issue when we get to the vows. Dais." I chuckle.

"Ugh. I'm fucked."

"I still love you, but you should definitely make sure that mascara is waterproof."

"Well, Mr. Romantic, I might have something to top all of your"—she waves her hands around me—"sweet words."

"Oh yeah?"

She walks over to her luggage and pulls out an envelope. My brows furrow in confusion.

"I know we were conflicted about whether or not to find out, but I had the blood test done and got the results. We can keep it in this envelope and never open it," she adds quickly, but I can't take my eyes off the envelope.

"That has what we're having inside of it?"

"It does."

"Do you want to find out?" I look up and ask.

Her watery smile tells me before her words do. "I really do. But if you don't want to, I'm fine with that."

"Open it," I whisper.

Her hands shake as she goes to slide her finger under the seal. I wrap my hands around hers as she pulls out the card.

"I'm so nervous, and I don't know why," she says softly.

"It's because you're afraid to lose the bet." I smirk, trying to help her nerves.

"God, I fucking hope I lose, honestly." She laughs.

"On the count of three," I offer, and she nods.

"One. Two. Three."

We open the card, and the word written in clear print almost knocks me on my ass.

"It's a girl." I sniff, trying to keep the tears at bay. I fall to my knees, unable to hold myself in check. My hands go to her stomach immediately before pressing my lips to it. "Hi, my love," I murmur as my thumbs stroke her soft skin.

Sobs from Daisy above me, and her hands holding my head to her, steady me.

I make a vow to always be the man my daughter can be proud of. One she's excited to see every single day. One who'll show her how a man should treat her when she grows up because of how I treat Daisy.

I've lived for myself. I've lived for Daisy, but now I live for them both. Everything I do from here on out is for them.

"You better start planning that foundation," Daisy says through her crying, making me laugh.

"On it." I stand up, pulling her in a tight hug.

"I think I'm in shock," she mutters.

"I think I'm so damn happy."

"We're supposed to be getting ready to head down there." She laughs.

"They'll wait for us. We just found out we're having a girl. Let me have a minute. I need to soak it in with you." My hand moves to her stomach, barely protruding but enough to notice if you know what you're looking for.

We soak in utter bliss for a few minutes before she pulls back, wiping under her eyes.

"I kind of want to tell everyone at dinner. Not that it's a girl; I want to keep that to ourselves a little while longer," she says.

"You know I'm on board with whatever you want to do."

"Then let's tell them."

"Perfect. We'll tell them that in all my retired glory, I knocked you up—"

"Stop! Oh my God, why are you so ridiculous?" She laughs.

"Because it makes you laugh like that, and it's the best sound in the world," I tell her honestly. I'll say stupid shit all day long if I get that laugh out of it.

"I feel like I shouldn't even wear makeup at this point." She sighs.

"You'll still look perfect. Now, come on. Let's go do this shit." I kiss her cheek before walking to the closet, feeling like I'm on cloud nine.

I've had many great days in my life. A lot of them were spent in a race car. But

I have a feeling that all of those will pale in comparison to the day our daughter is born.

I put on my linen suit quickly, never taking my eyes off of Daisy as she covers that beautiful bump with a loose, flowy, cream dress. You can't tell she's pregnant with it on, and I have to say, it annoys me more than I thought it would.

I've barely been able to keep my hands off of her stomach since we found out. And since it popped? I'm obsessed with it. A visual representation that our baby is growing in there is mind-blowing.

"You ready to do this?" she asks softly.

"So ready."

We walk down to the beach and down the aisle together, never disengaging from each other's touch.

And then we recommit our love and relationship in front of every single person we love, including our daughter.

"Daisy. We've been through the wringer the past couple of years, and we not only survived but are now thriving. I can say with complete confidence that I wouldn't be here today without you. You make me stronger; you make me want to be better every single day. You've let me chase you when I've failed, and you've never given up on me. I can't thank you enough for that. Our love can weather any storm. No matter what gets thrown our way, as long as you are by my side, we'll get through it. I can't imagine spending my life with anyone else. I'm so excited—no, ecstatic—about what our future holds. The anticipation of what's next, of the life we get to live together, is the greatest feeling in the world. I love you so much, and I recommit the rest of my life to you." I let go of her hand and dig into my pocket for the ring I put there secretly.

"Luka..."

"I didn't know what to get you to mark this day. Nothing felt like enough, but this is what I came up with." The infinity band I slide on is dainty and looks like flowers floating on her finger, pairing perfectly with her wedding and engagement ring. I already have the jeweler on standby to make one for when our kid—daughter—comes.

She lifts up on her toes and kisses me before lowering down and clearing her throat.

"Luka. My God, we've been through so much. It's been hard, harder than anything I've been through, and I still wouldn't change it for anything. We've grown stronger together. We're better together. You are my soulmate; I know that without a doubt. There's no one in this world I'd rather live life with. I can't wait for what's next." A sly smile plays on her lips. "I can't wait to continue to grow with you by my side, taking on new adventures and new projects. I'm looking forward to lazy days, crazy days, playful days, and everything in between. I love you so much it hurts sometimes, but I am so thankful that you are the person by my side through it all."

I don't know how she made it through that in one go because I'm practically bawling my eyes out. I don't hesitate. The second I know she's done with her side of the vows, I cup her cheeks and kiss her with everything I have.

Cheers sound around us, making me smile against her lips.

"I love you so fucking much," I whisper.

"I love you too." She kisses me again.

We turn to our friends, who all have tears in their eyes, even people like Felix and Nate whom I've never seen cry or get remotely emotional before in my life.

I grab Daisy's hand and hold it up. "Let's party!" I yell, breaking through the high emotions.

A gorgeous table set up nearby holds seats for everyone, with a massive spread of food. It's not a quiet affair. People are talking, laughing, and enjoying a celebration of Daisy's and my life together.

Once the evening settles in and the food has been eaten, I look at Daisy, and she nods in return.

I stand up, tapping my glass with a nearby spoon, which gets everyone to quiet down.

"Hey, we just wanted to thank all of you for coming and celebrating with us. I know most of you have a long season coming up, and we're thankful you could take time out of your busy schedules to come hang out in this gorgeous resort with us. Thank you, Pierce." I nod to him. "It's been a long journey, and I'm grateful for all the support and wake-up calls." I look at Beck. "It's meant more than you'll ever know." I reach down to grab Daisy's hand, and she stands up next to me. "We wanted to share..." I clear my throat of the emotion taking over. "We wanted to share some happy news. Daisy's pregnant." I barely get it out without more emotion clogging my throat. They say women are the emotional ones when pregnant, but I'm not far behind her, honestly.

The cheers and gasps turn to congratulations and happiness. Everyone takes turns hugging Daisy and clapping me on the back. It's by far the best day I've had in a long time.

Eventually, the night dies down and talk inevitably turns to the upcoming seasons.

"So, Sydney, is Empress ready?" Felix, the team principal at Legacy Racing, smirks.

"I feel pretty ready. What about you, Dais?" she asks.

"So ready. What about you, Toni?" she asks, making my head dizzy with all the women smirking and fucking with Felix. I wouldn't want to be on the other end of their wrath.

"Oh, so ready. You sure you can keep up?" Toni asks Felix with a sly smile.

"You don't need to worry about me. I'm just worried you might not be up to the task. The offseason isn't real long to make significant changes, you know." I may not know Felix well, but Beck's always liked him and touted him as a fair boss, even if he was a little pretentious.

"Now, Felix. We're friends. Don't make me turn against you." Sydney narrows her eyes at him.

He puts his hands up, his eyes not leaving Toni, which makes my eyebrows go sky high. Well now, this *is* interesting.

"I'm just making sure you all are ready, is all. I want real competition this year."

Toni and Felix have a staring contest as those of us in the conversation take note of it.

Daisy leans closer to me. "Do we think they're fucking already, or do they need to fuck? I can't tell," she whispers.

"It's a toss-up. Speaking of which, you ready to get out of here, mama?"

"Hell yes, I am. But I really want another one of those passionfruit drink thingies." She sticks her bottom lip out like I'm not going to get as many as I can carry to bring upstairs.

"Well, it's been a lovely evening. Thank you all so much for coming out, but I've got to take my wife to our room and get her off her feet." I smirk.

"Like, why even attempt to make a riddle out of it? We all know what's going down. That's why we're all on the other side of the resort," Beck says with a roll of his eyes.

"Because 'I'm about to fuck my pregnant wife senseless' sounds less romantic, and it's a vow renewal, dick," I counter.

"Ooookay, and that's our cue. Love you, guys! Thanks so much for coming out, and I'll see most of you tomorrow." Daisy blows a kiss to the group before dragging me out of the room.

"Wait!" I stop and head back.

"Luka ... I want an orgasm," she whines.

"I know. Give me second." I race back in and grab a couple of premade glasses from the drink table. I happen to be lucky enough to catch one of the servers on my way out. "Hey, can I ask you to get, like, a pitcher of these brought up to our room? The woman in the green dress, Sydney, can fill in the blanks." He nods, and I race back out to Daisy.

"Oh, good fucking call. I forgot about that." She snags one and sucks down half of it before we reach the elevators.

"God, I love you." I sigh, leaning against the elevator wall as she drinks her newest drink obsession like the happiest woman in the world.

"I love you too. And next time, let's not tell Beck and all of our friends that you're about to fuck me, okay?" She smirks, telling me she really didn't mind it.

"I believe I said fuck you senseless."

"Yep, you sure did, so you better put out." The bell dings, and she races out of the elevator, giggling as she looks behind her as I chase her.

There's never a day where I don't chase Daisy Tomic, and there won't ever be a day where I won't.

The New Formula One Season Brings Plenty of Drama to Race Week One

Bahrain saw the resurgence of Empress Racing, and it's already made the season an exciting one. Team Principal, Antoinette (Toni) Bailey, and Legacy President and Team Principal, Felix Karlsson, were seen in a heated argument moments after the trophy ceremony.

No word yet on what it was in reference to, but it is surmised that the almost-crash between two of their drivers early in the race was a catalyst for the tension. With Legacy taking the top spot, and Empress taking second and fourth, it could shape up to be quite a contentious Constructor's Championship if it stays competitive between these two.

We'll be eagerly awaiting to see how this plays out between the two team principals and their drivers' standings this Formula One season.

Buckle up, folks. I have a feeling it's going to be an explosive season.

Acknowledgements

To Karolyne and J- You both have kept me sane writing this book. It was a hard one, but you helped push me to bring it to life. I'm so grateful to you both.

To Nina- You always have my back. Your faith in me is humbling and I am so grateful to have you on my team.

To my hubs- There's a lot of truth and emotion in this book. It's about things we've both had to work through and I'm thankful every single day that you are the person I get to work through the hard things with. I wouldn't be here without you. I love you.

To my readers- THANK YOU! This story is hard and personal, and I hope I did it justice. Your support means the world to me, and I couldn't do this without you!

Also By

The Catalyst Series

The Beginning
Meet the women of The Catalyst Series a decade before the series takes place!

The Detour
Bea and Riggs

The List
Penelope and Andy

The Case
Larkin and Theo

The Vacation
Jane and Pierce

Bluebell Falls

Second First Impression

Ainsley and Ledger

For the Thrill of It
Willow and Oakley

What You Broke
Rina and Arlo

Redefining Strength
Roxy and Lennox

Qualifiers of Love

Serendipity
Beckett and Sydney

Be sure to join my newsletter to stay up to date on new releases and all other things me!
http://www.samanthamthomas.com

If you enjoyed Fuse, please think about leaving a review! I would be so grateful to you!
Review Here